THE LAST ECHO

Also by Kimberly Derting

THE BODY FINDER
DESIRES OF THE DEAD

Kimberly Derting

THE
LAST
ECHO

HARPER

An Imprint of HarperCollins*Publishers*

Library of Congress Cataloging-in-Publication Data
Derting, Kimberly.
    The last echo / Kimberly Derting. — 1st ed.
        p.   cm.
Summary: Violet, a high school junior, discovers the body of a teen
killed by "the collector" and is determined to solve the case, but the
serial killer is on the lookout for a new "relationship" and Violet may
have caught his eye.
    ISBN 978-0-06-208219-0
    [1. Psychic ability—Fiction.   2. Serial murders—Fiction.   3. Dead—
Fiction.   4. Best friends—Fiction.   5. Friendship—Fiction.   6. High
schools—Fiction.   7. Schools—Fiction.   8. Washington (State)—Fiction.]
I. Title.
PZ7.D4468Las 2012   2011044633
[Fic]—dc23   CIP
                                                                   AC

Typography by Andrea Vandergrift
12 13 14 15 16   LP/RRDH   10 9 8 7 6 5 4 3 2 1
❖
First Edition

To Connor, Amanda, and Abby. My everything.

CHAPTER 1

VIOLET STRAINED, SEARCHING FOR THE SENSA-
tion through the suffocating blackness. It wasn't the kind of
thing she could see or hear, making it all the more difficult
to pinpoint. She didn't know how exactly to describe what
was leading her—pulling her. But it was definitely an echo.
That much she knew for certain.

Her fingertips tingled, her toes too. And even though it
wasn't painful, or even uncomfortable, it was still . . . odd.
Like the prickling sensation of sitting on your foot for too
long.

She followed it by its intensity. If she turned one way, the
sensation weakened. The other, it grew stronger.

It was almost completely black in this part of the abandoned warehouse. Her feet crunched over broken glass, the sound slicing its way through the calm that had settled over her, blanketing her fears and dulling the rhythm of her heart. She paused, her stomach tightening as her eyes searched the shadows, trying to discern one shape from another, trying to convince herself that she was all alone in here.

"I'm okay," she whispered into the emptiness around her, telling herself she should stop. That she'd already gone too far. But after a moment, when the need to follow the echo became too strong, she started moving again, her feet shuffling over the concrete and kicking debris out of her path. The last thing she wanted to do was to trip and fall on the glass-littered floor.

She reached a doorway and the prickling shot through her arms and legs, surprising her and making her gasp. She gripped the exposed wood of the doorjamb to steady herself. "What the hell . . ." She wheezed as she reached up to knead the puckered flesh of her arm so hard she worried it might bruise.

She shook her head, ignoring both the sting and the concerns that refused to be silent now.

Moving more slowly, but still cautious of her surroundings, Violet continued toward the echo. It hadn't always been like this; she hadn't always been so careful. But she was learning . . . trying to think past the overpowering need to find the dead and be aware for her own safety.

But it wasn't easy. Especially now, when the echo was so strong, and she was so close. When a body was calling to her . . . begging to be found.

Ahead of her, she could see something in the darkness. Something solid and out of place in a building that had been stripped all the way down to its studs.

Violet's heart raced and her entire body itched as if she were being gouged by a million tiny thorns. She wasn't sure what to do now: Her training told her to walk away, call for help, and bring them back here. But her instincts demanded something different.

She took a single step closer. She had to be sure. Her skin was pierced and stabbed, although whether those sensations came from inside of her or outside, she was no longer certain. She took another step forward, wincing from the discomfort as she rubbed her arms and gritted her teeth.

When she was within reach, she held out her hand and ran it along the surface of what looked to be a box. But her fingertips stilled when she felt how smooth it was—how firm, how solid. She'd been right when she'd suspected it was out of place here. It hadn't been there for long, she could tell just by feeling it. It was clean; there was no dirt corroding it, no layers of dust and grime coating its glossed surface. Her hand moved down, finding the latch.

Even without opening the top of the freezer her fingers brushed across, Violet knew it was her: the girl they'd been searching for. She was in there.

"I found her." Violet spoke quietly, reaching up with one hand to brush her hair away from her face, her fingertips settling over the earpiece still firmly embedded in her ear. The gesture was unnecessary; she knew they were listening. "I'm in the old Pacific Storage building."

She took an uncertain step back and waited, ignoring that part of her that wanted to peek inside—to see the girl, to confirm that her intuition wasn't mistaken. Instead, Violet decided to give her a few more moments of peace, to let the girl lay silently, peacefully, in the darkness . . . before the others came and disentombed her. Before they prodded and poked and probed.

Before she became evidence.

Violet heard their shouts, and their boots grinding over the glass. For a moment, she thought about not answering them, about just remaining quiet and waiting. She knew eventually they would find her there, in the gloom of the huge warehouse, even if she didn't respond. But *they* didn't have an echo to follow, and it could take them considerably longer than it had taken Violet to find the body.

"Dude, even I can hear them now." Krystal's voice practically shattered Violet's eardrum. She'd nearly forgotten her earpiece was still in place. "If you don't answer, they're going to pull their weapons and start blasting down the walls."

Violet smirked, not answering Krystal, but getting the point of the warning. "I'm over here!" she finally called out, although not quite loud enough. And then, knowing that she had to, she called again, louder: "Back here!"

She saw the beams of their flashlights bobbing through a doorway on the other side of the warehouse and their footsteps grew closer, more disorganized, chaotic.

"Are you safe?" It was Sara this time, although not through her earpiece. Her voice came from the frenzy the police officers brought with them.

"I'm fine," Violet answered, biting her lip and wishing she'd taken those extra few minutes. "She's in here. I'm sure it's her."

A shaft of light reached her face, blinding Violet, and she turned away, shielding her eyes with her arm. The beam dropped to the ground—no apologies—as another fell on the freezer behind her.

Violet stepped out of the way and let them work. This was their operation, the local police department. And at least for the moment, Sara Priest had become one of them.

But not Violet. She was part of another team altogether.

She stood back and was immediately forgotten. She watched as procedures were followed: The room was cleared and the dogs were brought in; they had to be careful to not taint any potential evidence.

The stinging sensation continued; it would for as long as Violet remained near the body. And it *was* a body, Violet knew. She didn't need the dogs to tell her that—she had her *gift*. The ability she'd inherited to find those who'd died at the hand of another. Those who'd been left with a unique sensory signature—an echo—that only Violet could find.

For this girl, it was the tactile feel of pins and needles.

From behind, Violet felt a strong hand reach for her. Its gentle tug pulled her back to reality, reminding her of where she was and what she was doing. The tingling that rippled through her now had nothing to do with the echo coming from the girl. She allowed herself to be drawn away from the mayhem and farther into the shadows.

"Why didn't you respond when Krystal asked for your location?"

Violet didn't need to see the expression on his face to know Rafe was glaring at her.

She pulled her hand from his, ignoring that weird crackling of electricity that sparked between them whenever her skin so much as brushed his. It was so strange, that sensation, like static, and she was, once more, left with just the needling barbs from the girl's echo. "I did. I distinctly remember saying I was in the old Pacific Storage building."

His voice tightened. "Before that, V? When you were ignoring her questions? Why the hell did you wander away from the team? From me?"

She didn't bother trying to explain that some of the cops were distracting her, that at least two of them had distinct imprints that interfered with her ability to track the girl's echo. Because not only could she sense the echoes of the dead, she also felt the imprints left behind on their killers. She doubted Rafe even realized he was wandering into slippery territory with this line of questioning. She still wasn't comfortable discussing what she could do. It was just too weird. It was hard to undo years of secrecy.

But of all people, Rafe should understand that. Despite working together for the past two months, she'd learned that

6

he didn't like prying questions about how his ability worked either. Or about anything, really.

"I found her, didn't I? Why do you think it's your job to keep track of me anyway? Sara didn't put you in charge. You're not my boss."

If there'd been enough light, Violet was sure she would have seen the slow smile spread over his face, because she knew it was there . . . she could feel the change in the atmosphere as he reached for her hand again, this time to lead her away. "C'mon, let's get out of here. It's too dark. Besides, it's more fun if I can see you while you're bitching me out."

Violet didn't pull her hand away this time; she was secretly glad she'd had Rafe around these past months. Someone who'd been willing to show her the ropes. With Rafe she felt like she'd met someone who really understood her . . . someone who knew what it felt like to be truly *different*.

But it wasn't just Rafe. They were all different.

"I'll be right with you," Sara said, raising her finger in the universal sign for "give me a minute," although in this case Violet thought it probably meant "stay put" instead. She watched as she rushed across the lot to talk to a man who'd just emerged from the warehouse. Judging from his jacket and tie, she guessed he was one of the detectives in charge.

Violet could only imagine what the three of them must look like to the man, and to the officers and crime-scene investigators who'd taken over once the body had been located: a trio of misfit teens who had no business being at the scene of a murder investigation. She wondered how they'd feel if they knew what the three of them could actually do. If they'd earn any respect for their unusual abilities, or if they'd simply be treated like any other tools of the trade. Like those drug- or bomb-sniffing dogs they used in their canine units. Or in her case, she supposed she'd be more of the cadaver-sniffing variety.

She smiled inwardly as she turned to Krystal. "How'd you draw the short straw for this assignment?"

It made sense for Violet to be here—she was the resident body finder, after all. But Krystal was the self-proclaimed medium of the group, talking to spirits and getting messages from ghosts. It wasn't like her specific talent was all that useful on this case. At least not today.

Violet recalled the first time she'd met Krystal, the same day she'd first been introduced to the rest of the team. She'd never really shared what she could do with anyone besides her family and Jay, and suddenly it wasn't just Sara and Rafe she was expected to open up to, it was Krystal and Sam and Gemma too. But everyone else had become background noise to Krystal during that first meeting. At twenty-one, and the oldest of the group, Krystal was tough to ignore. Yet even though her outward appearance screamed: *Emo chick with issues and attitude,* her entire demeanor shouted: *Let's hold hands and be friends!* At least that's the way Violet felt whenever she was around Krystal. And she found herself drawn to her brand of openness, especially since Violet wasn't exactly an open book. She found Krystal's noncynical approach to life refreshing.

Krystal looked at Violet now and tapped the headset she wore, the one that made her look more like she belonged onstage at a pop concert than as part of a high-tech tactical response team, especially with her heavily kohl-lined eyes, bright purple tights, and Harley-Davidson boots. "Someone's gotta be in charge of Comm. Sara's"—she waved her hand in Sara's general direction, where Sara was just closing the file she was holding and shaking hands with the detective— "doing whatever it is Sara does. Liaising and whatnot. And it's not like Rafe's gonna do it. In case you hadn't noticed, he's not much of a talker." She cast wide, innocent brown eyes at Rafe when he turned to glare at her. "Well, I'm not lying, am I?"

He just shrugged, shoving his hands deeper into his pockets. "Whatever."

Sara joined the three of them near the edge of the parking lot, where they'd been trying to stay out of the way of the police who swarmed the building. "Good job, Krystal," she said, interrupting them. And then she shot a meaningful glance in Violet's direction, her eyebrows rising slightly, and it wasn't hard to tell she was annoyed. "Rafe, Violet, would you two mind staying behind for a minute? I'd like a word."

Krystal pursed purple lips that were the exact same shade as her tights, her eyes widening. "Ooh, sounds like someone's in trouble. . . ." The *I-told-you-so* in her voice was obvious. "Should've answered me when I asked where you were."

"Whatever," Violet whispered back to Krystal as discreetly as she could. "We found her, didn't we? Neither of us did anything wrong."

But Krystal just snorted, as if Violet was being ridiculous. "Except you broke contact with your team. And Rafe was supposed to keep track of you." As she stripped off her headset, her collection of necklaces—long chains strung with healing crystals, stones, and charms—clattered noisily together. "Later, losers. Hope you don't have to stay in detention for too long."

Violet shook her head as Sara walked with Krystal across the blacktop, toward the car Krystal had affectionately dubbed "Roxy," her heavy black boots looking oversized for her scrawny legs. A crowd had already gathered, probably people who worked in the area, those who'd heard the sirens and wanted to know what was going on. Violet knew it wouldn't be long before the news crews arrived too, and started asking questions.

She waited until Sara and Krystal were out of earshot, then turned to Rafe. "What did Krystal mean?" she insisted. "Did Sara ask you to *watch* me?"

Rafe just shrugged. "Does it matter?"

"Um, yeah, it sorta does. I'm a big girl. . . . I don't need you babysitting me."

Rafe's blue eyes glittered mischievously, but before he could respond, Sara was already coming back.

She crossed her arms, looking first at Rafe, and then to Violet, her gaze serious. "What happened back there, Violet?

I thought we talked about this? You said you were ready."

Violet let out a gusty sigh, stalling as she tried to decide whether to defend her actions, or to outright lie to Sara. Looking at the woman standing in front of her, always starched and no-nonsense, Violet finally lifted her shoulders, settling on the truth. "I honestly don't know. I thought I could handle it, but then I was there . . . and I could feel it. . . ." She glanced uneasily at Rafe, who stood beside her, no longer holding her hand but making her just as uncomfortable. "*Her* . . . I could feel *her* pulling me to find her and suddenly nothing else mattered." Her shoulders sagged again, defeatedly. She knew she'd let Sara—and her team—down. "I'm sorry."

Violet waited for the reprimand about leaving the safety of the team, especially after how often they'd talked about that very thing.

But it was Rafe who Sara turned to, her blue eyes narrowing. "I asked you not to let her out of your sight, didn't I?"

Rafe just shrugged again, in his usual Rafe-ish way, like he didn't really care what anyone else thought. "I told you she needed more time," he retorted, his quiet voice never rising.

Violet's cheeks grew hot as she stood there listening while they talked about her . . . as if she were completely invisible.

She winced when Sara continued, "It wasn't your decision, Rafe. When we're out in the field, you need to follow orders, just like everyone else."

Rafe's shoulders squared, his jaw flexing almost imperceptibly. "It's hard to follow orders when they don't make sense." And then his eyes shifted, only slightly, to Violet, who watched them in chagrined silence. "Besides, I didn't mean to lose her. I only turned my head for a second, and when I looked back . . ."

Now they were both staring at her, and Violet felt the heat in her cheeks creeping down her neck, coiling into an angry ball in the pit of her stomach. She shook her head, not sure what more she could say.

"Part of being on the team means we look out for each other. *Especially* in high-danger situations. We had no idea if the tip was legitimate, or if the killer was setting a trap—baiting us so he could ambush us when we got there."

Sara was right. Of course she was right. And, more importantly, she was in charge. Violet had known she was breaking the rules when she'd wandered off. Besides, she'd only barely been allowed to be there at all, and only because Sara had pulled some strings and promised to keep "her people" in line.

Violet had forced Sara to break that promise the moment she'd followed the girl's echo without telling anyone else what she was doing.

"I'm sorry," she repeated numbly.

Sara's curt nod told Violet there wouldn't be any more lecture. And then her face softened. "How are you feeling? Do you still have the CDs Doctor Lee gave you?"

Violet nodded. She knew she'd need to listen to them when she got home; already she could feel the girl's death—her unsettledness—weighing on her. Pulling her down and making her head throb.

"I'm going to make an appointment for you to see him again, so you can talk about what happened tonight. Does tomorrow work for you?"

Again, Violet nodded. "Sure. I can make it tomorrow." Not that she really had a choice. She'd broken the rules, after all. Besides, Dr. Lee could help. He'd been teaching her how to cope with finding the dead.

With some bodies, she was left with a persisting heaviness that clung to her until the body was buried or cremated . . . until that body was *at peace*. That feeling blanketed Violet, deadening her to everything else. Normal function could be difficult, even impossible.

But Dr. Lee offered Violet techniques to help her stay focused, to remain anchored in the real world. He taught her breathing exercises and had given her meditation CDs. He used hypnosis, telling Violet to "imagine" herself staying in control while the dead tried to keep her with them.

And it was working. Even now, after finding the girl, Violet felt more . . . *secure* than she would have before. Clearer.

Sara nodded, accepting Violet's response, then turned to Rafe again. "Why don't you walk Violet to her car?"

Violet started to protest, but then thought better of it. Wasn't that what Sara had just talked about, about being a team player, about looking out for one another? This probably wasn't a good time to complain.

She watched as Sara marched away, going to join the

buzz of activity that surrounded the crime scene. "Sorry about that," she muttered to Rafe.

"About what? About wandering away, or getting me in trouble?" The glint was back, mocking her from his deep blue gaze. His dark eyebrows were raised challengingly.

She thought about telling him "both," but then changed her mind. She wasn't sorry for following the echo, because it had led her to the girl. Who knew how much time she'd saved them from aimless searching? She shrugged as they reached her car. "For getting you in trouble." Violet unlocked the door and got inside, but Rafe grabbed the top of the door before she could close it.

He looked at her, his eyes finding their way inside of her, his intense gaze making her feel exposed. "Yeah, that's what I thought. I'll see you later," he finally said right before he slammed her car door shut.

The house was dark by the time Violet got there. Peaceful. She was careful not to make any noise as she crept up the stairs to her bedroom. There was no point disturbing her parents . . . or letting them know just how late she'd been out. They were already giving her far more freedom than she probably deserved, allowing her to come and go, even keep unusual hours, as long as her grades didn't suffer. And as long as she promised to be careful.

They knew she was working with Sara now, and even though they didn't entirely understand what it was that she did, they knew enough to be concerned. But they'd also been reassured by Sara that Violet's safety would always come first, that Sara's priority was to keep her team out of harm's way. And it was. Sara was nothing if not cautious, and she'd spent the past several weeks trying to instill in Violet the importance of following the rules.

But sometimes Violet found it difficult to ignore that undeniable drive to find the dead. Sometimes that need was stronger than her resolve.

Like today.

She undressed quickly, changing into a pair of sweats and a threadbare T-shirt before reaching for her iPod, where she'd uploaded the CDs Dr. Lee had given her.

It wasn't until she was about to press Play, just as she was climbing under her covers, that she noticed it, the envelope tucked beneath the edge of her pillow. She frowned as she reached for it, her fingers lingering for only a moment before pulling it free. The plain white envelope was blank, but she suspected who it was from.

She tore the top apart and unfolded the paper inside, her heart fluttering when she recognized the handwriting.

I miss you like crazy.
Jay

Violet grinned. It was just a note—a single line, really—but even his notes made her pulse race. *Ridiculous,* she thought as she ran her fingertips over his words, committing them to memory.

Then she tucked the note back where she found it, beneath her pillow, and collapsed into her bed. Pressing Play on her iPod, she listened as the sounds of ocean waves drifted through the earbuds, accompanied by a man's easy, melodic voice, reminding Violet to breathe deeply as he walked her through the stages of relaxation, instructing her to release the tension in her shoulders, her arms, her fingertips, and her toes.

But when she finally fell asleep, she wasn't thinking about the voice whispering in her ears or the quiet solitude of an island beach. Or even the haunting echo of the dead girl she'd discovered in a warehouse.

Instead, she fell asleep dreaming of secret notes and soft kisses. She fell asleep dreaming of Jay.

CHAPTER 2

VIOLET FELT BETTER THE NEXT MORNING. NOT A hundred percent exactly, but if Dr. Lee had been there, Violet was pretty sure she'd have kissed him on the mouth for making this part of her ability somewhat bearable. Unlike in the past after she'd found a body, she was able to think clearly, without the mantle of disorientation hanging over her like a stifling shroud.

But that didn't change the fact that she'd overslept.

"Sit down with me," her mom said as Violet poured hot coffee into a travel mug.

"I can't, Mom," she answered hastily, reaching into the fridge to pull out the creamer. "If I don't get going, I'll be late."

But her mom didn't relent, and as Violet swirled the vanilla-flavored liquid into her mug, she saw her mom reach out and pat the stool beside her at the kitchen counter. "Don't give me that. You can spare a minute." When Violet opened her mouth to argue, her mom insisted, her voice leaving no wiggle room. "It wasn't a request, Vi."

Violet exhaled dramatically, but dropped her backpack and slouched onto the seat. "Happy now? What's up?" she sighed, wondering if her parents had finally had enough of her sneaking in at all hours.

"Nothing really." Her mom blew on her tea, steam drifting up lazily from the delicate teacup with pink and yellow rosebuds painted on it. But Violet wasn't fooled by the cavalier attitude. *Nothing* was the last thing this was; otherwise she'd already be out the door and on her way to school. "I just wanted to check in. See how things are going. You've been working a lot lately and we haven't seen much of you. Is it so strange that I'd want to know if everything's all right?"

Violet flashed her mom a skeptical frown, and then grinned. "What's the matter, Mom? Do you miss me?"

Her mom shot a humorless glance her way. "Of course I do. Does that really surprise you?" Then her lips curved into a wan smile—weak at best—and Violet realized she really *was* worried. "I just want to make sure Sara's keeping up her end of our arrangement. That she's keeping you safe."

"Haven't you asked her yourself when you've called to check in?" Violet didn't see the point in pretending she didn't know about the almost daily phone calls.

18

Her mom's eyebrows lifted and she studied her daughter as she set her teacup down on the table. "Of course I've asked her, but now I'm asking you."

They stared at each other for a long, strained moment, Violet thinking it should bother her that her parents were checking up on her. She was seventeen years old and deserved more freedom than that, didn't she? But then she remembered what she'd done last night, in the warehouse. And she couldn't help wondering if Sara had already told her mother.

Maybe her mom was right to be concerned.

"Everything's okay," Violet finally promised, smiling a little too eagerly, but feeling the beginnings of a headache coming on. She resisted the urge to press her fingers against her temples. "There are a lot of people looking out for me, Sara included. They won't let anything happen."

Her mom's gaze narrowed as she studied her daughter, and Violet felt like a fraud. What if Sara couldn't always keep her safe? What if Dr. Lee couldn't teach her to control her *gift*? What if she put herself in danger again?

She thought of the girl in the freezer as she wrapped her hands around the travel mug filled with hot coffee, trying to chase away the bitter chill that slid through her veins at the thought.

Violet lagged behind the other girls who'd left the locker room. She'd changed slowly, pretended to forget something in her locker, and now, as she sat on the sidelines of the gymnasium watching everyone as they paired up, she dropped down and retied her shoes for the fifth time. They were probably the best-tied shoes in the gym by now.

Basketball wasn't exactly Violet's thing. She knew she was just as likely to injure herself trying to play a game of one-on-one as she was trying to locate the echoes of the dead. Maybe more so.

And unfortunately, everyone else knew it too.

Today, at least, they were only doing drills. No one-on-ones, scrimmages, or team play. Just plain old, ordinary drills. She could handle that, couldn't she?

But even now, Violet watched as the girl with the back brace for scoliosis picked someone else to be her partner. And, one by one, everyone around her paired up, until Violet was the only one left standing.

Violet left her spot on the white line and eased closer to Chelsea. "Come on, you guys, can't I just play with you?" She hated that she was whining, but she hated it even more that she was a basketball leper. Chelsea ignored her as she and Jules executed perfect, high-velocity chest passes between the two of them. Violet flinched when the ball came flying back to Chelsea.

Chelsea's lip curled as she caught the ball, and she shook her head at Violet disappointedly. "No. And *that's* why. You're afraid of the ball, Vi. You can't catch it and you can't throw it." Chelsea holstered the ball at her waist and looked dubiously at her friend. "Can you even dribble?"

Violet shrugged. "Not really," she admitted. "But I don't wanna be stuck playing with the coach again. She throws

20

too hard, and she yells at me when I miss. Everyone stares at us."

Chelsea shook her head, launching the ball back at Jules. "I'm sorry, I really am. But you suck at basketball."

Violet did her best not to shrink away this time when the ball came hurtling back to Chelsea, trying to show that she could be part of their team. "*Please.* Just until we start dribbling drills?"

Chelsea closed her eyes as she dropped her chin to her chest. She clutched the ball in both hands and let out a long, dramatic sigh. Violet didn't even need her to answer now—she knew Chelsea was giving in. Chelsea was her best friend, after all, and while she tried to be indifferent—to everything and everyone—Violet knew she couldn't resist her friend's puppy-dog eyes for long. Jules wouldn't be thrilled—Violet would *definitely* slow them down—but if Chelsea agreed, Jules wouldn't argue either.

The whistle sounded, interrupting Chelsea's melodramatic scene.

"Ambrose!" the coach barked out warningly.

Violet's head snapped up as she tried to explain: "I didn't have a partner, and Chelsea and Jules are letting me join them." The last thing she needed was to get in trouble for disrupting drills. It was bad enough that she had no talent on the court; she didn't need to lose points for being a trouble-maker too.

"Well, it looks like it's your lucky day. I found you a partner. Ambrose, Sorrells, pair up!"

21

Violet's stomach sank.

Perky and athletic, Jacqueline Sorrells joined Violet at the line, her gleaming ponytail swaying behind her as her hips wiggled in her snug-fitting gym shorts. "Great," Jacqueline complained. "This is what I get for being late; I get paired with you." She was already holding a basketball and she tossed it gently—as if Violet was somehow handicapped—across the few short feet that separated the two of them. "How's that?" she cooed in baby talk. And when Violet caught the ball, she clapped her hands, her shimmery pink lips squeezed together to form a mock *O*. "What a big girl!"

"Knock it off, Sorrells," Chelsea chimed in from beside Violet as Jacqueline found her spot beside Jules.

Jules stared down at Jacqueline, her eyes narrowing. The look on her face—the unabashed distaste—was more than enough to let the shorter girl know what she thought of her. Jules might not say much, but she gave the best dirty looks, and her support for her friends was unwavering.

Jacqueline tried to glower back but she was no match for Jules, and she was the first to look away. She flipped her ponytail and lifted her hands, signaling to Violet that she was ready.

Violet shoved the ball away from her as hard as she could, trying to mimic what she'd seen Chelsea and Jules doing. The ball was supposed to go straight to her partner, landing directly in Jacqueline's hands—a clean line from one player to another.

Instead, it listed to the right and bounced about four feet in front of her partner.

"Nice job, Special Ed." This time there was no pretend good cheer in the other girl's voice, just bitter sarcasm.

Jacqueline took off after the ball and when she returned, finding her spot again, she shot it straight at Violet, this time holding nothing back.

Violet flinched as much outwardly as she did inwardly, and she fumbled to make the catch but the ball hit her squarely in the chest. On the other side of the key, Jacqueline snickered.

Violet inhaled deeply, getting ready to throw the ball again. But before Violet had the chance to throw it, she watched as a ball—not *her* ball—flew through the air and smacked Jacqueline in the face.

She didn't mean to, but her hand shot up to cover her mouth so no one could see her openmouthed gape as Jacqueline cried out in shock and pain, bending over to cover her nose. Violet had seen exactly where the ball had come from, and she was sure Jacqueline knew too as the cheerleader looked up, accusation in her dark gaze as she noted that neither Chelsea nor Jules had a ball any longer.

Violet's eyes went wide as she turned to Chelsea, who just shrugged. "Oops," was her one-word explanation. And then she jerked her head toward the exit, where the double doors were propped open to let fresh air in the gym. "Your boyfriend's here. You might wanna get him outta here before Sorrells tattles on you to Coach."

Jay stood in the opening, leaning against the doorjamb as he studied her, a grin curving his lips.

Violet glanced to where Coach was already escorting Jacqueline to the locker rooms so she could put some ice on her nose—she wouldn't want one of her star cheerleaders to swell or bruise—so Violet took her opportunity to jog over to the entrance.

"What are you doing here?" she asked, looking around to see if anyone was watching them. "Shouldn't you be in Chem?"

"Yeah, but this is way more entertaining than the covalent bonds. I can't stay long, though, I'm supposed to be getting my homework from my locker."

Violet grimaced. "*Ugh!* How much did you see?"

Jay's eyes glinted knowingly. "Enough to know you probably shouldn't be playing any sport that involves a ball."

Trying to defend her athleticism was pointless, Violet realized, her shoulders deflating. They both knew he was right. She'd stopped playing softball in junior high when it had become clear to everyone she was afraid of the ball and had no other redeeming skills, like hitting or pitching. "Yeah, I guess I should just stick to running, something I can do alone."

"And without a ball."

She punched him in the arm. "Yes. *Without* a ball." But she had to bite her lip to stop herself from giggling.

Jay reached out and absently wrapped one of Violet's curls around his finger as he changed the subject. "I missed you this morning."

"I know, I didn't hear my alarm go off so I got up late."
She pointed to her ears. "I had my headphones in."

She didn't have to explain and he moved in closer, his
voice dropping. "Did something happen last night? Were
you listening to those things your shrink gave you again?"
He looked at her more closely, examining her for signs of
strain.

Glancing up, she met his worried gaze. "Yeah," she
admitted. "I found a girl last night—a body. But it's okay. I
feel . . ." Her brow furrowed as she tried to put it into words.
"I don't know . . . not terrible, I guess." A nervous laugh
bubbled from her lips. Since when did "not terrible" become
the gold standard she aspired to?

"So you think this shrink stuff is really working?" She
ignored the skepticism in his voice. For the most part, he'd
been pretty supportive of her work with the team, not com-
plaining too much about the time she'd been spending with
them as she tried to figure out if her ability was truly useful
or not. Especially how much time she spent with Rafe. But
she knew how he felt about her seeing a psychiatrist: She
didn't need therapy; there wasn't anything wrong with her.
He thought it was a waste of time for her to see a doctor
whose job it was to treat "crazy people."

Violet couldn't help finding it sweet that he didn't consider her at least a little crazy, her being the girl who found
dead bodies and all. That was enough to unbalance anyone,
wasn't it?

She nodded. "I do, Jay. I don't know that I've ever felt
this *in control* before a body was buried."

Jay mulled that over for a second, and then asked, "Is this a case you're working on"—his eyes shifted around, making sure no one was listening to them—"with your team?"

Violet thought about the prickling sensation and squeezed her fists. "You know I'm not supposed to talk about it." She nudged him with her shoulder then, and grinned deliberately up at him. "But yeah, it is."

Behind her, she heard the coach's whistle and knew she'd run out of time. The idea of going back to basketball drills made her stomach tighten, but she stood up on her tiptoes and leaned into Jay, whispering against his cheek. "I got your note last night. Would've been better if I'd have found *you* in my bed instead."

Jay groaned and grabbed her by the shoulders. There was the hint of accusation buried behind his breathy chuckle as he set her away from him. "You're playing with fire, Vi. You shouldn't tease me at school. Besides, I think if I hid in your room, your father—check that, *your mother*—would skin me alive."

Violet heard the coach shouting her name, and she knew she'd be getting a demerit for slacking off. But she didn't care.

She flashed him her most wolfish smile. "Next time, you should totally take that chance. It could've been fun," she promised before sauntering away.

ATTRACTION

HE SAT AT THE TABLE IN THE CORNER, KEEPING
*his head low, his eyes down. He didn't want to draw attention. Not
today. Not yet. Not because he didn't want to be seen, but because
it didn't matter. Even if they saw him, they wouldn't be worried.*

*He took a bite of his sandwich, turkey on whole wheat, hold the
mayo. Same thing he'd ordered every day for the past week. Same
order, same restaurant, same table. He set the sandwich down again
and lifted the newspaper, holding it in front of his face as he dared a
quick glance at the girl behind the counter.*

*She smiled sheepishly at the man she was helping, her gaze
darting away quickly when he smiled back at her, her hand nervously
lifting to tuck a nonexistent stray hair behind her ear as she turned
to get his change.*

Even from where he sat, he recognized the gesture, the difficulty maintaining eye contact, the awkward glances and tight-lipped smiles. The girl was shy—painfully so.

That's what made her perfect for him. That's why he'd been coming here, day after day, working so hard to make her notice him, to make her comfortable with him. Hoping to coax a real smile from her. An effortless, carefree smile.

He understood her. He could help her. If she let him, he might even be able to fix her.

Still, he hated watching as her hands brushed over theirs, as they passed her money and credit cards and she handed them coffees and bags filled with pastries and sandwiches. He felt an instant surge of jealousy. It was familiar and deep and painful. That was the same, too, the resentment he felt when he watched her interact with the customers.

No, not all the customers—the men who came in to see her. He didn't know why she encouraged them, why she let them come, time and again. Why she tried so hard to smile at them, when he knew . . . that what she really wanted was him.

The newsprint crumpled in his fists, and he dropped his gaze again, breathing deeply, reminding himself that this was her job. Reminding himself that she had to make a living.

He glanced up again, quickly, briefly, feeling relieved as he saw the man take his white paper bag and step away from the counter.

He had no business being jealous, he told himself. She didn't belong to him. It wasn't like she was his girlfriend or anything.

His girlfriend was gone. He'd broken up with her, and now he was alone again. Probably why he was feeling so lonely, so bitter.

He took another bite of his sandwich, setting the newspaper aside, but just for the moment.

He suddenly felt claustrophobic within the space of the café, like he needed to get outside. He felt anxious thinking about the girl behind the counter, thinking about his ex-girlfriend, and glancing at the front page of the paper out of the corner of his eye. He stared instead at his lap, trying to get his emotions back under control.

And that was when he saw it, the flash of pale purple beneath his right thumbnail. He couldn't believe he hadn't noticed it before, that he'd missed it when he was cleaning up.

Keeping his hands hidden beneath the table, he used the nail of his left index finger to dig at the polish, cursing himself for being so careless, so reckless. He hoped that no one else had noticed it. He ran through the list of people he'd come in contact with already that day.

He retraced his steps in his head, trying to remember who he'd spoken to, who might have had the opportunity to see his hands up close.

His eyes shot upward, widening—a little too much at first— and then he narrowed them, keeping them trained on her, the girl behind the counter. Had she seen it? Did she notice the sliver of nail polish he'd forgotten to scrub away?

It was then that she looked up at him, and for a moment time seemed to freeze as they stayed like that, staring at each other. His heart was racing as his mind worried over what she might have witnessed. And then her lips parted, her brown eyes fastened on his, sparkling as she smiled at him. Fully. Without inhibition.

It was the loveliest of smiles.

His mouth curved in response, daringly. Boldly. Telling her that *he, too, was ready, even as his heart hammered recklessly.*

She involuntarily licked her lips, reaching up to tuck that invisible strand again, before turning back to the next customer in line. He knew he was still smiling, but he couldn't help himself. It was soon—too soon after his breakup—but there was no accounting for love, after all, was there?

When he was sure he'd scraped away every last trace of the shimmering purple lacquer, he carefully folded his newspaper and tucked it beneath his arm. He was done here for now. He would have to come back later, when the girl's shift was over. Maybe he could even have a chat with her. Maybe they'd hit it off.

Maybe it was time for him to get a new girlfriend.

CHAPTER 3

VIOLET GLANCED AT THE ASSORTMENT OF SCIence journals and *National Geographics* on the table in front of her. She always wondered why doctors and dentists didn't fill their waiting rooms with more interesting reading material like fashion magazines or entertainment news. Even tabloids would be better than the assortment in front of her. It looked like school . . . on steroids. She reached for a copy of *Scientific American* with a cover article about dark matter, and she absently flipped through the pages, not really noticing them.

A faint headache pulsed at her temples and she knew what it was . . . it had been there all day, taunting her. Just enough discomfort to remind her that she wasn't entirely in control of her ability. Which was why, of course, she was sitting here now, at the appointment Sara had scheduled for her for this afternoon. Violet knew Sara only had her best interests in mind. That she wanted Violet to be safe. And *safe* meant learning to curb her impulses . . . to stop the echoes from consuming her, especially in the days after finding a body.

Dr. Lee opened the door to his office and poked his head out. "Ready?"

Violet tried not to sound too morose as she muttered, "As I'll ever be, I suppose." She dropped the magazine back on the coffee table as she got up to follow him.

Inside his office, she went to her usual spot, a chair across from the couch and adjacent to Dr. Lee's. Funny how they'd already established a routine after only a few sessions. Funny, too, how Violet refused to sit on the worn leather couch, no matter how inviting it looked. Somehow the couch made it feel more . . . *shrink*like.

Dr. Lee gave Violet an easy smile as he crossed his legs, setting her file aside and giving her the impression he'd just been brushing up on her case. "How are you today, Violet?"

There was no point mincing words—wasn't it kind of his job to know if she wasn't being completely honest? "A little better today. The breathing exercises and CDs have helped, but I'm still feeling . . . uneasy."

He settled back but his eyes never left her face. His bushy, salt-and-pepper eyebrows drew together. "And when did this *uneasiness* begin?"

Violet smiled. It felt like a dance they did. He, pretending he didn't know about the body in the warehouse, that he wasn't in contact with Sara at every turn. And she, pretending she didn't know he knew.

"Yesterday," she answered. "I found a body yesterday."

"Murdered?"

There was no need to nod—he already knew the answer—but she did anyway.

"A girl. Stuffed in a freezer in an old warehouse. We found her last night. We were following up on an anonymous tip that she was in the area."

Dr. Lee pressed the fingertips of both hands together. "Yes. I saw the story about her in the paper. Did you see it?"

Violet shook her head. Even if she read the paper, she would've avoided it today, not wanting to see anything about the girl. Sometimes rehashing things like that made it worse for her.

He considered her response the way he seemed to consider everything—patiently, thoughtfully—his foot bobbing up and down in an even rhythm. Violet concentrated on the toe of his shoe. White sneakers. Practical, but not very professional. She wondered if Dr. Lee dressed out of comfort or in a conscious effort to put his patients at ease. Maybe he thought a suit and tie would make him seem stuffy and unapproachable.

"Did anyone happen to mention how long until she'd be buried?" he asked, understanding that that would bring Violet peace—real peace—at last.

"Sara said that as soon as they could confirm the girl's

33

identity and perform the autopsy, then she could be released to her family. That way they can make funeral arrangements."

"And then you'll be . . . better?" He'd asked these questions before, and Violet suspected he'd be asking them each time this topic came up.

"Pretty much." She shrugged.

He smiled. "But not all the way?"

She chewed the inside of her cheek, drawing a deep breath. "It'll just happen again, the next time a body . . ." She shifted, anxious about which word to use. She wondered if she'd ever get used to talking about it. ". . . you know, *calls* for me."

His head bobbed now, matching the tempo of his foot. "And that bothers you?"

Violet wasn't sure how to answer. It's not like she'd never considered the question before: Did it bother her to find those who'd been killed? Would she rather not be drawn to unsettled bodies? That depended, she supposed. She liked helping, being useful, and the team had given her the ability to do some good with her strange talent. And she didn't *mind* the dead, necessarily; they certainly deserved to be at peace.

But would she rather be like everyone else? Maybe.

Probably.

She picked at a hangnail on her index finger, making it worse when she tried to rip it free and leaving an angry red strip of raw skin in its place. "I don't know," was all she could come up with for a response.

Dr. Lee let it pass. "Okay. Well, how's everything else going this week? Anything happening at home? Is there anything with your friends or your boyfriend that you want to talk about?"

This time the smile was genuine and Violet's cheeks flushed as her eyes lifted to meet Dr. Lee's gaze. "Everything's good. Really good. Especially with Jay. He gets me, you know?"

"And you mentioned before that he knows about what you can do?" He'd picked up her file and was leafing through it now, looking at old notes he'd written. "You two have known each other since you were seven?"

She nodded. "He's the only one of my friends I've ever told."

Dr. Lee leaned forward, his pale eyes intense. "So you trust him with your secrets?"

There was a note in his voice, something that made Violet hesitate as she tried to place it. "Completely. Jay would never betray me."

"What about other people's secrets? Have you told him about the team? What the others can do?"

Violet stiffened now, wondering what Dr. Lee was insinuating. Did he think Violet was revealing top-secret information to Jay? She understood that she needed to be discreet; Sara had been more than clear that what they did at the Center was confidential.

"He knows I'm working with Sara, but he doesn't know

what I'm doing. Or what anyone else is doing either. I haven't told him *anything*." She hated feeling like her loyalty was being questioned. Dr. Lee was supposed to be helping her. He was supposed to be on *her* side, wasn't he?

His face smoothed over once more, his expression becoming placid, unruffled. He was obviously satisfied by her answer and he leaned back, running his palm over his too-crisp, too-blue jeans as if there may have been a wrinkle that needed straightening. "What about the other team members? You've said before that you don't think some of them care much for you. Do you still feel as if you're having trouble fitting in?"

Violet was flustered by the change of topic, and she wondered if her confusion—and her misgivings about his questions—were simply other side effects from the dead girl she'd discovered the day before. Clarity wasn't exactly her strong suit in the wake of finding a body.

Besides, she supposed it was Dr. Lee's job to dig into her personal life, to pry. And she reminded herself that he *had* been making things easier for her.

An image of Gemma flashed through Violet's mind. Gemma Kidder was the one team member who had gone out of her way to make Violet feel unwelcome in the two months since Violet had joined their group. Violet kept hoping that something would change between them, that maybe Gemma was one of those people who had a hard time warming up to new people, and that eventually her cool exterior would thaw and they'd find a way to get along. Or at least be civil to each other.

But so far, all she'd gotten from Gemma were icy stares and cold shoulders.

On the flip side, there were Sam and Krystal and Rafe.

Violet didn't know Sam all that well yet—she'd only met him a few times—but what she knew of him, she liked. With Krystal, it was different. She'd felt that instant connection. In some ways, Krystal reminded Violet of her best friend, Chelsea. Well, in the sense that she was loud and sort of obnoxious. But that was pretty much where the similarities ended. Where Chelsea didn't mind being thought of as overbearing—and probably tried to be, for the most part— Krystal was oblivious to it. She would probably feel terrible if she realized how disruptive she tended to be. Even when she was trying to be quiet, Violet realized early on that Krystal seemed to be almost incapable of whispering. Add that to her loud sense of style—her constantly changing hair colors and lipsticks, her brightly colored tights and biker boots, and multiple ear and eyebrow piercings—and Krystal stood out like a sore thumb. But she was also very calming. Her presence was reassuring, soothing. It was a strange combination.

Rafe, on the other hand, was not soothing. His intense blue eyes made her feel like he could look right through her, boring into her whenever he watched her. And even now, her fingers tingled as if they'd just brushed against him, despite the fact that he was nowhere near. . . . That phantom spark.

What was that all about anyway? That static she felt whenever their skin met? She didn't understand it, yet she knew she wasn't the only one aware of it. Rafe had to sense it too. She'd seen it in his reaction, watched him flinch in response. But neither of them ever mentioned it, like an unspoken secret.

"It's better," Violet lied. "I think I was just nervous at first." She purposely avoided saying Gemma's name. She didn't want to talk about her; she'd had enough drama for one day, she thought, recalling the incident in PE with Jacqueline.

Gemma was another matter altogether, but Violet was sure she could handle the situation on her own. She certainly didn't want to tattle to the team's shrink about it.

"And Sara?"

He was definitely covering all the bases. "Sara's fine," Violet assured him. "She's easy to work with, and I trust her. That's important to me."

He tipped his chin forward, a curt nod. "All right, then, back to this uneasiness you're feeling. What about sleep, Violet? Can you sleep when you're feeling this way?"

Normally she couldn't, but with Dr. Lee's help—using the CDs he'd made for her—she had. This was new.

Still, she had to admit she didn't feel totally rested. "I did, but I'm still exhausted," she finally admitted, sighing as she said it. "I dreamed about her . . . the girl."

He studied Violet, and then stood and went to his desk. Pulling a set of keys from his pocket, he unlocked a drawer and reached inside. When he returned, he held his hand out to her, giving her a transparent brown prescription bottle. "These will help. Take one if you have trouble again tonight.

It won't do you any good to lose sleep." Then he scribbled on a pad of notebook paper before tearing a sheet free. "Here's a prescription for more if you need them. If your parents have questions, they can call me," he explained, handing her another one of his business cards. He scrawled a phone number on the back. "And this is my mobile number, in case it's after hours." His eyes held hers. "You can use the number, too, Violet. For anything. At any time."

Violet nodded as she slipped both the note and the bottle into her pocket.

Sleep would be good, she decided. Sleep might be just what she needed.

Violet stood outside, watching as the lights went out, row by row, inside the auto parts store where Jay worked. She probably should've felt guilty about showing up unannounced, but truthfully, she didn't. The only thing she felt was that familiar thrum of anticipation in the pit of her stomach whenever she was about to see Jay. When the door finally opened and she heard the key slide into the lock, she smiled, stepping out of the shadows.

"Jesus, Vi, you scared the crap outta me!" Jay jolted, but even in the washed-out light coming from the store's sign, Violet could see the easy smile that found his lips as he stuffed the bulky store keys in his pocket. "Although I have to admit I knew you wouldn't be able to stay away."

She made a face at him. "Whatever! You don't know anything." She lifted both hands in front of her, as if he hadn't already seen the two cups she was holding, her version of a romantic gesture. They were Jay's favorite, cherry Slurpees from the 7-Eleven. Violet always teased him about having such simple taste, but secretly, she loved them too. Drinking the red, slushy drinks reminded her of the long summer days they'd spent loitering on the hot blacktop parking lot in front of the run-down convenience store, waiting for something interesting to happen. But it was Buckley, after all, and the best thing that ever happened was a street race between two hotheaded teens trying to show off for a girl. Or maybe a shoplifting incident during which the police would be called. Every so often it was her uncle who would show up, and she and Jay would talk him into giving them a ride in his police cruiser to town where they would hang out in the park instead.

Jay grinned, reaching for one of the cups. Violet sat down on the curb, just like they used to do as kids, and lifted her straw to her lips.

"I'm glad you came," he said, serious now, following her lead and dropping onto the curb beside her.

Violet leaned against him, just enough so their shoulders were touching, and she felt a different kind of spark, the kind forged from years of connection. This was where she belonged. This was where she should always be. With Jay.

"So how was your appointment? With the shrink?" He was frowning as he stared down at her, his lips already turning red from his drink. His face was creased with worry.

"It was good," she said, taking a long pull from her own

straw and swirling the sweet, syrupy ice around her tongue. "It—it helped to talk to him." She didn't tell Jay about the pills Dr. Lee had given her, the ones in her pocket, pressed against her thigh at this very moment. Pills felt like failure to her. Like admitting she couldn't handle this on her own. That willpower wasn't enough . . . even though, clearly, it wasn't. "But, you know, I still don't feel great. I was hoping that seeing you might make things . . ." A tiny smile tugged at her lips as she shrugged. ". . . better," she finished.

She knew he'd understand what she was telling him: that the echo of the dead girl was weighing on her still.

After a hesitant pause, Jay set the wax-coated cup on the sidewalk next to him. He leaned down and pressed the barest whisper of a kiss against the top of Violet's dark curls. Despite the icy sensation of his lips, heat unfurled in Violet's belly, licking through her. "I hate this, you know." Absently, he reached for her hand, lifting it and flipping it over as he studied her palm. His thumb ran along the grooves there, and then his eyes moved up to meet hers. "I hate that you have to do all this without me. Maybe it would be better if you spent less time there . . . *with them*."

Violet wished he'd just say it, what he really meant. "He's not that bad, Jay. He's just trying to help." She knew that neither of them was talking about Dr. Lee now. This was about Rafe.

She looked at him, taking in a face that was almost more familiar to her than her own. His golden features, his warm eyes, his slightly too-long hair with the faintest curls

41

dropping past the tops of his ears and brushing his neck. He looked so hurt, so vulnerable, and she blamed herself.

He touched her cheek, his hand as cool as his lips had been. "I just worry that he's careless. I don't know if I trust him, Vi."

"He saved me once. What more do you want?"

"I want to know that he'd protect you the way I would if something happens. That he has your best interests in mind." And then he sighed, a ragged, defeated sound. He ran his hand through his already rumpled hair. "That's a lie. I want my girlfriend to stop spending so much time with another guy. I wanna know that you two don't share some sort of bond because of what you can do. But what I really want is to know that he doesn't have feelings for you."

Violet was speechless. She had no idea how—or what—to say to any of that. She could defend her relationship with Rafe by saying that they only worked together, but it wouldn't matter. Partly because she'd be lying. Of course they shared a bond, one Jay would never truly understand. And she certainly wasn't going to quit the team because of that.

But it was that last part, the thing about Rafe having feelings for her, that really made her pause. Rafe didn't *like* her, not in the way Jay meant.

Fortunately for Violet, she didn't have to speak because Jay wasn't finished yet. "But, honestly, you know what bothers me more than anything?" She shook her head, and he continued, his voice so low it sounded like a whisper

42

rumbling up from his heart. "It's that I can't do anything for you when you're in this kind of pain, Vi."

Eyes wide now, Violet released the shaky breath she'd been holding.

Jay leaned forward, resting his forehead against hers while he scooped up both of her hands and squeezed them tight. As their breath mingled Violet wondered when she'd set her own cup down. They remained there like that—like marble sculptures—frozen nose-to-nose, mouth-to-mouth.

Then she felt his lips move against hers, and she closed her eyes when he whispered, "I wish I could make things better. I wish I could stop you from hurting."

Speechless, Violet tipped her head back, just enough so that their lips were no longer just brushing, so she could *make* him kiss her. She needed to taste him, to draw strength from him as she pressed herself nearer to him, straining to be closer still. She freed one hand from his and cupped the back of his neck, her fingers digging into his hair, telling him—without words—not to pull away.

He kissed her back, in response to her restless request, giving her only what she needed. He stayed cool and restrained, never pushing her for anything more than what she asked for.

Violet's toes curled inside her shoes and she wished that they were somewhere, anywhere, besides sitting on the edge of the sidewalk in front of the auto parts store. Finally, when she peeled her cherry-flavored lips from his, they still burned from his touch. "You do make things better," she exhaled, her voice sounding faraway even to herself. "You make me feel . . . *normal*."

Jay laughed, hauling Violet against his chest. She felt safe with his hands spanning her back. "And that's good?" he laughed. "Most people want to be anything but normal."

Listening to the rhythm of his heart, she smiled, feeling the deep fog lift from around her, over her, as she concentrated—focused—just like Dr. Lee had taught her. "Trust me, normal's good. Very, very good."

She felt suddenly shy about what she was about to ask but she let the words tumble from her lips anyway. "Can we go back to your house for a while?"

Jay squeezed tighter, his arms still wrapped around her with the unspoken promise of never letting her go. "For as long as you want, Violet."

EXCLUSIVITY

IT HAD BEEN HARD TO WAIT ALL DAY. HE'D BEEN impatient, anxious. Excited.

He loved that butterfly feeling deep in the pit of his stomach, the fluttering sensation that came with the birth of each new relationship. He felt giddy just thinking about her, dizzy with the anticipation of every new first they would soon share as a couple.

The first time their eyes would meet, and hold—ripe with understanding. The moment their skin would graze—accidentally at first, and then once more, with purpose. Their first kiss—tentative and slow, and then again more passionately.

All of those firsts they had to look forward to . . .

He watched as she opened the back door to the café, the one leading to the alley where her car was parked, just as she did at the end of each shift. Though it was barely dark yet, her gaze flitted in every direction, watchful. Wary.

She wasn't stupid; he would never have chosen a stupid girl-friend. As she released the café door behind her, he saw that she gripped her keys in her fist, a defensive maneuver that he easily recognized.

Definitely not a dumb girl, *he thought, smiling to himself.*

She darted quickly, her footsteps purposeful, determined. It was less than fifteen paces to her car—he knew because he'd already counted them—and he watched as she reached it easily while he stayed low, tucked away in the shadows and out of sight.

He waited until she was safely inside, keeping his breathing low and in check, until he heard the click of her locks. Until he knew she felt safe.

Now all he had to do was wait for his part.

Listening, he heard her engine struggling to catch. Trying and trying again, she turned her ignition. Without even peeking, he could picture her pleading with her car to start.

But it wouldn't start. Not tonight.

After a few minutes, he stepped out from the shadows, his back-pack slung over his shoulder. He knew how he looked from her vantage point: He was just an ordinary guy—a student, probably—parked in the same lot she was.

He had to be careful, to time his actions perfectly:

First, he ignored her, pretended he didn't realize her predicament as he unlocked his own car.

Second, he started his engine. No problem there. His ignition switch was fine.

And then, just as he was about to go, to leave the girl stranded, he had a change of heart. Lucky for her.

When he reached the last step, the crucial one that would bring his plan home, he turned his car off and got back out. Lifting a hand, he waved uncertainly as he made his way timidly across the lot. "Sorry. I don't mean to pry, but it looks like you might need a hand." He stayed back, though. Far enough so she'd feel comfortable, so she felt like she was the one in control.

At first she hesitated. But then, even though she didn't actually voice it, the sudden shift in her expression said it all . . . the slight lift at the corner of her mouth, a hesitant smile. She recognized him.

It was a positive first step in their budding relationship.

She rolled down her window, watching him with her big, trusting brown eyes. Another first. "It won't start," she explained. She leaned forward now, feeling more comfortable.

He thought about it for several seconds, not wanting to appear too eager, too desperate, and then finally, he said, "I'd offer to take a look, but . . ." He smiled sheepishly. "I don't know a thing about cars. The best I can do is call you a tow truck." He pulled out his cell phone.

She wrinkled her nose. "I have my phone. You don't have to . . ."

He glanced around at the alley, wearing a practiced expression of concern. "At least let me wait with you."

She looked too, her brow creasing as her hand shot up to her neck, nervously fingering the necklace she wore . . . a vintage locket with a small pearl inset at its center. He knew the look on her face: She was worried about what—or who—might be out there. In the shadows. "Are you sure?" she asked at last. "I don't want to put you out."

He just smiled at her, telling her in their new implicit way that it was fine. "How about you buy me a coffee next time I come in?"

Her lids lowered and he could practically hear her thoughts: He remembers me too. "Yes . . . next time. Of course."

Satisfaction coursed through him: Next time would have been their second date.

Except that the moment she unlocked the passenger side door to let him in, the date had become unnecessary. She'd just agreed to take their relationship to a whole new level. She'd just agreed to become his.

He reached across then, surprising her as he threw himself on top of her. He cupped his hand over her face as he held her down, covering her mouth and nose with the plain white cloth he'd been clutching in his fist.

She struggled—they always struggled—but in that moment, their eyes met, and held.

He wondered whose heart beat faster, harder, as he leaned closer. "Shhh," he crooned, pressing the cloth firmer against her face. Her eyes widened in response, and he knew that she'd understood his unspoken reassurance, he knew that already they were developing a wordless rapport.

He held her like that, embracing her until she stopped struggling, until she relaxed, succumbing to his adoration, his devotion. Until she accepted that she belonged to him.

Then he gently unbuckled her and carried her to his car. He tucked a loose strand of hair behind her ear for her, just as he knew *she'd have done. And when he leaned in close, his lips hovering right above her cheek, his heart fluttered and his stomach tightened. It was another first: the kiss.*

He pressed his lips to her cheek, savoring the sensation of her soft skin beneath his mouth. It was warm, soft, supple.

He could hardly wait until she kissed him back.

CHAPTER 4

SOMETIMES VIOLET FELT LIKE A FRAUD, LIVING A double life the way she did. One part of her life was so normal, her days filled with school and homework, family and friends. The other half was riddled with secrecy and death. This had definitely been one of those days, as she'd been forced to sit through World History listening to Ms. Ritke's lecture about Charlotte of Belgium's tragic life, wondering how much hair spray it took to keep the teacher's tall bouffant from losing its shape. Ms. Ritke was a student favorite and taught history as if she were giving a recap of her favorite soap opera, not focus-ing on dates and locations, but including all of the scandalous details like affairs, conspiracies, and incest.

But even Ms. Ritke hadn't been enough to hold Violet's interest after she'd gotten the text from Sara:

Need you at the Center. Can you come after school?

She didn't tell Sara that she'd come whenever she asked. How could she not? If it hadn't been for Sara and Rafe, Violet probably would've been killed that night at the cabin, when Mike and Megan's dad had discovered she'd known the truth about how his wife had died. She owed her life to them.

But it was more than just the fact that Sara and Rafe had saved her life that made Violet want to be there, she admitted. There was something about that place—and the team—that made her feel *normal*. Not like such a freak.

Her friends Mike and Megan had moved away after that night at the cabin when their father had confessed to killing their mother and then turned the gun on himself.

But they weren't the only ones whose lives had been changed by the events of that night. Violet's life had changed too.

She had found a home that night. A safe place where she could put her gift to good use. With Sara's team of misfits.

Violet parked her Honda next to Krystal's oversized, gas-guzzling Chevy. It didn't matter that Roxy was about thirty years out of style, or that she took up nearly two parking spaces on her own; the car totally suited Krystal's eclectic style.

She navigated the nondescript hallway that led to the state-of-the-art facility the team referred to as "the Center." If you didn't know better, the building was just another warehouse in the middle of the industrial section of Seattle. But Violet knew better. Holding up her keycard, she waited until the light on the panel outside the inner entrance turned from red to green, signaling that her access had been granted, and she slipped quietly inside.

Everyone was already there, gathered in the oversized space where a cluster of chairs and couches had been pulled together for their meeting. Violet took the opportunity to look around at their group. They were an odd collection, with very few outward similarities.

Gemma was a throwback to old Hollywood glam, and Violet envied the other girl's heart-shaped face, golden blonde hair, and bowed lips that were perpetually painted a vibrant poppy red. She wondered how it was possible that Gemma was only sixteen. But the effect of her doelike brown eyes was lost once you recognized the hardened air she wore like armor. She seemed jaded. Cynical. Caustic.

Or maybe it was only Violet who got that vibe from her.

Her gaze moved to Sam Abolins, the youngest member of the team. He claimed to be *almost* sixteen, but Violet had a hard time believing he was a day over fourteen. Granted, he was tall, but he was too gangly by half . . . still waiting for puberty to fill out his lanky body. In the two months she'd been with her new team, Violet had only met Sam a handful of times, most of those during the first investigation she'd been involved in, an arson case. It had been awkward for Violet since she was brand-new, and her ability hadn't been useful. But unlike Gemma, Sam had made it easy for her, making an effort at small talk and trying to make Violet feel welcome. Violet had watched him then, as he'd touched the charred remains from the fire when they were brought into the Center, his face twisted in concentration.

Now Violet saw Krystal standing in the space they called the break room. She was just closing the door of the industrial-sized refrigerator when she noticed Violet at the entrance and her mouth split into a wide grin. "What took you so long? We were waiting for you," she whisper-yelled as she popped open a bottle of sparkling water. Violet wondered if she actually thought no one else could hear her, even when everyone stopped what they were doing and looked up at her.

"You know, school," Violet answered, doing her best to ignore the look of disgust Gemma shot her from her place on the couch. She made her way as inconspicuously as she could to where the rest of the team was gathered, hoping not to draw any more unwanted attention.

"Yeah, well, maybe if you didn't live so far away, you'd be here on time like the rest of us," Rafe said, his voice quiet and mocking as Violet took the open spot next to him. "Nice entrance, by the way. Way to be low-key."

Violet made a face at him as Sara gave her a brief nod and flipped through a manila file. "Now that everyone's here, let's get started." Violet cringed at the reminder that they'd all been forced to wait for her. "Here's what we know so far. . . ." Sara's voice began in its usual controlled and clipped way—what Violet considered her work voice. "The police

53

have confirmed that the girl Violet found was Antonia Cornett. She'd been missing for almost two weeks." Sara pulled a photo from her file and handed it to Sam, who was sitting in the seat closest to her. "Her friends called her Toni."

Sam studied the picture for a moment before passing it to Gemma.

"I've also been told that she's not this guy's first victim. In fact, the police are dubbing him 'the collector.' Apparently, this is the third body they've found in this condition."

Violet wondered if she'd missed something, and she raised her hand uncertainly.

Her lips turning up slightly, Sara shook her head. "Violet, this isn't school. If you have a question, just ask."

Violet dropped her hand, her cheeks flushing. "Sorry. What did you mean by *in this condition*? What condition was she in?"

Sara nodded as she explained to the group. "Apparently his MO is to try to preserve the bodies. The first two times he used large coolers, but this time . . ." She looked at Violet again. "Well, you saw, he put her in a freezer instead. Since there was no power and it was still cold, it was obvious it hadn't been there long. The girls are killed by suffocation; there are signs of strangulation. But each of them is treated with the same care: hair washed and styled, nails freshly painted, makeup applied, and clothes immaculately cleaned and pressed. Like they've just gotten ready for a date."

Violet felt sick. Whoever this guy was, he was clearly spending far too much time with the bodies *after* they'd died.

She couldn't help wondering what else he'd done with them.

Shuddering at the thought, she curled her feet beneath her and glanced up at the skylights in the ceiling. The sun was moving down the sky, tracing a fiery path toward the waterfront. Already Violet could feel the effects of a restless night catching up with her, and she stifled a yawn with the back of her hand. She blushed again when she caught Rafe watching her. It seemed like he was always watching to see how she was handling all this.

Violet widened her eyes at him, letting him know she was fine. She turned away, forcing herself to focus on Sara's words.

Krystal interrupted then, disruptive and unrepentant as usual. She dropped onto the couch, squeezing into the narrow space between Violet and Rafe without even trying to be quiet, oblivious that she was disturbing anyone. Sara didn't acknowledge the disturbance; she just kept talking like nothing had happened.

"Wow. What a sicko, right?" Krystal tried to whisper. She toyed with one of the clear healing crystals that dangled from a chain around her neck, as if she were rubbing for answers.

Violet kept her voice considerably lower than Krystal's. "Totally."

Sara shot a pointed look at Krystal, and Krystal rubbed her stone even harder. It was on the tip of Violet's tongue to ask if Krystal was her *real* name, or just a nickname because of her belief in the powers of the stones she wore.

She opened her mouth to ask, but Sara drew her interest.

"We have some of Antonia's things—some of her personal effects—if any of you would be willing to stay behind for a bit and check them out for me. Tell me if you sense anything?"

Violet sat up a little straighter, eager for the chance to watch the rest of them in action. Everyone on the team—at least everyone but her—was in some way psychic. They all had certain "sensitivities" to things that weren't *exactly* tangible.

She supposed she did too; her gift just didn't work the same way theirs did. Hers wasn't useful at a moment like this. But that didn't stop her from being fascinated by the others.

"Any chance we can go to her place? Check it out in person?" Rafe asked.

Sara cocked her head, her brows raised. "You think that wasn't my first question?" she asked, addressing Rafe directly. "Sorry. Her home is off-limits. Once the police give us the go-ahead, I'll see if we can schedule a little field trip. But until then, we'll have to make do with what we have."

Violet's part of the investigation had pretty much finished the moment she'd discovered the girl's body in the warehouse. Or at least it was finished until they had a suspect in mind. That was when she could try to match the echoes from the dead girls they'd already discovered to the imprints on whoever might be responsible for killing them. For now, all she could do was stand back and watch while the others did their thing.

She hovered near the edge of the large conference table where Sara placed a cardboard box and opened the flaps. Already several of her teammates were reaching inside, pulling out the girl's belongings. Violet felt like she was eavesdropping on something that they probably didn't share with many outsiders.

This was how it worked for some of them—maybe all of them to some degree, Violet thought as she stood back, watching as items were passed from one set of hands to the next.

Psychometry. It was what she'd seen Sam doing when she'd first met him. Violet had learned the term soon after she'd joined the team, and she'd Googled everything she could about it. From what she'd gathered, it was the ability to "read" the history of an item—or the person who owned the item—simply by touching it. Of course there was nothing "simple" about it. And like her gift, there didn't seem to be a lot of hard and fast rules to it. Each of them seemed to have their own way of doing things. It certainly wasn't a science.

But it had a name, and Violet felt a flash of envy that they, at least, knew what to call their ability. Hers continued to remain nameless. For all she knew, she was unique in her ability to seek out those who'd been murdered.

She eased closer, trying to get a better look at what was happening in front of her, until she unwittingly became part of the circle, handling objects that were passed around. She paid less attention to the personal effects and more attention to those who held them. Beside her, Krystal closed her eyes whenever she was given something, seeming to concentrate on the feel of each item in her hands, while Gemma scrutinized the pieces like a detective, as if she were searching for physical clues that might have been left behind on the objects themselves. Rafe, on the other hand, barely paid attention to any of them—the objects or the others. He was passed an item, glanced haphazardly at it, and then passed it along, almost as if he were playing a bizarre game of hot potato.

From outside the circle, Sara supervised, taking in all their reactions.

Sam caught Violet watching him and he winked at her, catching her off-guard with the gesture. And then he glanced away again, his face almost childlike, right down to the spray of freckles across his nose, as he ran his fingers over an ordinary hairbrush.

Violet watched him as he closed his eyes, concentrating once more. She wondered what he sensed that she didn't.

She reached inside the box for a small photo album with a brushed black velvet cover. She drew it out, untying the satin ribbon that held it closed as she flipped to the first page. Inside, she got her first real glimpse into the girl's life— before it had been stolen away from her.

Antonia Cornett looked barely older than Violet. She was just twenty-one, an art history major at the university. The last time any of her friends had seen her alive was just two weeks earlier, when she was leaving the off-campus rental house she shared with her best friend to go to class.

Violet studied Antonia's big brown eyes and her thick curtain of dark hair, and wondered if she looked like the other girls who'd been discovered before her. The ones they suspected had been murdered by the same person.

As she looked at the smiling images in the photo album, it was hard not to notice how pretty the girl was. There was a quiet sort of laughter in her eyes, buried behind her shy smiles. But what really struck Violet was that this was a girl who'd had friends, a family . . . a life.

Her heart ached. People missed her, this girl. And whoever the killer was, he'd taken her away from them. Violet wished she could do more to help her team find him, to stop him from doing this to anyone else's daughter . . . sister . . . friend.

She closed the book and glanced up to find Rafe watching her just as she felt a tear slip down her cheek. She hadn't even realized she'd been crying.

She watched as he tucked something into his pocket, something small and silver. She swiped at her face with the back of her hand and pretended not to notice the concern on his face as she turned away again, setting the album aside. This was hard, she realized, peering into the private life of a dead girl. It was one thing to find her body, to know where she'd been discarded by her killer. It was another thing altogether to know *her*.

Slipping away from the solemn congregation, Violet

wandered to the kitchen and grabbed a can of Coke from the fridge. She found a chair, one away from the others, and she curled up, tucking her feet protectively beneath her.

"Wanna talk about what happened back there?" Violet glanced up to find Rafe staring back at her. "Did that freak you out? It can be kind of intense."

"No." But the denial came a little too quickly, and then she frowned. Sighing, she chewed on the inside of her cheek. "Sort of, I guess," she admitted hesitantly. Softly. "How do you do it?"

He sat down in the chair across from her, leaning forward on his elbows and studying her intently. "Do what?" His quiet voice was even quieter now, an uncertain breeze.

"Try to understand them? Try to get inside their heads?" she whispered.

"Who? The killers, or the victims?"

"Either." Violet shrugged.

"It wasn't like I've ever had a choice in the matter," he answered cryptically. And just when Violet thought about asking him to explain what that was supposed to mean, he spoke again, his blue eyes unguarded, his expression almost daring. "I'm guessing that's the way it was with you too. You were never asked whether you wanted to find the dead, were you, V?"

Violet's heart stopped. She felt cornered, like an animal trapped. It was new to her to talk openly about what she could do; the team had given her that. And even though it wasn't yet completely comfortable for her, she was trying.

She shook her head, her unblinking eyes never leaving his.

But she wanted to know more. So much more. "So is that how it works, then? You sense things from touching them?"

"It's different for everyone," Krystal announced as she snuck up on them, seeming to materialize from out of nowhere and dropping onto the arm of Violet's chair. "You know that show *Medium*, where the lady talks with the dead? You know, ghosts and spirits and stuff?" She shrugged. "That's kind of how it is for me."

Violet's face snapped up to meet Krystal's, her expression dubious. "Seriously? I knew you . . . you know, got messages from . . . ." She hesitated, not sure how to word it. "Beyond." It sounded so stupid when she said it out loud that she cringed a little. She tried to shrug it off. "I guess I sorta thought you did what the others do—you know, touch things." She hated the uncertain edge in her voice. Why should she doubt that Krystal could talk to the dead, when she herself could find them by the sensory echoes that were left on their bodies?

Krystal grinned, and Violet could smell the familiar scent of jasmine—Krystal's perfume—as she stared into her dark, honest eyes. Krystal shrugged again. "We all *touch things*, Violet." But the way Krystal said it, was in the most obvious way, as if Violet hadn't meant the whole psychometry thing. "And it's so not as cool as it sounds. Mostly the ghosts or whoever come to me in my dreams. A lot of times I don't even understand what they're trying to tell me. It's all very mysterious. I'd way rather have what Rafe has."

"Which is . . . ?" Violet asked, so curious that she nearly forgot Rafe was sitting right there with them.

"That"—Rafe scowled at Krystal, and Violet got the sense that sharing time was over—"is really no one's business."

Krystal's lip curled as she stared challengingly at Rafe. "By the way, Houdini, I saw what you did back there," Krystal accused. "Don't think you're going without me."

Rafe looked genuinely puzzled by her words. "I don't know what you're talking about."

Violet glanced between them. Rafe's expression remained blank, while Krystal's was impassive, her stare narrowed. "Bull. I saw you slip that key in your pocket, and we both know what it opens. I'm just saying, if you go, I go."

Now Violet was the one who was confused. She'd noticed it too, but she'd been too preoccupied with the fact that Rafe had caught her crying to realize it was a key he'd pressed into his pocket. "What does it open?" she asked, not sure who she expected to answer her.

"Her house," they both said at once.

And then Krystal clarified by adding, "Her front door."

Violet's eyes widened and her voice dropped. "You *stole* the key to Antonia Cornett's house? But Sara said we couldn't go there. You aren't planning on breaking in, are you?" She wanted no part of this, no part of Rafe's stupid plan to break into a victim's home and go through her things without anyone's permission. "You're both crazy."

"V, *wait*." Rafe reached across the space between them and grabbed her arm, closing his hand around the sleeve of her hoodie. "Just hear me out," he begged, his voice softer now, quieter even than usual.

She reluctantly turned to face him. She didn't want to meet his gaze, but she could feel his thoughtful eyes on her, penetrating her, and she couldn't stop herself from glancing upward. She sighed, her only audible response, but it was enough and Rafe knew he had her attention.

"I need to get in there, to see if there's anything . . ." He didn't finish, but his brows drew together and Violet could see he was trying to choose his words carefully. "I want to do whatever I can to help. Hopefully *before* it's too late for someone else."

And that was it, the one thing Violet couldn't do that Rafe and the others could. He and Krystal might actually be able to stop this killer from striking again. They might be able to use their ability to do something good. Something very, *very* good.

Just like Rafe had done for her.

She felt herself waver as she bit her lip. "God, Rafe, I don't know. You could get in so much trouble if you got caught."

His serious expression faded, and even though his voice remained calm and quiet, everything else about him—the mischievous glint in his blue eyes, the half grin that challenged her, the dark slash of his brows—looked defiant and dangerous. "From who? The cops? Sara practically has them eating out of her hand. And what's Sara gonna do, ground me? I don't think so, V. I think Sara wants this info as much as we do. I think if she could give the order herself, she would. She'd probably thank me for going in there to look around."

"Yeah, somehow I doubt that," Violet said.

"So you're coming, right?" he asked.

"I don't know," she answered slowly. It was a terrible idea, but she wanted to know as badly as he did if they could find anything useful.

Rafe and Krystal stared at her, waiting for her to make up her mind.

After a moment, Krystal turned to Rafe again, acting as if Violet didn't exist. "When are we going?"

"I was thinking tonight. That way I can put the key back before anyone realizes it's missing."

"Fine. I'll drive. No way I'm getting on that metal death trap of yours." Violet wanted to shush Krystal, to tell her she was being entirely too loud—especially in light of the fact that they were talking about becoming felons and all.

At last, Violet's voice ripped like dry paper from her throat. "I'm in."

Rafe jumped up from his chair, a wide grin on his face, his teeth a brilliant flash of white. Violet didn't think she'd ever seen him so . . . *so enthusiastic.*

Violet swallowed around the grit forming in her throat, which threatened to smother her if she waited too long to speak again. "I'll meet you in front in five minutes."

UNCERTAINTY

HE STEPPED CAUTIOUSLY INTO HER ROOM, NOT *wanting to disturb her too soon. She needed her rest. He knew she was exhausted.*

It was dark, but the lack of light didn't indicate night or day. It was always dark in here, just the way she liked it.

He stopped briefly, deftly balancing the tray on one hand as he pulled the lighter from his pocket and lit the small candle on the dresser that stood just inside the doorway. The candle's light infiltrated the space, casting flickering shadows over every surface, into every corner. In the pale glow, he could also see that he wasn't disturbing her at all; she was already awake, her eyes wide. Alert.

He balanced the tray in both hands, smiling broadly. "I'd say good morning, except you slept most of the day away. It's dinner-time." He glanced self-consciously at the tray, suddenly nervous, his palms sweating and his heart racing. *"I brought you some soup. I figured you must be starving."*

She didn't answer—not out loud—but he knew she was glad to see him. Her eyes darted around the room, first one way and then the other, searching, appraising.

He followed her gaze as he set the tray on the bedside table and sat on the bed beside her. He took in the details of his handi-work, trying not to smile, reminding himself that too much pride was an ugly trait. *"Do you like what I've done with the place?"* His gaze roamed over the thick black foam that covered the windows and walls, absorbing both sound and light. *"I did it just for you. I wanted you to be comfortable."*

The mattress shuddered violently, and he turned back to look at her, confused. She thrashed wildly, her body convulsing beside him, and he wondered if she was trying to get closer to him. They always did.

But he was worried she might hurt herself, so he leaned down, his lips grazing her ear as he spoke. Her entire body went still, every muscle coiled as she waited on his words. *"Be still now. There's plenty of time for that later. Let's get to know each other better first . . . take things slow."* He sat back, feeling more relaxed know-ing that she was as eager as he was. *"Besides, you don't want to make sores,"* he explained, his fingers gingerly brushing the ropes around her wrists. *"Infections can get nasty if we're not careful. And I don't like infections."*

He couldn't stop himself and he reached for her fingertips,

caressing each one in turn, inspecting the ridges and curves of her nails. "I brought lilac for you. It's a pale shade of purple with just the faintest shimmer." He picked up the bottle of nail polish from beside the bowl of soup and held it up so she could see. He wished he had something more to give her—a gift. He liked to give them gifts. But he'd lost hers and this was all he could offer. "It will be beautiful on you. Now, are you ready for some food?"

She stared at him, her eyes still wide.

He took her silence as consent; she didn't understand the rules yet. "Good, but you need to know. . . ." The warning in his voice was clear. "If you scream, I leave. No food, no water, no . . . treats." He set the polish down with a meaningful crack. "Understood?"

Her brow creased into a frown. She understood.

"Good," he repeated, this time more cheerfully. He freed her mouth and turned to get her some water. They always wanted water first.

That was when he heard her. Her raspy voice warbled behind him as her body went rigid with effort, screaming—or at least trying to. "Help!" she croaked, her parched voice trying to find purchase. "Someone! Please . . . help me . . ." Her last words drifted away on a sob, as she realized, belatedly, that her own voice had failed her.

But he wasn't concerned with her voice, or with her tears. She had failed him. She had screamed. He hated it when they screamed.

He stood abruptly, reaching for the gag and jerking it back over her mouth. He was rough—too rough probably, and he'd have to apologize later. But for now, she deserved it. She'd hurt him.

Tears burned in his eyes, stinging, but he blinked them away. He couldn't let her think he was weak or fragile.

"I warned you," he admonished sharply. "Now you get nothing."

He kept his back to her as he gathered his things and hurried toward the door. He needed to get out of there, to be alone—away from her—so he could collect his thoughts and breathe again. So he could stop trying so hard not to cry.

On his way out, he blew out the candle, leaving her alone. In the dark.

CHAPTER 5

VIOLET WAITED WHILE KRYSTAL SHOVED ASIDE
magazines and wadded-up drive-through bags, clearing a
space for her. Roxy's white interior was some sort of leather,
or more likely vinyl, and smelled musty in the way old cars
did, like mildew and oil and damp carpet. And, of course,
lingering with all of those smells Violet could also make out
Krystal's jasmine perfume.

Business cards were strewn across the dashboard, each one
identical to the next, and Violet reached for one. Big rainbow-
colored print spelled out the words *The Crystal Palace* on shiny
black cardstock, and beneath that, in smaller print, it read:
"Psychic Readings, Spiritual Advice, Numerology, Tarot, Tea

Leaves. By Appointment or Walk-in."

Krystal had handwritten her name—Krystal Devine—
and her cell phone number on each of the cards in sparkly
silver pen. Violet slipped one of the cards into her purse,
grinning as she imagined Krystal waving her hands in front
of a crystal ball, a jewel-encrusted turban perched on her
head.

When Krystal climbed into the driver's seat, the car
creaked and dropped at least half a foot on her side. Violet
clutched the door handle to steady herself as she wondered if
the ancient car was even street-legal. She pictured the steel
body dragging across the road as it drove, sparks shooting
up in its wake. Krystal didn't seem to notice the dip, but
then she reached down to the clunky console mounted on
the floorboards between them and tapped the black plastic
wastebasket that was sitting there. "If you feel sick, puke in
there, will ya?"

Violet scrunched her nose, suspiciously eyeballing her
friend. "Why would I get sick?"

Krystal started the noisy engine as she draped her arm
over the back of the bench seat and turned to watch while
she backed out of the parking space. Violet noted the sheer
volume of rings on the hand closest to her, taking up space
on every finger. "Bad shocks," Krystal stated flatly as the
car hit a tiny pothole and they were both pitched harrow-
ingly close to the car's ceiling, making it more than clear
how useless the 1970s lap belts that strapped them in actually were.

"Oh," said Violet, everything seeming to make sense now. The car leveled out, and Krystal shoved the gear into drive as she pulled onto the main road, heading in the same direction Rafe had gone on his motorcycle. "Is that why Rafe didn't want to ride with us?"

Krystal snorted. "Nah. Rafe's just kind of a lone wolf, if you know what I mean?"

Violet was confused. "Not really. What *do* you mean?"

"You know," Krystal answered, pursing frosty blue lips that made her look practically corpselike. As she reached the entrance to the freeway, she frowned, glancing at both of the overhead signs, looking completely lost. "Wait! Which way was it again?"

Violet looked down at the directions they'd printed from one of the computers at the Center. "You need to head north," she explained. And then she turned back to the topic of Rafe. "No, I *don't* know. You've known him longer than I have."

"That's kinda the thing, I guess. No one really knows him. He doesn't let anyone get close. Mostly, he keeps to himself. The only one who ever really tries with him is Gemma."

Violet understood that much, at least. She knew exactly what Krystal meant about Rafe keeping to himself. She'd felt that same thing whenever she was around him . . . that he would only let her get so close before he pushed her away again, putting up his defenses to keep her out. "So . . . she *likes* him? Gemma, I mean," Violet ventured, hoping Krystal didn't

71

read more into the question than there was. It was normal to be curious about the people you worked with, wasn't it?

"Mmm . . ." Krystal frowned, reaching up to rub one of her necklaces absently. "I'm not sure anyone *likes* him. None of us really knows Rafe that well, I guess."

"So why does she try, then?"

Krystal just shrugged. "I don't know. Gemma's had kind of a shitty life. I think she just wanted to fit in somewhere, to have friends. I think she thought Rafe would be . . . some sort of family to her."

"Family? I thought she wanted to date him."

Krystal's booming laughter filled the car, and Violet half-expected to look up to find her twirling her handlebar mustache like some sort of evil cartoon villain. "God, no. Gemma's not interested in hooking up with Rafe . . . any more than I am. And, trust me, Rafe's definitely not my type, if you know what I mean." She glanced at Violet, her eyes glinting wickedly.

Violet *didn't* know, but after being laughed at, she felt too stupid to ask. When she didn't say anything, Krystal's eyebrows inched all the way up until they looked like they were part of her hairline. "You do know what I mean, right?" Her eyes grew larger. "That he's a dude? Not my type . . . ?" She let the words drift off, ripe with meaning.

Violet rolled her eyes. "Got it. You're into girls. Why didn't you just say so?"

Krystal snorted again. "Because this was way more fun." She flipped on the radio and dialed the tuner until she found

72

a station without too much static. "Damn, you're easy to mess with. This is definitely worth a B&E charge."

Violet wouldn't even have needed to see Rafe's motorcycle to know that he'd driven faster than they had, and probably ignored any traffic rules that were *inconvenient*. In her head, she pictured him zigzagging in and out of traffic, with no regard to speed limits or personal safety. His or anyone else's. He was reckless. Jay was right.

Still, she felt a bubble of relief swell up from her chest when she realized his bike was there. And in one piece.

Krystal avoided the need to parallel park since there were no other cars around, and Violet shoved the massive door open while Rafe leaned against his motorcycle, a cocky smirk on his face. "I can't believe that hunk of junk actually made it. I'm surprised it even starts in the mornings."

Krystal glared at Rafe. "This car's seen more action than you can possibly imagine. She was at Woodstock, I'll have you know."

A skeptical expression crossed Rafe's face. "I sorta doubt that. I think Woodstock was before *her* time."

"You don't know. Besides, that's what the guy who sold her to me said."

"Yeah? Did he also tell you she was part of the moon landing? Sounds to me like you got taken."

Krystal's face fell, and Violet moved to stand in front of her, so Krystal wouldn't be able to see the derisive expression in Rafe's eyes. She scrunched her nose and shook her head, trying silently to tell Krystal to ignore him.

She thought about what Krystal had told her, that no one really liked Rafe. As she stood there, listening to his cynical tone, it wasn't hard to figure out why. Violet didn't know what she felt about him. She didn't hate him, but she didn't actually know if she liked him or not. More than anything, she felt grateful to him. And drawn to him. As if, in some strange way, the two of them shared a connection. And she supposed they did. But shouldn't she feel that same connection, then, with the others on her team . . . since they all shared a secret?

"Whatever." Krystal sniffed, patting the hood of her ancient Impala. "Roxy's a great car."

"Totally," Violet assured her friend. "Come on. Let's see if we can find anything useful in there."

They moved across the street to where Rafe strode confidently toward a row of unimpressive-looking houses . . . older homes in an older neighborhood, some well kept and others in desperate need of landscaping and repair.

Violet stood still for a minute, trying to decide if any of them felt different from the rest. If there was something to indicate that the girl who'd been living in one of them had been murdered by a serial killer. But there was nothing special. Just ordinary houses on an ordinary street.

Yet, without even glancing at the house numbers, Rafe knew exactly which one belonged to Antonia Cornett. "There," he said, pointing out the small white house with a stucco exterior and drab brown trim.

Violet tried to sense whether there was something out of place—anything only she might be aware of. Maybe the person responsible was nearby—a neighbor or a landlord. Didn't they say that most victims were attacked by people they knew?

She didn't know if that was a real statistic or not, but after a moment of concentrating she realized that her ability wasn't going to help her this time. She would have to depend on Rafe or Krystal.

Approaching the house, Violet could see the crime-scene tape, hidden beneath the metal mesh of the screen door. It had been left as a warning, and even though it hadn't been completely evident from the street, Violet couldn't believe she hadn't noticed the bright yellow strips sooner.

She hesitated. She was about to break the law.

Unlike her, Rafe didn't stop. He ignored the warning and yanked the tape away so he could unlock the door.

Violet stood at the top of the steps, glancing one last time over her shoulder to make sure no one was watching them, but the street was practically deserted.

When she turned around again, she placed her hand against Rafe's back, not sure if she was pushing him to hurry, or silently begging him to stop before it was too late. All the while, she pretended not to notice how warm he was beneath her fingertips.

But the unsteady rhythm beating within her chest had nothing to do with Rafe. "Are you guys sure about this?" Violet worried, gnawing her lip.

Rafe shrugged her hand away. "If you don't want to go in, then you should wait in the car. If you stand out here someone might notice." He sounded irritable as he dropped the key back into his pocket and reached for the handle. But when the tumbler clicked, he turned to grin at the two girls triumphantly. "I won't be long," he promised, slipping inside and leaving the door open behind him.

Krystal had no qualms about following him, and she just shrugged at Violet before she trailed after Rafe, leaving Violet to make up her mind. Violet stood there, staring into the open doorway.

She poked her head inside as she gripped the doorjamb, not yet willing to let her toes cross the threshold as she watched Krystal and Rafe stroll boldly into the living room.

The interior of the house was small, and it was fascinating for Violet to watch Rafe, who looked as if he'd been there before, as if he knew what he was doing . . . what he was searching for. He stroked his hand across the back of the couch—a couch on which Antonia Cornett had sat, not so long ago. He stopped every so often, picking up items and examining them. But they weren't the items most people would even look twice at.

He didn't sift through her mail or pick up photos and knickknacks she'd collected, the sentimental items. Instead, he chose random things: a jacket, his fingers brushing over the wool; a stack of magazines that he thumbed through absently; a laptop, powered down now, but he paused there, settling his palm over the keys.

Krystal, on the other hand, dropped onto one of the chairs and closed her eyes, almost as if she were meditating. Violet studied her for a moment, envious of her urban fashion sense, the edginess of her bold clothing and makeup. But there was something else about Krystal, a prettiness that was almost lost beneath the indigo streaks—Krystal's color of the week—that shot through her gleaming black hair. Her hair framed skin that was such a pale shade of olive that Violet wondered if only one of her parents was Asian. Her dark eyes were both exotic and expressive, and her full lips were almost always smiling.

Even now, deep in concentration, they curved upward.

Violet wondered if she was listening for something, waiting for the spirits to speak to her.

Rafe moved deeper into the house, out of Violet's sight, and Violet leaned farther through the doorway, not wanting to miss what was happening. There was no way she was going to wait outside while Rafe was in there discovering the girl's secrets, maybe learning something that might help them find the killer.

She took one tiny, insignificant step inside, and was surprised when she felt no different standing *inside* the doorway than she had when she'd been outside it. Except that *now* she was most certainly breaking the law.

And there was a part of her, much larger than she cared to admit, that found it thrilling, as adrenaline coursed through her.

She pulled the door closed behind her, deciding that she

might as well not draw any added attention to what they were doing. She walked more quickly now, slipping silently past Krystal, not wanting to disturb her trance, or whatever it was. Following the path Rafe had, Violet let her fingers brush over the things he'd touched.

When she'd read about psychometry, one of the articles had said that everything carries energy vibrations and that those who are sensitive to them are aware of those ener-gies. Some of those people know how to interpret what they sense. Violet stopped at the laptop and settled her hand in the exact same place Rafe's had been.

She waited, but felt nothing. Just cold, still computer keys.

"I wondered how long you'd last." Violet jumped. "I was starting to think you were really planning to stand guard out there the whole time."

When she looked up, Rafe was grinning at her from behind a cutout in the wall separating the living room from the kitchen. He shoved his black hair to the side before he went back to digging through one of the drawers. Violet heard the tinny clattering of silverware.

"I should've just called 9-1-1 and turned you in myself," she retorted as she turned in a complete circle, taking in the house around her. "So?" she asked, pivoting back to face him. "Find anything?"

Rafe shook his head. "Not yet. But I'm gonna check out the rest of the house. I don't want to miss something important."

Violet moved absently toward his voice . . . toward him.

There was enough light coming in from outside, through the curtained windows in the living room, that they didn't need to turn the lights on. Better, since they didn't want to draw attention to the fact that they were in here.

She followed Rafe into the short hallway, leaving Krystal behind. He slowed as he approached a door, and Violet stepped closer, leaning forward until she was practically pressed against his back, as she tried to see past him to the room beyond.

Inside was a bedroom. The bed was unmade—messy and rumpled—with pillows and blankets cascading haphazardly onto the floor. Clothes dangled from open dresser drawers. There was a framed black-and-white print of a sailor kissing a nurse hanging on the wall above the bed. It was a familiar poster, something Violet had seen in frame shops and print stores dozens of times before.

Rafe didn't stop.

"Don't you want to look in there?"

"It's not her room," he told her, leaving Violet to wonder once more about his ability. How could he possibly know for sure?

They passed an open pair of accordion doors that revealed a mismatched washer and dryer. The washer was avocado green, its enamel dull and chipped, and the dryer was stark white and shiny, brand-new. On top of the dryer was an overflowing basket of rumpled laundry.

It all looked so normal, like Antonia had just stepped out for a bit and would be back to fold the clothes soon.

But Violet knew she wasn't coming back.

Rafe stopped outside a second door, this one only slightly ajar, and Violet watched as he tentatively touched his fingertips to it, nudging it open. The blinds covering the window were closed, and it was far too dark to see exactly what they were looking at. Violet strained against the shadows to get a better view. She settled her hand against Rafe's shoulder as she eased forward, trying to see around him. Reaching inside, Rafe flipped on the light switch, filling the room with harsh overhead light.

That was when Violet saw the black smudges, like ebony feathers that coated nearly every surface. She'd never actually seen sooty film before, but she knew exactly what it was: fingerprint dust.

"You shouldn't touch anything," she told him, worrying about everything they'd already come in contact with. Would the police find their fingerprints and know they'd been there? She thought about wiping the light switch with the sleeve of her jacket, but when she turned to look at it, it too was smeared in a layer of the sticky black powder.

Rafe ignored her warning and barged inside, already sliding his hands—his fingers—over nearly every surface of the bedroom.

"This is it." Violet's voice rasped against her throat. "This is her bedroom."

Rafe nodded, as if she'd been asking him a question as he reached for the top drawer of the nightstand and started sifting through bras and underwear. He probably didn't hate this part of the job, Violet thought wryly.

The furniture in this room looked more like it belonged to a little girl than a college coed. Stark white and carved with flowers, the twin-sized headboard, the dresser, and nightstands were all part of a matched set. Violet guessed that Antonia had moved to this house from her parents', bringing with her the bedroom set she'd grown up with. The comforter was more sophisticated, bright jewel tones made from raw silk, with matching throw pillows and satiny sheets.

Antonia's room was tidier than the other one had been. Even in the aftermath of an investigation, with her belongings ransacked, there was a sense of order to the chaos. Her closet was neatly arranged, divided by clothing types—sweaters in one section, T-shirts in another, jackets and dresses each in their own designated spaces. Her jewelry was neatly organized in a polished lacquer jewelry box perched atop her dresser. And even her makeup had been compartmentalized in a tray on her vanity. Violet didn't need Rafe's special skills to tell her that Antonia had been a bit of a neat freak.

Violet watched as Rafe left his fingerprints on nearly every possible surface, but she was much more cautious with her own. She kept the sleeves of her hoodie pulled down over her hands. When she opened the vanity's drawer to get a peek inside, she used the fabric as a barrier between her and the knob, trying to avoid leaving any physical evidence that she'd been there at all.

"Are you almost finished?" she finally asked, when they seemed to be getting nowhere. She watched as Rafe thumbed through the pages of a paperback romance novel.

"Or do you have a thing for sexy, half-naked pirates?" she asked, pointing to the book's cover.

Rafe scowled as he flipped the book over, sparing only a superficial glance at the shirtless swashbuckler with flowing blonde hair. "Not yet." He frowned.

"Not yet, you don't have a thing for pirates?" She grinned meaningfully. "Or not yet, you're not finished?"

Rafe shook his head, ignoring her pitiful attempt at cracking a joke as he flipped to the back of the book, fanning through the pages, his concentration rapt. "Hold on. I think there's something here."

He didn't have time to find what he was looking for, as Krystal came bounding breathlessly into the bedroom. "Someone's here! I think we've been caught."

But it was already too late. A deep voice boomed from over Krystal's shoulder, and Violet saw Krystal's eyes bulge so far she thought they were going to pop.

"What are you kids doing here? This is a crime scene. Didn't you see the tape?"

Flinching, Violet watched as Rafe hid the paperback behind his back. Her heart catapulted into her throat as she turned and saw the police officer in his uniform, framed by the doorway to the bedroom, eyeing them suspiciously.

Krystal stood beside Rafe with her hands up, like she was already under arrest. "I swear we weren't doing anything, sir. Just trying to help."

That was when Violet saw it. A tiny slip of paper drifting gently to the floor from between the pages of the book Rafe was concealing. No one else seemed to have noticed it.

"Helping, huh?" He glanced at Rafe, his voice demanding. "What do you have there, son?"

Rafe sighed but withdrew the paperback, holding it out to the officer. "A really good romance novel," he drawled as he tossed the book on the floor between them. It landed on the carpet at the man's feet with a dull thud.

Violet moved quickly then, bending down to pick up the book with one hand, and discreetly snatching the small slip of paper with the other one. When she stood back up, she held out the paperback, her expression earnest. "Here you go."

The officer took the book from Violet, turning it over to examine it as Violet went to stand beside Rafe and Krystal. The man's lips thinned with impatience. "Do you mind explaining why you kids are in here?" His gaze fell on Violet this time as she wadded the paper into a tiny ball and shoved it into the pocket of her hoodie. She wondered why he'd singled her out. Did she really look that honest? Or just like she'd be easier to break than the others? "And I want the truth this time."

Violet wanted to glare at Rafe for putting her in this position in the first place, for forcing her to lie to the police. Sweat beaded across her forehead as she pictured her uncle Stephen, the chief of police in Buckley, and wondered what he'd think of her if he knew what she was doing now, where she was. She swallowed, wishing the knot in her throat wasn't choking her.

She opened her mouth, grasping—flailing, really—for the first excuse she could think of, but it was Rafe who stepped forward. "Fine," he said, his voice smooth and his expression unruffled. "We get it, we're in trouble. You caught us."

"You got that right," the cop said.

"Listen, just do me a favor. Can you call Agent Sara Priest for us?" Somehow he managed to say the words without smirking, despite the smugness Violet could hear in his voice. "She's with the FBI. She'll explain everything." Rafe pulled a business card from his front pocket as if he kept them there at all times, for just such an emergency. He handed it to the officer, who looked at the three of them standing in front of him with unguarded suspicion, probably wondering why in the world someone with the FBI would bail them out of the mess they were in.

They'd been taken to the police station, but since they weren't handcuffed, and hadn't been fingerprinted, Violet assumed they weren't actually being arrested or anything. At least not yet.

But she knew she was in trouble. Even though they'd been told Sara was on her way, she was still a minor. She wasn't stupid; she knew her parents had probably been called too.

They would *not* be happy about this.

Violet chewed on the side of her fingernail as she played out a dozen different scenarios in her head . . . none of which included being allowed to keep her cell phone, or possibly even her car.

Still, they were lucky, she supposed. Apparently they hadn't done anything bad enough to get themselves locked in the holding cells, where all the real criminals were waiting to be booked into jail.

Rafe didn't seem to care that they'd been caught. And Krystal was just . . . caught up in all the commotion around them.

"This is your fault. If you hadn't stolen that key . . ." Violet let the accusation hang there, both of them knowing what she meant.

A devious half smile lit Rafe's face. "Then you'd be clean and safe and warm at home, wouldn't you?" he offered, looking at Violet with blue eyes that were anything but contrite. "How boring is that?"

Violet shook her head. "It's not boring, it's . . ." She struggled, trying to find the right words, trying to find a way to make him realize he couldn't just go around doing whatever he wanted. "It's about doing the right thing. About *not* breaking the law."

From the other side of Rafe, Krystal snickered, and Violet turned to glare at her. "I don't see how this is funny," she practically choked out. "Besides, I thought you'd be on my side here. I mean, look at us, we're in jail!"

"We're not *in jail*." Rafe leaned back on the bench, stretching his arms across the top of it. His stance was far too casual, which only infuriated Violet even more. "Sara will spring us. Then you can go back to your safe, suburban little life."

Violet was about to tell him where *he* could go—where they could both go—when she felt something in the air shift, making it suddenly hard for her to breathe. Hard to blink.

It took several heartbeats before she realized what was happening as she sat there, openmouthed, waiting to see who it was. Her chest tightened with each second that ticked by, constricting until she felt as if her lungs might implode.

And then she saw him. The source of her sudden discomfort.

A killer hiding in plain sight.

Unlike the three of them, this boy was most definitely being arrested. He was surrounded by three uniformed officers as he was pushed through the station doors. He didn't bother struggling. It would have been futile, she supposed. His hands had been cuffed, and all three of the men escorting him were armed, as was nearly every other officer in the station.

Time slowed as Violet watched, and a chill gripped her. Instinctively, she wrapped her arms around herself, leaning closer to Rafe, seeking out his warmth. She could hear her own pulse as it established an eerie backdrop to the rhythm of each footstep the boy took.

Imprints clung to him like a thick layer of fog, so intertwined that it was almost impossible to distinguish one from the next.

Violet was stunned that the boy in front of her could be

responsible for carrying so much death. He couldn't possibly be much older than she was, hardly qualifying as a man. At first she thought she must be wrong, that she was confused . . . she had to be sensing imprints coming from the officers too. Surely these were men who had killed in the line of duty and were wearing those reminders on their skin.

But then she looked at the boy . . . really looked at him. He should have been too young to be so hardened, so dangerous. Yet Violet knew better. She knew that sometimes evil was born.

He was covered in tattoos that were almost tribal-looking, finding space on his forearms, hands, neck, and his face. Every place his skin was exposed. His black hair was short as if his head had once been shaved, but was now growing back, springing up lightly over his scalp . . . thin, like new grass.

Somewhere nearby, she heard the hum of Rafe's voice, trying to break through to her, to reach her, but she was too distracted to make it out clearly.

The moment was surreal, as Violet felt immediately detached from everyone around her. It was just her . . . and the boy. And the echoes—the imprints—that whispered to her.

One was a haunting choir of voices, constant and eerie.

Simultaneously, candied apples, sweet and tart, licked across her tongue, making her mouth water. That was another.

And then there were the tattoos. She almost didn't notice

what was so unusual about them at first. One seemed to blend with the next—those were the ones that were real, the ones that were visible to everyone, and not just to Violet. But then she saw some of them move, shifting and slithering like black vines just beneath the surface of the boy's skin. They snaked in and around his permanent tattoos, the ink that would never move or change. They stopped now and then to form a new pattern or a shape: interlocking circles, a rose, smoky swirls, a dagger dripping with blood. But then, before her eyes could fully adjust, they'd moved again, reshaping. That was the third distinct imprint, these ever-changing tattoos.

There were other imprints too. Some she could make out, and some that were too tangled with the rest to distinguish clearly.

"What're you lookin' at?" The man-boy wearing the imprints of the dead snarled at her, and Violet's skin puckered, chilling her all the way through.

She glanced away, trying to decide if the icy blast she felt was yet another imprint or if it was just the sensation of being so near a killer.

Violet glanced nervously, first to Rafe and then to Krystal, both of whom were watching her now, even as she saw one of the officers shove the boy: "Shut up! Don't talk to her."

"I'll talk to whoever I want, bitch," he shot back, his voice bold and full of menace.

He turned to Violet then, his stare intense. The creeping vine of a tattoo wound its way around his brow, framing

88

his black eyes with dark tendrils. The whispering chant remained steady, filling the small space with its ghostly cacophony.

Violet pressed herself closer to Rafe, trying not to look at the boy, but unable to look away from the ink curling and creeping beneath his skin. She shook her head, her heart racing, bruising her ribs.

He was directly in front of her now, being led to wherever they were taking him.

At last, Rafe's voice broke through Violet's reverie and she heard him talking to her softly. "V, look at *me*."

"I'm okay," she tried to say, but the words didn't quite reach her lips.

She could see in the boy's eyes that her fear incited him, and he jerked toward her, throwing his body in her direction, struggling against his restraints like a madman. He held her gaze as he tried to get to her. "You like me, girl? You like what you see?"

But he didn't get far.

Two of the officers pushed him down, forcing him to his knees. "I said shut up!" One of them was yelling as they gripped his handcuffs, hauling him upward until his shoulders were so contorted they looked like they might snap.

Violet squeezed as far back against the bench as she could. When the boy lifted his head, she found herself staring into his black eyes. A menacing smile curled his lips as his gaze roved from the top of her head down to her feet, pausing only momentarily over her chest. "You'd like me even better if we were alone," he promised, licking his lips lasciviously.

Violet glared at him. She hated that he could see her fear, that he knew he'd gotten to her.

He laughed then, a vulgar bark that sounded like a growl. "I knew she liked me. Me and her would get along *just fine*," he said to the cop as he was yanked to his feet again and dragged away.

And then everything was moving again, in real time. Voices rose around her, returning to their normal, fevered pitch. She would never admit how her pulse choked her, or how her breath felt hot and shallow, hard to find like the air was suddenly too thin in that cramped space. But she was grateful when Rafe's hand closed over hers . . . when she felt the familiar spark from his touch. She didn't care that he practically hauled her up from the bench, his body shielding her from the boy being taken into custody.

By the time Sara arrived, she looked as if she could spit fire at the three of them. Her gaze leveled on Rafe as the door closed behind her.

And then she paused when she saw Violet—when she saw the way Rafe stood in front of her like a sentinel—and the furious scowl she was wearing cracked, fracturing into something . . . softer. "What? Did something happen?"

"It's Violet. Some guy just threatened her," Rafe explained, his voice hard and filled with lingering menace.

Violet had just barely managed to control her shaking, and the unearthly choral voices had vanished. She realized she could have left it at that. That she could have let them both believe that the boy had simply frightened her. But now that he was gone, his imprints tucked away somewhere deeper in the building, she could feel her pulse steadying. "No. That—that's not it," she stammered. "He was . . ." She felt stupid for faltering, for her fear.

Violet felt Krystal's hand on her shoulder, and felt her fingers tightening. It was reassuring in a way Violet couldn't explain, and she relaxed. Despite what they'd been through tonight, these were exactly the people she could talk to about this.

"He was a killer, with imprints all over him. Strong ones. Almost overpowering . . . like they are when they're new." Violet swallowed, waiting to see what Sara would say.

But Sara didn't say anything. She just gave a brief nod, and then left them standing there as she marched assuredly toward the officer already heading in her direction, the same guy who'd caught them at Antonia Cornett's house and brought them there in the first place. Sara coolly revealed her identification . . . ID that looked suspiciously close to a badge, Violet noted, despite the fact that Violet now knew that Sara was no longer *actually* in the FBI. She showed it to the officer, while her other hand compulsively smoothed over her hair, which was pulled into a flawless ponytail fastened at the nape of her neck. As usual, there wasn't a single strand out of place. It was Sara's tic.

"I'm Sara Priest. And these three"—she glowered in the direction of her team—"are with me." She turned her attention fully on the officer then, smiling as she leaned in conspiratorially. "Can we talk privately for a moment?"

Violet watched as the officer grinned back at her, an almost too-eager expression on his face. She seemed to notice, for the first time really, how Sara's sapphire eyes stood out against her ivory skin, and the way her auburn hair, always so sleek and severe, captured light in its fiery strands. Strange how she'd never realized those things before.

Sara reached for the officer's arm, just the barest of touches, as she expertly drew him away from her team.

"Can you hear what they're saying?" Violet whispered, stepping closer to Krystal.

Pursing her full lips in concentration, Krystal shook her head. Violet could make out the voices as Sara and the officer spoke, but not a word of their conversation.

"Maybe you should ask one of your spirits to eavesdrop," Rafe stated flatly. "Shouldn't they have warned you this might happen?"

Krystal stuck her tongue out at Rafe, but then her face broke into a huge grin. "He's right, you know?" She elbowed Violet. "Here we are, a bunch of psychics . . . you'd've thought at least one of us would've seen this coming."

Violet let out a breathy giggle. She didn't try to explain that she wasn't really a psychic; she sort of liked feeling like she belonged in their ranks, that she was one of them. On the other side of her, she nudged Rafe. "Yeah, where were your superpowers when we needed them? Or do they only work if you're wearing your cape or something?"

Rafe rolled his eyes, and Violet thought he might be annoyed that they were making fun of him. And then his lips twitched. "Clearly you don't know anything. It's not the cape, it's the tights."

Violet had to cover her mouth to stifle a giggle. The idea of Rafe in a cape, let alone tights, was hysterical, but she wasn't sure Sara would appreciate their timing.

Watching, they saw Sara shake the officer's hand and then turn her back on him as she strode purposefully toward them. Rafe, as always, seemed unaffected by her withering stare, but Violet could already feel herself squirming, wilting beneath the white-hot intensity that was Sara Priest.

Sara stopped in front of them and inhaled deeply, almost as if she were mentally counting, collecting herself before attempting to speak to them. After a moment, she explained, "I've gotten things straightened out here. You three are lucky. They won't be filing charges against you." She stretched her hand out—palm up—to Rafe. "I need the key back." Violet wondered, although only briefly, how Sara had known it was Rafe who'd taken the key, but then she figured it probably hadn't been that difficult to sleuth out.

Besides, the apathetic look on his face pretty much confirmed her accusation.

He just shrugged when he pulled the silver key from his front pocket and dropped it into her hand, as if it didn't really matter to him one way or the other. The muscles around Sara's mouth tightened when she added, a heavy note of exhaustion in her voice, "I'm too tired to deal with this tonight. I'm going home. I expect to see all of you at the Center tomorrow."

Violet winced. It was almost worse that they'd have to

wait. She'd rather just get it over with, to know now what kind of trouble they were in.

And then Sara paused. "Violet, I'd like to talk to you about the boy who threatened you. Would you be willing to take another look at him if I can set something up?" Beside her, Violet was sure she felt Rafe's disinterested veneer crack. "From behind the two-way, of course."

Violet hesitated. She'd tried this before, tried to sense imprints from the other side of the mirrored glass they used at police stations. Sara had used the same technique to test Violet's ability, to see how much she could discern, and how accurate her gift was. She knew that sometimes the glass dulled the sensations, but it was better than the alternative. Better than facing the boy one-on-one again. "Of course," she agreed. "I'm happy to help." She wasn't sure that was entirely true. In fact, the boy's imprints made her feel cold and dirty. Violated. But wasn't that the point? Wasn't that the reason she'd joined the team in the first place, to help stop killers?

"I'm coming too." Rafe's voice left no room for argument as he glared not at Violet but at Sara. "If she has to see him again, I don't want her doing it alone."

"Look, I'm right here," Violet interrupted them. "You don't have to talk about me like I'm not."

Rafe directed his gaze to her, his eyebrows lifting. "Fine. If you have to see him again, I don't want you doing it alone," he repeated as he faced her. "Better?"

But Sara didn't seem to be paying attention to either of

them. She seemed unaware of them for a moment as she weighed Rafe's words. "You can go, but if I tell you to step out, you need to listen. Understood?"

Rafe's eyes narrowed. He shoved his hand in his pocket once more, and Violet waited to see if he was going to argue. But when he spoke, his voice belied the frustration she could see smoldering behind his eyes, and she wondered where it was coming from exactly—what Sara had done, or said, to incite that kind of irritation. "Understood," he bit out at last.

And then he turned on the heel of his boot and strode toward the door, leaving the rest of them behind.

CHAPTER 6

SOME DAYS THE RAIN JUST SEEMED TO FIT, AND today felt like one of those days. The morning sky was dark, layered with the kind of thick black clouds that promised showers. Violet didn't mind; it suited her mood. Despite the weather, she'd gotten up early, needing to clear her head the only way she knew how.

And now, running on what she considered a path, but what was really more of a thinned-out passageway between the trees surrounding her house, she could feel the dense fog in her head lifting. Something even the repeating loops of Dr. Lee's hypnosis tracks on her iPod hadn't been able to do.

She didn't want to think about last night, so she didn't

think at all, just concentrated on her pace as her feet landed heavily against the compacted forest floor. She listened to her breath steady in her ears, hypnotic in its own way, and it helped. She felt less jumbled. Less fuzzy.

She'd barely noticed when the rain finally started. It wasn't until she was soaked, until tiny rivulets of water trickled into her eyes and she had to blink them away, that she realized it wasn't just a drizzle that fell from the sky, but a full-on downpour. Yet even that couldn't sour her improving mood. Instead, she went out of her way to find every puddle on her way home. She felt like a little girl . . . jumping in them just so, sending sprays of muddy water splashing up her legs until her shoes were drenched all the way through, and her rubber soles squeaked with each step she took.

By the time she tumbled through the back door of her house, into her kitchen, Violet was laughing and dripping and filthy. She slipped off her waterlogged shoes and grabbed a sweatshirt from the hook by the door, doing her best to towel off with the thick fleece, but it was a poor substitute for a real towel.

Her dad was sitting at the table, watching her curiously. "You're in an awfully good mood this morning for someone without a cell phone."

Violet shrugged. Her parents had been waiting for her when she'd come home last night. They'd gotten the call from the police, just as she'd suspected they would. "I can't really say I didn't deserve what I got, I guess." She tried to smile, to lighten the mood, but he wasn't buying it.

His fingers tapped against the tabletop, his eyebrows raised as Violet dropped onto the chair, water puddling onto the floor beneath her. "Jay called while you were . . . out," her dad said, changing the subject. "And Chelsea too. In fact, she's called three times already this morning. I forgot how exhausting it was before you had your own cell phone." He shook his head at the receiver sitting in front of him. "Just tell them they don't have to *keep* calling. I promise to give you the messages."

Violet smiled at her father, feeling guilty for putting him in this position. He was supposed to be the good cop in their household, and here he was playing the part of enforcer. Violet knew, just from the strained expression on his face, it wasn't a role he cared for.

The phone rang again, as if on cue, and he sighed as he glanced at the caller ID.

"I gotta get ready for school," Violet said, jumping up and patting her dad's sagging shoulder. "Don't worry, I'll tell her to stop calling. Maybe we'll get some walkie-talkies, or learn smoke signals." She snapped her fingers. "Or, I know, we can tie some cans to a really long string and go old-school."

"Or maybe," he drawled impatiently, "you could try staying out of trouble and we'll give you your phone back."

Cocking her head to the side, Violet pretended to think about that, and then she winked at him. "Yeah, but how boring is that?" she said, and then caught herself, realizing those were the exact words Rafe had used the night before. "I'm kidding. I'll behave," she amended before her dad could say anything. She kissed him on the forehead as he lifted the receiver to his ear, answering it on the third ring. "Cross my heart."

Getting up early meant Violet made it to school with plenty of time to spare. Slamming her car door and tugging her hood over her head to keep from getting drenched as she raced toward the building, Violet avoided eye contact with everyone around her as much as humanly possible.

Running in the rain had made her feel a little less . . . *dazed*, but it didn't change the fact she was in trouble with her parents. Or that she'd gotten caught trespassing by the police the night before.

She really wasn't in the mood for superficial chitchat, even with her friends, and she kept her head low as she made her way to her locker.

"That bad, huh?"

Violet glanced up to find Jay leaning against the bank of metal lockers, amusement clear in his expression.

"Totally." She twirled the lock. "My parents took my phone, and I feel completely naked without it." She frowned when she heard him laugh under his breath. "It's not funny, Jay."

"I knew something was up when your dad answered and said I'd have to talk to you at school. So, what'd you do?"

She concentrated intensely on her combination, on lining the numbers up just so. As if she hadn't done it a thousand times before. As if she couldn't do it in her sleep.

She lifted one shoulder, trying to act as if it were nothing when she answered him. "I got picked up by the police last night." Despite her nonchalant tone, she cringed inwardly. It wasn't like she really expected him to just let that pass.

Jay didn't disappoint. "What the . . . ? What do you mean, *picked up by the police*? Where were you? Why?"

Violet sighed dramatically and threw her arms down to her sides, momentarily giving up on her lock. "Okay, so technically it was breaking and entering, but we didn't actually get charged. Rafe stole a key to the dead girl's house—the one I found in that warehouse the other night—and when we were there the cops showed up. Sara had to bail us out." She batted her lashes at him, trying to look as innocent as possible. She'd seen it work a thousand times on TV.

His voice came out sounding constricted from between his clenched teeth, but Violet had to hand it to him, he wasn't freaking out or anything. "If you weren't arrested, then why did Sara have to bail you out?"

"So, *bailed* out isn't precisely the right word, but you know what I mean. She had to come and rescue us. Plus, they called my parents."

Jay chewed on that for a minute, his eyes narrowing. But then his expression shifted, and he leaned casually against the locker. Violet started to wonder if he was enjoying this part. Seeing her squirm and all. "And they took your phone?"

"Exactly," she sighed.

He surprised her then by grinning. "C'mon, don't be like that. Think about it, it could've been so much worse."

Violet turned back to her locker and spun to the last number in her combination before lifting the lever. The door rasped metallically when it opened. "How? They might as well have teleported me back to the nineties."

"Did they ground you?" he asked, moving closer, so that he was right beside her now, leaning over her shoulder . . . his breath at her neck.

She scowled, refusing to acknowledge that they hadn't.

"And you said yourself you didn't get charged with anything." The levity in his voice was beginning to grate on Violet's nerves. No one should be so . . . cheerful.

She pulled out her books and slammed the locker shut again, not caring that she'd slammed it unnecessarily hard. She just wanted him to stop making it sound like her parents had done her a favor by taking away her cell phone. No matter how you looked at it, it was a bad move on their part. She'd tried to explain that to them, telling them they were putting her in danger by leaving her without any way to call for help if she needed it.

They'd countered with the fact that she shouldn't be putting herself in situations where she needed help that badly. They also threatened to pull her from the team, to force her to stop working with Sara altogether if she got in that kind of trouble again.

Violet supposed Jay was right: She should be glad it

was only a cell phone violation.

"Come on, jailbird," he said, leaning down and kissing the top of Violet's head. His breath tickled her scalp. "Let's get you to class before you add detention to your rap sheet."

ENGAGEMENT

HE CREPT IN QUIETLY, MORE CAUTIOUSLY THAN he had before. He knew he'd waited too long to return, but he'd been angry; her rejection had stung.

He desperately hoped she was ready now.

This time, when he lit the candle, he stood there longer than he needed to, watching as the flame sputtered and waved, casting luminous shadows on the wall behind it. He waited, letting the scent of the smoke reach him, settling his jangled nerves before turning to face her.

Just like before, her eyes were wide, her expression expectant. He prayed it was a good sign. A sign that she'd come around.

He smiled at her, a peace offering. It was small, bashful, childlike.

He felt butterflies erupt in his stomach as he watched her. She remained still, her gaze never leaving him. He clutched the tray in nervous fingers as he stepped nearer to the bed where she lay resting.

"I'm sorry I stayed away so long," he apologized, remorseful. "But I needed you to understand. You must follow the rules." He said the last part firmly, hoping he didn't sound like he was scolding her. He didn't want to frighten her.

But this time, she nodded, and he felt confidence swell within his chest. Tears of a different sort filled his eyes and he released a grateful breath from between clenched teeth.

"Thank God," he whispered, setting the tray on the bedside table. "I knew you'd get it. I knew I hadn't made a mistake by choosing you." He lifted his hand to the rag that bound her mouth. He raised his brows expectantly. "No noise, right?"

She shook her head, assuring him that he'd been right about her. That she was perfect for him.

His shoulders sagged in relief. "Good. Now, are you thirsty?" He tugged the gag away from her swollen lips. At the sight of them, his heart ached. He wanted to tend to them immediately. They were cracked and bleeding, and he needed to make them soft again, uninjured. But first she had to have water. Girls never survived long without water.

Her head bobbed eagerly, gratefully, the liquid brown of her eyes as smooth as melted chocolate. He brought the glass to her mouth, gently cradling the back of her head as he relished the feel of her silken hair beneath his hand. He watched her drink greedily, and then he drew the glass away even as she tried her best to follow it. She made a gagging sound as the rope at her neck reached its limit, choking her.

"Don't worry," he crooned, leaning close, whispering his

gentle reassurance hotly against her cheek. "There'll be more. And I brought you breakfast too. You can eat just as soon as we get you cleaned up." He reached for the bowl of warm water and squeezed the excess liquid from a washrag. He smoothed it tenderly, gingerly, across her forehead, and down her cheeks to her neck. He took his time, patiently taking great care with his task. He hesitated when he reached the top of her blouse.

She squirmed, and started to moan, but clamped her lips tightly as she turned her head away from him. She didn't protest. And she didn't scream.

"I'm sorry," he apologized earnestly as he unbuttoned the top buttons and slid the washcloth inside. He was nervous around her, and he reminded himself that they were still getting to know each other, that they were only dating.

His hands shook, and he kept his gaze averted while he worked, telling himself that this was necessary. He couldn't allow her to wallow in her own filth. He was doing her a favor.

When he finished, he released the breath he hadn't realized he'd been holding.

"There," he announced. Things were progressing well. They'd just passed another milestone. "That's better, right?" When she didn't respond, he lightly tugged her chin with his finger, drawing her gaze back to his. He scowled at her until the shadow of a smile touched the corner of her lips. It was tight and tentative, but it was a smile nonetheless. He was certain of that.

"Now, I bet you're ready for some food." He smiled back at her with no tentativeness at all. He felt elated. "And after that, a treat." He lifted the bottle of nail polish. "How do you feel about lilac?"

CHAPTER 7

"ARE YOU SURE YOU HAVE TO WORK TONIGHT?" Violet asked, leaning through the open window of Jay's black Acura. "Maybe you could call in sick. Just this once."

The sounds of other students and engines starting filled the lot. The rain had lifted just before lunch, and the sun was making intermittent appearances between clouds that drifted idly across the sky, warming Violet's back. Like the weather, her bleak mood had cleared as well.

"You know I can't. Al's counting on me. Besides, I need the money." He lifted her chin with his finger, compelling her eyes to his. "I have tomorrow off, though. We can hang out then."

Violet's lips pulled into a demure smile. "You read my mind."

"I'm starting to think maybe I got a little psychic thing goin' on too."

She crossed one foot over the other and leaned closer, so that her mouth was precariously close to his. She felt bolder now, her lips parting slowly, purposefully. "Then what am I thinking? Read my mind . . ." She let the words hang like a promise as her breath mingled with his.

Jay reached around her neck and slipped his fingers into her curls as he dragged her so close she was almost *inside* the car now.

She let go of her backpack, and it fell to the ground with a *thunk* as she balanced on her toes, leaning half-in and half-out of his window. She pressed the flat of her hand against his chest to steady herself, feeling his muscles bunch beneath her fingertips.

His breath was warm as his lips feathered over hers. Her pulse fluttered in the base of her throat. And before she knew it, they were kissing, heat uncoiling in the pit of her stomach, making her crave more. His lips and tongue moved with hers, until she felt fevered and restless.

When she pulled back and looked into his dazed eyes, she felt something stir within her, something fierce and feral. She felt like a cat toying with a mouse.

"I'll be at work until nine, nine thirty," he explained, his voice shaky. "Maybe you can stop by the store and visit me." And then he grinned at her, all lopsided and boyish, and

Violet realized *she* was the mouse in this scenario. Whenever he smiled at her like that she wanted to nod stupidly, agreeing to whatever he requested of her.

But this time she never had the chance, because all at once, his expression changed, a scowl shadowing his face. Violet knew something was wrong.

"What's the matter?" she breathed.

"What the hell?" Jay muttered. "What's he doing here?"

She followed his black gaze, craning her neck so she could see behind her.

Her breath caught when she saw Rafe standing near the edge of the school parking lot. His stance was casual as his eyes met hers, a red motorcycle helmet tucked beneath his arm.

Rafe lifted his chin, giving a cursory nod, and Violet couldn't help wondering if it was meant for her or for Jay. She didn't miss the smile that tugged at his lips.

Violet's grip on Jay's arm tightened. "I don't know." She wasn't lying. Rafe hadn't been to her school since the first time he and Sara had come there, searching out Violet in the parking lot after she'd discovered a missing boy on the waterfront.

And he fit in just as well today as he had back then, with his torn black jeans and his jet-black hair—basically, not at all.

Jay's gaze raked quickly over Rafe, taking him in before he turned back to Violet. His jaw clenched. "Well, I guess you better find out. I doubt he came all this way to ask about the weather, Vi." She was relieved when he didn't sound angry; his voice was resigned, passive. But the effect was just as painful for Violet. She hated that he was uncomfortable, even if he had no reason to be jealous of Rafe.

"I swear I didn't know he was coming. . . ."

But Jay just reached for his keys and started his engine. "I know." He gripped the steering wheel, his knuckles whiter than they should be. "I really do have to get to work." He put his car in gear and glanced at her wistfully before pulling away, leaving Violet standing in the spot where his car had just been.

She turned then, her mouth drawing into a hard line. She was frustrated that Rafe had shown up unannounced. And with Jay for being jealous, and for making her feel guilty, like she'd done something wrong.

She was mad at herself too. For not stopping Jay so she could tell him he was being ridiculous. For not explaining that it wasn't a competition between the two of them . . . that it would never, *ever* be a competition.

"Ever hear of a phone?" Violet stormed across the pavement, not bothering to keep her voice down. Even though the lot had mostly cleared out for the day, a few heads turned toward the commotion.

Rafe shrugged like he always did, as if he wanted everyone to know he didn't care . . . that nothing bothered him. But Violet saw the smirk concealed just beneath the surface of his invulnerable outer shell.

"You can't just show up whenever you want."

Again, he shrugged. "Looks like someone woke up on the wrong side of the bed this morning."

"You know what I mean." Violet glared, not exactly sure where all of her anger was even coming from. But she didn't like the way she felt inside, regret and remorse festering, and Rafe was the only one she could think to blame. If he hadn't shown up . . .

Then Jay wouldn't have left, not like that.

She crossed her arms over her chest. "I have a life here. And Jay doesn't like . . ." This time she was the one who shrugged, not quite sure how to finish the sentence. Jay didn't like what? He didn't like Rafe? He didn't like the two of them spending time together? Both, she supposed, but said neither.

"Relax, it's not like I came to cause trouble. Here—" He held out the helmet he'd been holding, the one Violet had assumed was his. "Sara was able to get an appointment to see that kid today, the one from the jail. We're supposed to meet her there so you can take a look at him."

Stubbornly Violet held her ground, refusing to take the helmet and ignoring the fact that her curiosity had been piqued by the mere mention of the boy from the night before. "I didn't get the message," she argued.

"I tried to call, but you weren't answering. All the calls went straight to voice mail." He lifted his black brows curiously. "Almost like you were avoiding me."

Her hand automatically went to her pocket, but she froze. *Oh right, my phone.* She still wasn't used to not having it.

"You're pretty full of yourself. Actually, it had nothing to do with you. Thanks to you, I got my phone taken away." She eyed the motorcycle behind him with the same suspicion she always did. "And you're crazy if you think I'm riding that thing."

His serious expression cracked, just slightly, and Violet knew he was toying with her. "C'mon, I'll have you back before bedtime."

He tried to hand her the helmet again, but Violet pressed her palm against the cool red fiberglass to keep it from coming any closer. "No thanks, I'll drive myself," she insisted, making a point of searching for her keys in her backpack so she could ignore the look of satisfaction that crept over his face.

"I'd give you directions," he quipped. "But if I'm not mistaken, you already know the place." He strapped the helmet he'd been saving for Violet to the back of his bike and grabbed his from where it was dangling from the handlebar. His helmet was a sleek polished black with chrome accents, nicer even than the motorcycle he rode on. Then he slipped his shoulders into a well-worn leather jacket and hopped on his bike. "Race you there!" was the last thing Violet heard before he sped away.

The closer she got to Seattle, the more Violet questioned what she was about to do. Generally speaking, she went out of her way to avoid places like prisons, juvenile detention centers, and jails. Those who killed carried imprints.

Sure, Sara had taken her to the county jail, and even to Juvenile Hall, so she could sit in on interviews. Or, more accurately, Violet had recognized early on, so Sara could have opportunities to study the way Violet's ability worked. Violet had almost gotten used to Sara putting her in situations where there was only one answer—*echo* or *no echo*.

And she hadn't failed a test yet. The problem wasn't whether she could sense the echoes, it was figuring out a way to make that information helpful to the team. Tracking bodies was one thing—useful only after someone had already been killed. Violet would rather track killers. To find them *before* they could strike again.

A far more difficult task.

CHAPTER 8

THE HAIR ON THE BACK OF VIOLET'S NECK TIGHT-ened, standing on end as she pulled into a tight space in the parking lot and took a deep breath. This was it, she told herself. She could do this.

She was relieved to find Rafe waiting for her in the parking lot, checking his watch as he strode assuredly toward her car. "What took you so long? Even if you went the speed limit, you should've been here like fifteen minutes ago."

She raised her eyebrows, unamused. "I had to stop and call my parents. No phone, remember? I told them I had a project to finish and I'd be out late." She grabbed her wallet before locking her car and she followed him through the parking lot.

"So you lied to them? Didn't really figure you for a liar."

"Funny. I didn't lie, exactly; it's just not a *school* project. And who wears watches anymore?" she shot back, eyeballing the thick leather studded watchband on his wrist. "Isn't that what cell phones are for?"

"Yeah? Then what time is it, V?"

Ignoring the jab, Violet reached out and grabbed his arm, stopping him before they made it to the building. Despite her bravado, her heart was hammering harder now. "Wait. What do you know about this guy? Did Sara tell you anything?"

Rafe shifted suddenly, and she realized he looked just as anxious as she felt. She wondered how she hadn't noticed that before. Swallowing, he said, "Gangbanger. Drug dealer. Pimp. Take your pick, apparently this guy does it all. He was picked up yesterday after a domestic violence call. When the cops got there, they found his girlfriend and their two little kids dead. Slaughtered. He claims it was some kind of retaliation thing—rival gang stuff. But they think he's lying." His eyes dropped to his feet and his hands were clenched into fists.

Violet thought about the boy she'd seen yesterday, and her throat tightened. "How—how old is he?"

"Eighteen," Rafe said, shoving his hands into his pockets.

She winced. That was only a year older than she was. "They were *his* kids? And they think he killed them?"

Shrugging, he kept his gaze down. "That's what Sara said."

Violet hadn't seen Rafe looking this uneasy since they'd first met, and she wondered if he was worried about the same things she was.

She thought about the things Rafe had just told her, and about seeing the boy again, someone capable of harm-ing—*killing*—his own children. She felt sick. She considered refusing, at least this time. About making up an excuse that she had too much to do: homework or chores. Something. *Anything.*

But Rafe glanced up at her then, his voice barely a whis-per. "Come inside, V. See if you can help nail this guy."

Goose bumps stood up from the tips of her fingertips all the way to her toes, and Violet rubbed her arms. She stared back at him speechlessly, her brow furrowed with worry. Finally, after a long moment, she held her breath and nod-ded.

Rafe sighed, his stance visibly relaxing. "Let's go. Sara's waiting."

She wondered what had gotten into him all of a sud-den. This wasn't the Rafe she knew, nervous and fidgety and unsure. She wondered if this case had somehow struck a nerve with him. It certainly had for her.

She had the feeling she wasn't going to like what she found in there.

Once inside, Sara got them checked in and through secu-rity quickly. The three of them were escorted by an armed officer who chatted with Sara about the specifics of the case.

Violet was grateful that the man was "clean" of imprints, since it would make it easier to discern the ones coming from the boy. It was also easier for Violet to be around him.

"James Nua. Three domestic violence calls in the past month alone. There was a restraining order in place," Violet heard the officer telling Sara. "His record goes all the way back to when he was thirteen. Breaking and entering, assault, assault with a deadly weapon, possession, possession with intent to distribute . . ." He continued to tick off the offenses that had been leveled against James Nua, and that feeling of restlessness persisted, setting Violet's teeth on edge.

Beside her, Rafe remained fidgety.

When they stopped, Violet glanced at the black door with a rectangular wire-enmeshed window set vertically in the top. It looked like it was made from steel, or something equally solid, but it had pit marks and scars as if its strength had been tested . . . repeatedly. Violet stood as far from the door as she could manage in the narrow hallway, her eyes avoiding the small window at the top.

He was in there. Even from out here she could sense James Nua . . . and his imprints.

"We're going in here," Sara indicated, pointing to a different door, and Violet followed, suddenly hoping she'd be able to tell them something useful.

"Are you ready for this?" Sara asked, turning to look over her shoulder.

Violet was about to say, "Yes," when she realized that Sara wasn't talking to her. It was Rafe she spoke to now.

Rafe, whose silent, brooding stare fixated on the white-flecked tiles of the floor beneath him. He didn't answer.

"*Rafe?*" she repeated, and when he glanced her way, she asked again. "Are you sure you can do this?"

He lifted his shoulder, not quite a shrug, not really a response at all, and he pushed his jet-black hair out of his eyes. "Of course."

But from where she stood, Sara didn't hear what Violet had, the hitch in his throat. The officer opened the door, and Violet stayed back, trailing in behind Sara and Rafe, not sure *she* was ready either. She felt a chill the moment she walked through the doorway, one that had nothing at all to do with imprints.

She was about to come face-to-face with a child killer.

At the sound of the door closing, the click, Violet forced her gaze up, focusing on the window before her. She took a step closer, forgetting for a moment that she wasn't alone as she looked through the glass to the room beyond it. Even though he couldn't see her, even though he was in an entirely different room, Violet released a grateful sigh that Nua was handcuffed to the metal table he sat in front of . . . and that the table was bolted to the floor beneath him. Even his feet had been restrained.

She concentrated on finding them, the echoes she'd felt attached to him the night before. The choral voices and the sugared apples. The tattoos were easy; she'd noticed them slithering just below the surface of his skin the moment she'd looked at him. There were others too, the ones she hadn't been sure about the night before, that were somehow easier to pinpoint now that she wasn't surrounded by police officers and other criminals who muddied the waters.

She smelled autumn leaves, still crisp and earthy as if they'd been raked into a multicolored pile and were waiting for a child to bound into them at any moment.

And something else. Something far less pleasant. It was the cloying stench of rotting flesh. She'd smelled that smell before . . . too many times for a girl of her age. Even though it was less intense than the scent of leaves, it was much more visceral, finding a hold in Violet's gut and making her want to recoil. She had to remind herself it wasn't real, that she wasn't actually *smelling* Nua's decaying family. It was simply an imprint.

Sara came to stand beside Violet while Rafe remained at the back of the room, staying as far from them as he could. "His twenty-four-hour hold is almost up and so far they don't have enough to arrest him. I was hoping—" Her blue eyes held a strange mixture of optimism and regret. "I was hoping you might be able to tell us how many people he's killed. Maybe who he's killed. If we know what to look for we might have a better chance of finding it."

Violet's heart sank. She thought Sara understood . . . that she realized Violet's ability didn't work like that. "I can," Violet said at last, a solution coming to her. "If you take me to the bodies."

"How are you holding up?" Sara asked Violet as she handed each of them a bottle of water.

118

Violet unscrewed the cap and took a long swallow, trying to shake off the slimy feeling that still clung to her, that sensation of James Nua's imprints that seemed to permeate her skin. She felt like she needed a shower.

"I'm fine," Violet finally said, taking another gulp. "Really," she promised when she saw that Sara was still examining her.

Sara slipped off her jacket and draped it over her arm. "What about you, Rafe? Was that too weird?"

They exchanged a look that Violet realized she wasn't meant to decipher, and Violet was suddenly aware that they seemed to understand each other a little too easily. She wondered how long they'd been working together to form a bond like that.

Rafe inhaled slowly before answering. "It was weird enough. But you don't need to worry about me." His brows lifted. "Really, Sara, I'm fine."

She studied him for a long moment, squinting at him with her lips pressed together, as if she didn't quite believe him. But then she handed him something. "Here." Rafe palmed it so quickly that Violet didn't see what it was, only that it was small. A coin? Maybe a piece of jewelry? He tucked it into his pocket. Another secret between the two of them.

She turned to Violet again. "What about you? I know you can't be specific, but I also know you sensed something back there. What *can* you tell me?"

Violet glanced at Rafe before answering. "He's definitely killed before. Several times, at least five or six."

"And you think if you can get in to see the bodies of his family, you'll know if they were among his victims?"

Violet nodded, choosing her next words carefully. "I think so . . . yeah. The only way I can tell *who* he's killed is by matching the imprint to the echo." Violet waited a moment, making sure that Sara understood what she was trying to tell her. She didn't look Rafe's way. She didn't want to know if he understood.

Sara gazed over Violet's shoulder, thinking, and then she nodded. "Well, let me make a call. I'll see if we can make a quick stop at the morgue."

Even though her stomach knotted, Violet knew it couldn't be avoided. If she was going to learn to help—really help—she'd have to do things like that.

Things like going to the morgue.

Sara left them standing in the hallway while she made the call, trying to get them a "viewing" right away.

When she was out of sight, Violet turned to Rafe. "What happened back there? You seemed sort of . . . I don't know, freaked out. Are you okay?" She knew why Sara hadn't believed him when he'd said he was fine; his face was still ashen.

Rafe just shrugged, and even though she wanted to, Violet didn't press him. Rafe didn't like to be pushed, and she didn't entirely blame him. If he wanted to talk, he'd tell her.

That was when the door to the other room, the one James Nua had been in, started to open. Violet's eyes bulged as she jumped out of the way, realizing belatedly what was happening.

James Nua was still in there.

And she was out here.

Rafe reacted before she did, and she felt her heart slam against the walls of her chest as his hand closed around hers, pulling her roughly behind him.

But it was too late. Nua was being escorted out, and he'd already seen her.

He carried himself as if it were a normal affair for him to be restrained and accompanied in that way, strolling with handcuffs and armed guards. And even when Violet saw the light of recognition flicker in his eyes, his step barely faltered.

Barely.

And then a knowing grin parted his lips while the black ink coiled and curled and crawled along his skin. "Hey, White River." His voice sent a spiderweb of fear shooting from Violet's core, radiating outward, firing tenuous threads that made her arms and her legs quiver. Its sticky webs reached into every crevice of her being. Somehow he not only recognized her, but he'd just mentioned the name of her school.

His smile grew exponentially, but there was something in the way he looked at her, something in his eyes as he watched her—a suspicion almost—that made Violet's breath catch.

He was shoved from behind then, forced to keep moving. He somehow managed to maintain pace with the men who escorted him, even though his neck craned to keep Violet in his sights for as long as possible. Violet didn't breathe again until he was no longer near her.

Until his imprints were no longer visible or audible to her.

Then she struggled to unravel the cobwebs that infiltrated her mind, making it hard for her to think . . . to find the missing puzzle piece. How did he know anything at all about her?

"Violet," Sara said, standing at the other end of the hallway, her startled expression making it clear she'd overheard what James Nua had said to her. "What were you wearing yesterday?"

Violet frowned. What did it matter what she'd been wearing? How could her wardrobe choice possibly be relevant? "Jeans and a hoodie," Violet answered. And then it came to her . . . painfully, brutally clear. Her throat went dry as she looked down at the simple black zip-front jacket she wore today. When she spoke again, her voice was just the ghost of a breath. "I was wearing my White River High School hoodie."

Violet glanced up at Rafe, who was waiting for her while Sara filled out some paperwork and chatted with the medical examiner. They'd all three arrived together in Sara's black SUV within half an hour of leaving the jail.

Now that she was here, Violet could feel her skin itching. Already—even from out here in the lobby—the echoes of the dead were calling to her . . . reaching out to her . . . drawing her to them.

She had yet to determine whether any of those echoes matched the imprints carried by James Nua.

"This is the autopsy suite," the technician assigned to escort them explained as they stopped in front of the large window. From her side of the plate glass, Violet looked at the stainless steel tables, sinks, and cabinets. Glaring overhead lights reflected off the polished silver surfaces, and she could practically taste the metallic tang from all that steel in one place. The oversized room was empty now, but she imagined that this was where bodies were brought to be examined for signs of foul play, to be scoured for clues and evidence. Calling it a *suite*—of any kind—felt odd, considering it was cold and sterile, outfitted with scales, hoses, lights, and state-of-the-art camera equipment. It was exactly as Violet thought it would look. Only the name seemed not to fit.

Barely acknowledging Violet or Rafe, the tech focused his attention solely on Sara as he gave her "the grand tour," leading them to where the bodies were stored. Violet was too distracted trying to extricate one echo from the next to notice the slight, and Rafe didn't seem to care.

He had fallen quiet on the ride over, and Violet was certain it had something to do with the object in his pocket. Rafe hadn't let it go since Sara had given it to him back at the jail.

"So, what is that?" Violet finally whispered, curiosity getting the best of her.

Rafe's gaze met hers, his eyebrows low, scrunched together.

"That thing . . . that Sara gave you. What is it?"

"Wouldn't you like to know," he answered, teasing her like a little boy with a secret.

Violet hated secrets.

She wanted to pretend she didn't care, to tell him it didn't matter what it was. But she'd be lying. She *did* want to know . . . more than she cared to admit. "Just show me," she demanded, trying not to appear too eager.

Rafe stopped walking, and Sara and the tech increased their distance by several steps. "You really wanna see it?"

Violet nodded, and this time she couldn't keep the interest from her face.

"I could really torture you, you know?" He started to pull his hand from his pocket, his expression playful, and Violet caught a glimpse of something shiny—something gold. She leaned closer. And then he shoved his hand back inside again, hiding whatever it was from sight.

"Cut it out," she complained, crossing her arms. "If you're not gonna show me, just say so. You don't have to be a jerk about it." Instead of waiting for a response, Violet turned on her heel and hurried after Sara, leaving Rafe standing there.

When he reached her, he tugged at her arm. "Come on, I was just messing with you."

But they were already there. And Violet barely heard his words as she stood rigidly outside the door that led to the storage lockers, the place where the bodies were kept.

Even from here, the echoes were strong, reverberating deeply and making her skin burn. She strained forward, not wanting to go closer but virtually unable to resist.

As the tech explained what they could expect to see, his gaze moved anxiously from Rafe to Violet . . . as if neither of them had ever seen a dead body before. He looked worried that one of them might be sick, that this was too much for kids so young. And it might have been for any other kids; maybe it was, even, for Rafe. She had no idea if he'd ever seen a body before. But it definitely wasn't for Violet.

At last he opened the door and let them inside. The bodies were still safely entombed within the stainless steel refrigeration units, and Violet faced a wall of small, rectangular doors, three high and six wide. Eighteen spaces. Eighteen units where bodies could be held. She had no idea how many of the spaces were occupied. From inside several of them, she could already sense the murdered dead.

Unable to stop herself, Violet stepped forward, ignoring the surprised look on the tech's face as she brushed past him, disregarding the warnings he'd given them about staying back. She tentatively pressed her hands flat against one of the closed doors. From where she stood, Violet could feel the heat trying to find its way out, as if there were a fire trapped within the steel vault. Impossible, she knew, since the unit was refrigerated, but even from out here, that door—and only that door—shimmered and rippled, the way heat did when it rose from the asphalt of a desert highway.

Heat was this person's echo.

"That's not the right one," the tech explained, his voice thick with criticism.

For an endless moment there was silence, and then Violet answered, "I know. But I hope you're looking into this person's death too." She stood back. She didn't have to be told that the body of James Nua's girlfriend wasn't behind that particular door, or that it didn't belong to one of his children. She knew because she'd already sensed their echoes . . . the moment she'd stepped into the room.

They were here. And Nua had killed them.

She stepped to her left and pressed her hand against another of the doors. "This is one of them," she said as the strange choral whispers filled her ears, echoing within her own head. Then she moved again, brushing her fingertips over the silver door just to the right of it. The distinct taste of candied apples was there too. "And this one."

And then she found the last one, that strange chill that she hadn't been able to distinguish as real or imprint when she'd been in James's presence. It was here too, clinging to the life he'd extinguished. She held her hand over yet another steel door and nodded, looking at Sara, and only Sara.

She had no idea who the slithering tattoos had belonged to. She had no doubt that killing came easily to a boy like James Nua.

Violet stepped back, this time reaching for Sara and finding the sleeve of her jacket. "I'm ready to go," she said softly, reverently.

She could see Rafe too, a gold chain wrapped around his hand as his thumb feverishly stroked a simple cross. James Nua's cross, Violet was certain of it. Sara had given Rafe one of Nua's personal effects, hoping that he might be able to pick up on something about the young killer.

Once they were in the parking garage again, away from the cloying overload of echoes from the dead, Violet sighed, trying to find her way from beneath the suffocating burden of those who were unsettled. She climbed into the SUV and strapped her seat belt around her. She barely realized when Rafe climbed in beside her instead of sitting in the front seat with Sara. She felt robotic, like she was just going through the motions of everyday life.

At last she said the words that struggled to find their way to the surface. "I'm just so tired." She let her head fall against Rafe's shoulder, and his arm slipped around her. The musky scent of his skin was mingled with deodorant and leather. "I need to go home now."

INTIMACY

SHE WAS SLEEPING. HE FELT BAD WAKING HER, *and he hoped not to, but sometimes it couldn't be avoided. It was dark and he couldn't bear to be alone.*

Instead of the candle, he used a small penlight. The bulb was nearly microscopic and the light was dimmer than a candle's flame, yet he found his way to her bedside without stumbling, even over his heavy clodhopper feet.

His face dropped, and his eyes moved downward as his cheeks burned with humiliation. Clodhopper. *What a terrible word. What an awful thing to tell a child. He flashed the penlight's glow over the top of his shoes, not wanting to look, but unable to do anything else. They weren't so big, he thought. They weren't* awkward or unwieldy. They were just normal feet, he assured himself. Just average, ordinary feet. There was nothing special about them.

Yet, he was angry for the shame he felt . . . that he could still be embarrassed in that way, even in the privacy of his own grown-up thoughts. His mother wasn't here, he reminded himself. She couldn't hurt him . . . she could no longer humiliate him.

He pursed his lips, bitter now instead of afraid, and wondered if this was really the best time to see his girl again. None of this was her fault, after all, and facing her when he was in one of his moods wouldn't do either of them any good. It never did.

But the idea of going back to bed, upstairs all by himself, made the acids in his stomach churn violently. He closed his eyes, trying to think clearly.

At last, he lifted the penlight and flicked it across the peaceful plains of her face, checking to see if she was still asleep. Her eyes were closed, her lids still, motionless. A dreamless sleep.

That's usually how it was after they'd eaten one of his "special" meals. He felt better knowing they would sleep peacefully, that waking wasn't an option.

He lifted a finger to his mouth to chew on the ragged edge of his fingernail, and then he remembered what a disgusting habit that was and dropped his hand away guiltily. He let the glow of the penlight move down over the blanket, finding the girl's limp hand in the darkness, as he studied her long, lovely fingers.

He felt himself relax when he saw the color, the shimmering lilac he'd painted on her fingernails.

She had beautiful hands. Clean and pretty and soft.

129

He wanted to be near her. He didn't want to be alone, not tonight.

He crept closer, hesitating as he reached the side of her bed, and he listened to the long, stretched out sounds of her sleep. Such a peaceful sound. Such a soothing sound.

The bedsprings creaked as the weight of the bed shifted. There was plenty of room for him, and he slid beneath the covers easily. He curled himself around her, finding her warmth and letting it surround him, lull him. Yet she never flinched, never moved.

She was ready for him, waiting for him.

CHAPTER 9

VIOLET STARED OUT HER BEDROOM WINDOW AT a black sky punctuated by a million effervescent white lights. She was trying to decide if it was too late to go to sleep or too early to be up. From where she stood, looking out, everything was so peaceful. Calm. Yet inside of her, a war waged, and sleep was overruled by torment.

She listened to the darkness, to the nighttime sounds that surrounded her: the furnace blowing air through the vents, the occasional creak of her house, a dog barking in the distance . . . too far away to be bothersome to anyone but those who were already awake. She knew it wasn't any of those things that troubled her. She knew it was James Nua's family—his girlfriend and their children, lying dead in the morgue, miles away—who kept her awake.

She'd tried to slow her breathing, to concentrate on finding that *inner calm* Dr. Lee had taught her to draw upon. But tonight, for some reason, inner calm was hard to come by, and Violet found herself struggling with the weight of the echoes cloaking her in a mantle of sorrow and despair. She hoped the bodies would be buried soon, hoped they would find peace at last.

Frustrated, Violet sighed and shoved away from the windowsill. She felt sluggish, as though she were wading through gelatin, gummy and sticky, while it sucked at her, dragging her down. Every movement felt slow and strained.

She wandered to her chest of drawers and pulled the top one open, peeling back a layer of clothing she'd used to conceal the pill bottle Dr. Lee had given her. She picked it up and jiggled it, letting the white capsules rattle together, like tiny graveyard bones picked bare.

Violet smiled; death was definitely on her mind tonight.

Everything would be so much easier if she'd just take one of the chalky pills. Maybe she'd sleep then. Maybe she'd feel some peace at last, even if it was only temporary.

The idea had definite merit.

But she sighed once more as she closed her eyes and let the bottle fall from her fingers. She just couldn't do it. She couldn't bring herself to even open the stupid bottle.

Yet here she was, sapped, a bone-deep kind of exhaustion that made her legs feel like rubber as she listlessly closed the drawer again.

She blinked, her eyes feeling gritty, abraded by her own eyelids as she shuffled back to her bed. She would keep trying. She refused to let the echoes consume her.

She collapsed heavily onto her bed and punched her pillow before rolling over. When the phone on her nightstand rang, she was reaching for it, checking the caller ID, and pressing Talk before the first ring had ended. It was one thing to have the home phone in her bedroom, a poor substitute for the cell phone that had been taken away from her; it was another to have it wake her parents in the middle of the night.

Violet glanced at the clock on her nightstand. 1:57. "What are you doing, calling so late?" She glared into the darkness, hating how easily her curiosity was pricked.

Rafe's voice was low and gravelly on the other end. "How come you can't just say hello? You give off kind of a hostile vibe, you know that?"

She curled her hand around her mouth, not wanting to wake her parents as she whispered frustratedly. "I wouldn't if you'd call at a decent hour. You could have woken me."

"Could have?" She could practically see the smug look on his face as he pointed out her poor word choice.

"Well . . . you know . . . I was just . . ." She faltered, and then shrugged as she gave up, sitting up and crossing her legs in front of her. She balanced her elbows on her knees and rested her chin in her palm. "I was having a hard time sleeping, that's all. But you didn't know that. I should have been asleep."

The silence dragged between them as Violet leaned

forward, waiting for him to get to the point. And when he did, his tone was somber. "Another girl's been taken, V." He paused, and his voice grew thick. "Sara thinks it was the collector."

Violet's head cleared instantaneously, her mind reeling with a hundred unanswered questions. "When? How? What makes her think it was him—"

Rafe seemed to know what she was going to ask even before she'd finished asking. "Nothing in particular. The girl was reported missing by her roommate, said she didn't come home after work."

"And that was strange?"

"Cops didn't think so. They assumed she went out with friends. Figured she was a big girl and didn't need to check in with her roommate. No one took it seriously at first."

"So why does Sara—"

"Krystal," Rafe stated flatly, cutting Violet off again.

Violet thought about that, and wondered what Krystal had told Sara exactly. "She knew?" was all she asked.

Rafe didn't answer the question directly. "Sara made a call and told the detectives what she suspected. She talked them into checking out the lead, and apparently, when they went to the girl's house, they found what Krystal said would be there. He'd dropped something . . . it was under her bed."

Violet's eyes widened, her heart pounding. "What was it?"

"It was a piece of jewelry. A ring. It was Antonia Cornett's. It was reported missing from her belongings."

Violet gasped, covering her mouth, not wanting to

wake her parents. "Did Krystal say how she knew it would be there?"

There was another pause, and then Rafe answered her. "A girl spoke to her in her sleep. She thinks it might have been Antonia, but since it was just a voice, she can't be sure."

Violet's blood turned to ice at the mention of the girl's name, a ghost now, and she reached for her blanket, pulling it up to her chin. "She . . . she spoke to Krystal?" But Violet already knew the answer. Isn't that what Krystal said, that the dead talked to her? "What's her name, the missing girl? Do you know who she is?"

"Her name is Casey Atkins. She goes to the university, just like Antonia did."

Violet felt sick. She wondered if there were any other connections between the two girls, other than the school they attended. She thought about this new girl, Casey, and tried to imagine what she was like, tried *not* to think about what she might be going through right now.

She hoped they could find her before it was too late.

"What about you?" he asked. "It was a rough day. How are you holding up?" Violet didn't want to talk about what had happened at the morgue, but it didn't matter—Rafe wasn't really asking after her feelings to be nice. "Can you come to the Center in the morning? Sara's trying to get some of Casey's things." He was asking if she could still work.

Violet shook her head. "I don't think so. Not yet." Squeezing her eyes shut, she tried to stave off the fogginess that threatened to steal over her once more. "Besides, there's not much I can do anyway," she added, as if that was the only thing keeping her away, her inability to do what the others could.

Rafe went silent again, longer than necessary, and Violet wondered if there was something else, something he wasn't saying. But then he just softly added, "If you change your mind—"

"I won't," she stated resolutely. She didn't want to know any more, not about Antonia Cornett and not about Casey Atkins. Not now. Not while she was feeling like this.

"Fine," Rafe said. "Good night, V. Sleep tight."

Violet hung up, ignoring the odd sensation that penetrated the leaden veil surrounding her. *Sleep tight?* she thought, wishing she had the strength to smile. *Who says that anyway?*

And what was that other thing? The barely concealed tenor she'd heard in his voice. Something like affection? Maybe tenderness?

Was Rafe going soft on her?

She shook it off, certain she'd only imagined the tone in his voice. She was disoriented, she reminded herself, as her thoughts once again drifted unwittingly to Casey Atkins.

Rubbing her temples, she wondered how on earth she was ever going to get any sleep now, with the fate of a missing girl weighing on her conscience.

After a few minutes, Violet got up and paced across the room once more. The pills were still there, lying on top of a pile of rumpled T-shirts in the top drawer, and she plucked them out, slipping the cap off without a second thought.

They were easier to swallow than she'd imagined they'd be, and for several long minutes as she lay in her bed staring at the ceiling she thought nothing was happening, that the pills weren't working. And then her eyelids fluttered, growing heavier and heavier. Until, at last, she could no longer hold them open.

And a dark, dreamless sleep claimed her.

At some point, during the early hours of the morning, the dreams found their way in. They were dark dreams, treacherous, submerging Violet in their murky depths until she was incapable of finding her way to the surface. At first the images were harmless, like some sort of crazy kaleidoscope, drifting in and out of focus, colliding and splintering and reforming again. Happy childhood memories, mostly. Flashes of Jay and her friends. Summer days spent climbing trees and playing flashlight tag. Slumber parties, camping, picnics, cherry Slurpees, and school carnivals. Just quick snapshots that meant nothing at all when pieced together.

And then the images became more gruesome. Glimpses of dead squirrels and possums. A cat with empty sockets where its eyes had once been, now gouged out. And the face of the first dead person she'd ever seen—a girl whose eyes had been wide and pleading. Although what Violet most remembered was the girl's echo, the haunting voice that had called her away from her father's side as they'd walked through the woods behind their home.

But it was the last fragments of the dream, images that made her feel as if she were drowning, reminding Violet that her ability was nothing less than a curse, where she saw the faces of killers. The two men who'd hunted in her hometown just months before, killing violently, brutally. Mike and Megan's father, a man who'd murdered his wife years earlier, and then killed himself in a final act of desperation. And her uncle, someone she loved almost as much as her own father, whose imprint had been earned simply by saving the life of his own niece from the hands of a serial killer. She saw too the sadistic James Nua, who'd ended the lives of his very own children.

Finally, the last man she saw didn't have a face in her dream; she simply knew him as *the collector*—but he was there too, a dark, featureless mass, coming closer and closer to where Violet flailed, struggling to remain afloat and desperate to find her way to the surface and break free from the waters that threatened to drown her.

She gasped at the same time she jolted upright, her body gripped in the spasm of an unvoiced scream. As if deprived for too long, oxygen savaged her lungs as she gulped mouthfuls of air, waiting until enough time passed that, at last, her breathing finally found a rhythm that felt steady and calm.

And the tormenting visions faded, becoming nothing more than a memory. Enough was enough, Violet thought. She had to take control. She needed to go to the Center after all.

★ ★ ★

"Are you sure you're okay with this?" Violet asked once more before reaching for the door's handle.

Jay scowled, but not at Violet. He was gazing uncertainly at the neglected façade of the warehouse they were parked in front of. "Are *you* sure this is the right place?" It was impossible *not* to notice the grime and the desolation in this part of town. "*This* is where all the magic happens?" He chuckled, but Violet could hear the concern and couldn't help wondering at his use of the word *magic*. She was suddenly nervous about him being there, about having him so close to her team.

"But you understand why you can't go inside, right?" She shifted in her seat, blocking his view of the building and forcing him to look at her instead.

Jay grinned, the corner of his lip riding up just a bit. "I know you have work to do, and that it's top secret or something. That you're some sort of super spy, right?" She didn't stop him when he closed the gap between them, his lips finding hers in a deep—and territorial—kiss. She couldn't help wondering who he thought might be watching.

She'd called Jay first thing in the morning, to ask if he could drive her to the Center before school. She hated that he had to wait outside, but she didn't trust herself to drive this morning. Not after the pills . . . and the nightmare.

Besides, she was still feeling foggy from the pills Dr. Lee had given her, and she'd been worried about driving herself.

Inside the warehouse, Rafe was already in the hallway and Violet wondered if Jay hadn't been right to think they

139

might be being watched. She eyed Rafe curiously but he was already leading the way. "We don't have much, but Sara wanted to fill us in on all the latest." Violet followed him, feeling strange about leaving Jay outside.

In the Center, Sara had started the debriefing, and Violet and Rafe slipped silently into the gathering.

"—I was able to get photos of the first two victims, and a little more information about them. The first of the girls was from Ballard and had been doing an internship at a local advertising agency. She was twenty-three. The second was a twenty-one-year-old preschool teacher from the Green Lake neighborhood. Not much to link them—either to each other or to the two college students—except for their looks." She passed the photos to Violet, and there was no denying that the resemblance was striking. Both girls looked like Antonia Cornett. "I'm still working on getting the file for the missing girl, Casey Atkins, and some items from her home, including the ring they found." She smiled at Krystal when she mentioned the ring they'd discovered in Casey's home. "I do have some things from the other girls, though, if you don't mind taking a look at them."

Everyone started to jump up, but Sara stopped them. "Oh, and guys. Just so you know, the police suspect that he's the one who's been calling in the girls' locations."

"What d'you mean?" Sam asked, his lip curled in disgust. "They think *he's* the anonymous caller who told them where to find the bodies? Why would he do that?"

Sara's mouth pulled into a tight line as she shook her

head. "They have no idea. But so far the phone numbers he called from have been tracked down to disposable cell phones, and the receipts have been dead ends. Whoever he is, he's careful, that's for sure."

Beside her, Rafe let out his breath, and Violet felt the way he sounded. Disgusted.

"Violet, can I talk to you for a minute? Alone?" Sara asked as the rest of the team descended on the box sitting on the conference table.

Violet got up and followed Sara to her private workstation. When Sara turned around to face her, she frowned. "Didn't I just say *alone*?"

But behind her, Violet heard Rafe, his voice low. "I wanted to talk to her too. I figured it was better to do it here than in front of everyone else."

Sara crossed her arms but released a resigned sigh. "Fine." She turned to Violet. "I just wanted to see how you were doing, after last night with James Nua. You look . . . you look tired, Violet."

Violet glanced self-consciously over her shoulder at Rafe. "I am, sort of." She shrugged. "I mean, you *did* call me in the middle of the night."

Rafe swiped at the back of his neck, looking apologetic. "Sorry about that. I thought you'd want to know."

Violet managed a weak smile. "Of course I did. But I'm still tired."

"But you're okay?" Sara interrupted. "Other than that, I mean?"

"Yeah. I'm a little groggy from the pills Dr. Lee gave me, but I'm fine."

Violet watched as a silent look passed between them, something she didn't quite grasp. And then Sara reached for an envelope on her desk, handing it to Violet. "I almost forgot. This is yours."

Violet slid the flap open and peered inside, her stomach coiling. She felt strange taking a paycheck for an ability she had no control over, but Sara reacted before Violet could protest . . . again. "Violet, we've talked about this. It's your job now. I couldn't ask you to do these things and not expect to compensate you. Besides, how else are you supposed to afford all your gas money? Buckley's not exactly around the corner." She smiled patiently. "Now try to get some rest. Who knows, I might need you again tomorrow."

Violet shook her head but stopped short of arguing. She folded the envelope and stuffed it in her pocket. It wasn't until she turned around that she nearly gasped, surprised to find Jay sitting in the kitchen. He was across from Gemma at one of the small Formica tables, and she was cupping one of his hands in both of hers, her fingertip grazing the creases that ran through his palm. Neither seemed aware of Violet, and she watched in stunned silence as Gemma first glanced at Jay's face, and then closed her eyes, as if deep in concentration.

Violet was about to storm over and put a stop to whatever Gemma was trying to pull, when Rafe grabbed her by the sleeve, jerking her to a halt. "Wait a sec, will ya? I wanna see where this is going."

142

Violet frowned, turning her glare on Gemma once more. "You've got to be kidding. She's not really telling his fortune, is she?"

"What an amateur," Krystal tried to whisper, sneaking up on the two of them from behind and draping her arms around their necks.

But Jay and Gemma had heard Krystal too, and they looked up to find the three of them standing there, watching as they huddled over the top of the table. Jay jerked his hand away from Gemma's, hiding it in his lap while his cheeks burned red.

Gemma just smirked at Violet, cocking her head. "Look who was sitting out in his car . . . all by himself." Her voice was pouty, as if she were talking about a lost puppy.

Violet narrowed her eyes at the other girl as she swallowed the lump that had formed in the back of her throat.

Rafe sauntered over to the table and flipped one of the chairs around so he was straddling it. "Did you see anything interesting?" he queried, propping his chin against the back of the chair as he glanced from Gemma to Jay.

Gemma's perfectly painted lips upturned in a slow, evocative smile. "Sure, a lot of stuff. I'm sure you'd be very interested," she finished, letting the words hang between them, her brown eyes locked with his blue ones.

Krystal's arm was still wrapped around Violet's neck and she tugged her closer, so that her mouth was right at Violet's ear. "That one's like a snake. She'll strike if you don't watch your back," she managed in the first quiet voice Violet had ever heard her use.

But Jay was already jumping up, rubbing his palm nervously on his jeans. "You all done?" he asked, his eyes widening in a silent plea. "We should probably get going—it's getting late."

Violet decided to let him off the hook; it wasn't his fault Gemma had it out for her. Besides, she didn't want Sara to see him and think she was the one who'd invited him inside. "He's right," she agreed. "We've got school."

Violet grabbed Jay's hand and dragged him through the Center, watching his reaction and remembering how she'd felt the first time she'd been there. High-tech didn't begin to describe the wide-open interior with its oversized plasma displays mounted on the walls, state-of-the-art computer workstations, and security cameras that tracked movement throughout the Center.

"Surveillance, huh?" Jay breathed, his eyebrows inching up a notch. "Pretty high-tech." This time, unlike when he'd first seen the outside of the building, he actually sounded a little awed.

"Pretty cool, isn't it?"

Jay leaned down. "I forgive you." He grinned enthusiastically.

"For what?" The rest of her team was just steps away, and Violet's stomach knotted angrily.

His voice dropped. "For ditching me all the time. This is way cooler than hanging at the Java Hut."

ANGER

*THE SCREAMING HAD STARTED EARLY, AND EVEN
though he couldn't hear her from upstairs—not with all of the pre-
cautions he'd taken in preparing her room—the speakers on the
monitor he looked at still blared with her staticky cries. He covered
his ears as he rocked himself . . . forward and backward . . . forward
and backward. He watched as she pounded on the doors, the walls,
and even precariously balanced on her bed as she strained to reach
the ceiling overhead, beating her fists against it. She had no way of
knowing that no one could hear her, that her every effort was in vain.*

*Maybe it had been too soon. Maybe she hadn't been ready for
the freedom he'd offered when he'd released her from her restraints.*

But he'd hoped . . .

He uncovered his ears, once again letting her hoarse shrieks find their way into his head, letting the sounds echo inside the walls of his skull, reverberate through his skin. Making his hair stand on end.

The screaming was more than he could bear. It always was.

He reached out and turned the volume all the way down as he paced toward the kitchen. He reached into the sink, pulling out a dirty bowl, and rinsed it hastily beneath the faucet. Without even bothering to dry it, he filled the sticky bowl with soup—the same special soup he'd made for her the night before—and he shoved it into the microwave.

He waited only seconds before pressing the cancel button and jerking the bowl out again. Soup sloshed over the sides of the bowl. He didn't care if her food was warm. He didn't care if it was good or that the bowl was still dirty. She would eat it, whether she wanted to or not. She had to. He had to stop her from screaming.

And then he'd get out of the house for a bit. Get some fresh air so he could think again . . . and he had a lot to think about right now.

Maybe she wasn't the right girl for him after all.

CHAPTER 10

VIOLET HAD KNOWN BEFORE SHE WAS FULLY awake the next morning that she'd overslept, and she vaguely wondered why her parents hadn't come in to wake her. She'd heard a faraway buzzing sound—something that sounded strangely like her cell phone—but even in the fuzzy depths of sleep she knew that couldn't be it. It wouldn't have mattered, though; she'd been unable to rouse herself.

It was the dream again. The one from the night before, with the dark, faceless man. Only this time she wasn't drowning. This time he was coming after her, his fingers reaching for her . . . and she knew what he wanted. She knew he meant to choke her, in the same way he'd strangled all those other girls.

She awoke drenched in sweat, and released a shuddering sigh into her pillow as she clutched it in her hands. Blinking hard, she lifted her head and glanced down at the fabric she held. But it wasn't her pillow at all. It was soft fleece she gripped until her knuckles were white and her fingers ached.

The moment she recognized it, she threw it down, wondering how it had gotten there in the first place. And then she glanced at her nightstand and saw the phone there. Her cell phone. Beneath it was a note from her mother, and she realized it was probably her mom who'd folded her hoodie and placed it on her bed too.

She picked up the note.

You can have this back on a probationary basis. Mess up again,
and it's ours for good!
XOXO,
Mom

Of course Violet knew what this was really about. Her parents had hated being unable to reach her, not being able to call and check up on her. Still, the hugs-and-kisses were a nice touch, she thought; glad to have her phone back, no matter the reason.

She scrolled through the messages and realized that she hadn't been dreaming after all; there were calls and texts from Jay, Chelsea, and Jules, asking where she was. Already she'd missed first period, she realized as she glanced at the time.

Violet sent a quick text to Jay, knowing he'd spread the word for her:

Running late. Be there soon.

Then, setting the phone aside, she hesitantly reached for the sweatshirt, almost as if it might scald her, and she flipped over the fleece to examine it. There was nothing different about it than there had ever been before; it was the same White River High School hoodie it had always been . . . the one she'd worn so often it had lost its shape, the edges of the sleeves fraying and tattered.

Only now she didn't want to wear it. Now it was just another reminder of the night she'd first encountered James Nua in the police station.

Violet's face crumpled as she glanced once more at the sweatshirt she held. And then she remembered something. Something she'd very nearly forgotten about . . .

Slipping her hand inside the single front pocket, her fingers searched until they grasped the tiny slip of paper that was wadded into an almost unnoticeable ball. "There you are," she whispered, the sliver of a smile finding her lips as she smoothed it out. Her eyes were slower to adjust than they should have been. She guessed it was a side effect of the drug she'd taken the night before to help her sleep. Everything about her felt like that: slow to adjust.

When she finally recognized what it was she was staring at, she felt a burst of triumph, even though she had no idea if it even meant anything.

She recalled the way Rafe had been flipping through the pages of the book, sure he'd discovered something. And how she'd watched as the slip of paper tumbled from between the pages to the floor when the cop had interrupted them.

It was a receipt. A restaurant receipt from someplace called The Mecca.

Violet studied it, tracing it with her fingers, considering it. And then she put it away again, realizing she had somewhere she needed to go after school today.

"So, are you planning to tell me what Madame Gemma saw when she was reading your palm yesterday?" Violet stared up at Jay with wide, overly innocent eyes as they maneuvered through the hallways toward the cafeteria. She batted her eyelashes and dropped her voice. Jay didn't mention how bloodshot her eyes were, or that there were deep bags beneath them, even though she was sure he'd noticed. "C'mon, I won't tell anyone your secrets . . . even if they're really, *really* bad," she promised, raising an eyebrow.

"Mocking me will get you nowhere." But he leaned down, his breath tickling the side of her neck, and a rush of warmth flooded Violet's stomach. "There are other ways to break me, though."

Violet reached for his hand, drawing him out of the flow of traffic, away from the pushing and shoving of students, until they were tucked into a private pocket of space, just the two of them. "What do I have to do to make you talk?" She pressed against him, standing on her toes so her lips could reach his.

She didn't have to reach far; he was already meeting her halfway, his arm snaking around her waist. They didn't speak for several long seconds as Violet savored the feel of his lips against hers, soft and familiar and achingly tender. She shivered inwardly, both loving and hating the way her body reacted—almost instantaneously—to his. She had very little control over herself when he touched her. She felt like a puppet, at his command.

But they couldn't stand there for long, pretending that no one could see them, when everyone could. She kissed him one last time . . . lightly, softly, sweetly. "So, *now* are you gonna tell me?" she teased, slipping her hand beneath his T-shirt so she could feel the warmth of his bare stomach.

One side of his lip twitched upward. "There's really nothing to tell, Vi. I don't have any deep dark secrets or anything. What you see is what you get."

"How can you be so sure? What did she say exactly?" Violet's fingers danced along his waistline, tracing a path to his back.

Jay grinned down at her, reaching for her hand and leading her toward the lunchroom. "Nothing, really. She just kept saying 'interesting,' over and over again. If you ask me, she just noticed what everyone else already knows, that I'm incredibly interesting."

Violet stopped short as they reached their lunch table. "You've got to be freaking kidding me," she muttered under her breath.

Jay flashed Violet a puzzled look. "I didn't know you two were friends."

"We're not." Violet glared at Chelsea, Jules, and Claire, wondering what it was they were up to.

"Hey, guys," Chelsea chirped, entirely too cheerfully. "You remember Jacqueline, right?"

Violet clenched her jaw as she dropped her lunch on the table across from where Jacqueline stood beside Chelsea. Claire sat on the other side of her, daintily unfolding the plastic wrap around her sandwich, oblivious to the tension in the air. Violet searched Jacqueline's face for any visible marks where the ball had hit her the other day in PE.

Jacqueline ignored the halfhearted, quasi introduction and took a deep breath as if she were getting ready to start one of her cheer routines. Even her regular voice was . . . overly spirited. "I just wanted to come over and invite you guys to Hannah Sanders's house tonight. Her parents are out of town and she's throwing a rager. Everyone'll be there. And I do mean *everyone*." She directed her gaze to Jay as she said the last word, her eyes sparkling playfully.

Violet was biting down so hard now that she was worried she might actually shatter her own molars. She squeezed as close to Jay as she could manage on the cafeteria bench. She knew it was a possessive move, but at the moment that was the least of her concerns.

"Sorry, Jac, I have to work," Jay said, and Violet's stomach tightened, wondering when he and "Jac" had ever even talked before, when they'd gotten chummy enough to use nicknames.

Jacqueline's shoulders sagged. "Aw, that stinks, Jay! I was counting on you to be there."

"I can make it," Claire offered, her sandwich halfway to her mouth, as if Jacqueline were worried about a head count.

"Yep, me too," Jules added, leaning forward on her elbows. She lifted an eyebrow, a wicked smile dancing across her full lips. She knew this had nothing at all to do with how many people showed up. "Chels?"

Chelsea grinned with satisfaction. "Oh, I wouldn't miss it," she said, tapping her lip thoughtfully. "In fact, I think you should come too, Vi. It wouldn't be a party without you."

Violet scowled at Chelsea. "Sorry. I might've gotten my phone back, but I sort of doubt my parents will be letting me go to parties any time soon." She had no intention of admitting that the last place she wanted to be was at Hannah Sanders's house with a bunch of Jacqueline's friends.

"Your loss." Jacqueline shrugged, but she didn't sound all that disappointed to hear Violet wouldn't be attending. Again, she turned to Jay. "If you change your mind . . ."

Jay laughed off the suggestion as he cupped his hand around Violet's knee, squeezing it reassuringly. Violet thought of the way she'd seen Gemma cupping his hand the day before at the Center, and she couldn't help it; she felt something well deep inside her, something close to frustration and worry. She felt like she'd missed something important.

She knew Jay wasn't interested in Jacqueline—or at least she hoped he wasn't.

"What did you do, anyway?" Chelsea asked after Jacqueline had sauntered away.

Violet glanced up, confusion evident in her green eyes. "What are you talking about?"

"To get in so much trouble, what did you do?"

"It was nothing, really," Jay explained, dropping his arm around Violet's shoulder and pulling her closer. "Violet did a little breaking and entering the other night and got busted by the cops."

Chelsea frowned at him. "I don't believe a word you're saying. Violet doesn't even jaywalk—no offense, Jay," she said. "No way she was trespassing in someone else's house."

Jay just turned his wry gaze toward Violet for confirmation. "It's true, isn't it, Vi?"

She shook her head, trying to decide whether to laugh or to wring his neck for putting her in this position. Finally she sighed, her posture wilting. "It's true," she admitted. "But it's not like I was stealing anything. I was just looking around. Besides"—she gritted her teeth and glared at Jay— "I'm not sure we should be talking about this."

Jules interrupted her. "Oh, I'm totally sure you should be talking about this. This is the juiciest thing I've heard all week, maybe all year." She glanced meaningfully at Violet, her light brows arched. "Probably the juiciest thing I've *ever* heard about *you*."

If she only knew, Violet thought. And suddenly she

154

wondered if she'd been wrong to worry about Jacqueline. Maybe Jacqueline was *exactly* the kind of girl Jay needed.

The kind of girl who went to parties.

The kind of girl who *didn't* break into houses, or chase after dead bodies and serial killers.

An ordinary girl. A *normal* girl.

Violet hated parallel parking, so she decided that rather than embarrassing herself by even trying, she would drive around the crowded block several times, searching for alternatives. She finally found a spot in a small pay lot with spaces that were entirely too small, even for her Honda. It took some maneuvering but she managed to squeeze herself between a Toyota hybrid and a late-model Mercedes. From there, it was a walk to the main street where the café was, but at least no one had been watching as she'd backed in and out, and in and out, until she was straight . . . *ish*.

Making her way through the dingy alleyway lined with Dumpsters and discarded boxes, Violet had the distinct impression that this wasn't the kind of place you would want to be after dark. But it was still daylight, so it wasn't *so* bad.

Still, she walked quickly, tucking her hands into her pockets and keeping her head low. She glanced around, more wary of her surroundings than usual since she still felt groggy, a lingering effect from the pills that refused to dissipate entirely.

Since she didn't trust her dulled senses, she kept her eyes peeled, searching for signs that she wasn't alone. She peered into the shadows around each Dumpster and garbage can she passed, making sure no one was hidden there waiting to pounce on a girl who was all by herself in a creepy alley. She knew her imagination was working overtime, but even so, she breathed a sigh of relief when she reached the sidewalk and made a quick right-hand turn, joining the heavy foot traffic in the U District as she scanned the storefronts for The Mecca.

The café was really just a small soup-and-sandwich shop that, like so many others in the city, also served espresso and pastries. Outside, there was a cheerful red awning with *The Mecca* painted in swirling gold letters. It was inviting, Violet thought as she ducked through the entrance and the bells over the door jangled.

Inside, tables painted a glossy black were packed together, leaving little room to navigate between them. One entire wall was littered with a hodgepodge of framed paintings, each with a dangling, handwritten price tag, and Violet guessed they were probably on consignment from local artists. The paintings themselves ranged from generic cityscapes of the skyline and the Space Needle to the more exotic—and infinitely more colorful—paintings of fairies or pixies or other scantily clad, winged women. There was a large handwritten chalkboard above the counter that served as the menu, and a selection of coffee syrups littered the countertops around the industrial-sized stainless steel espresso machine.

Violet scanned the small late-afternoon crowd, not sure exactly what she'd expected to find, but hoping she'd be able to help.

She wondered if this was a place Antonia Cornett might have frequented, a usual hangout for her like the Java Hut was for Violet and her friends. Or if it was just a fluke that Violet happened across this particular receipt and it meant nothing at all, just a random slip of paper that the girl had been using as a bookmark. Meaningless.

Violet stood in front of the counter, examining the large corkboard covered in Polaroid snapshots. There were photographs of the café's employees, each with a drink recommendation listed below it. It was also handwritten with bold, colorful markers. There were lots of hand-drawn hearts and stars and flowers, and a drawing of a big coffee mug with swirls of steam rising from it.

Violet glanced at the red-haired girl behind the counter, and despite her puffy red eyes, she recognized her Polaroid from the board: She was the brown-sugar caramel macchiato.

"I'll have that," Violet said, pointing at the girl's drink recommendation. "Decaf, please," she added quickly.

The girl just nodded as she turned to the espresso machine. While she worked, Violet scanned the rest of the photos, thinking that maybe Antonia Cornett would be on there, that maybe she'd worked here before she vanished.

But by the time the girl was foaming the milk for the macchiato, Violet had given up. Antonia wasn't there.

She suddenly felt foolish for coming all this way over a simple receipt. How many insignificant receipts did she herself have lying around? More than she cared to admit.

She paid for her drink, took a sip of the sickly sweet concoction, and then dropped it in the trash can on her way out the door.

As she stood on the sidewalk once more, she struggled with what she should do next.

This area, the University District, was always bustling with activity, something Violet appreciated about the city. She could lose herself in a place like this, vanish in the rush of people and never even be noticed.

She stepped out of the way of foot traffic, students rushing past her with backpacks dangling from their shoulders and messenger bags slung across their chests. Even on a Friday afternoon, everyone had someplace to be. Everyone but Violet. She'd come all the way to Seattle hoping to find something useful, but had come up empty.

There was a bright red newspaper stand on the corner, and Violet dug in her purse for some quarters. She had no real plan, but maybe if she could find a place to sit and read for a while something would come to her, an idea. Dropping her coins into the slot, she pulled down the glass door and then paused.

Something felt off, and even though her first reaction was to dismiss it as just another strange side effect of the pills, she couldn't just ignore the way the hairs on the back of her neck prickled. Even the ones inside her nose felt suddenly itchy, tingly.

She glanced around, her hand still poised over the newspaper inside the metal box.

She couldn't describe the feeling exactly, but suddenly her chest felt tight, crushed. It was as if someone was watching her.

But everyone around her was moving, striding with purpose.

"Violet?"

She jumped at the sound of her name, catching her arm when she let go of the newspaper box's door. She turned toward the boy's voice and practically sighed with relief when she saw Sam standing there, looking at her curiously. Skinny, scrawny Sam, just another misfit in a sea of college students . . . in more ways than one. They were like peas in a pod.

"What—?" She grabbed her newspaper and let the door swing shut again, banging rustily. And then she turned to look behind her one last time, but there was nothing suspicious. Nothing out of place. "What are *you* doing here?" She glanced at him, at the button-down shirt that fit loosely from his gawky frame, and the messenger bag he gripped in front of his chest.

He smiled, making him look younger and even less like he belonged in the U District. "I could ask you the same thing. You don't live around here, do you?"

She concentrated on folding her newspaper and tucked it beneath her arm, ignoring his original question, not really wanting to explain *why* she was here. "No. Buckley, actually," she said. "What about you? Do you live nearby?"

He made a face, one that basically said: *You're kidding, right?* "You don't know?"

Violet shook her head, wondering what she'd missed. "Know what? Did something else happen?"

Sam laughed at that. "Wow, they really keep you in the dark, don't they? Don't worry, as soon as they know you're gonna stick, they'll let you in on all the cool secrets. But, to be completely honest, this hardly qualifies as cool." He raised an eyebrow and glanced purposely at his fingernails. She knew he was trying to look cocky, but it was a totally dorky move. "I live in the dorms. I'm just your average boy genius, that's all."

"Wait, you mean you . . . ?" Violet asked, not trying to hide her disbelief. "You go to school here?"

"That's pretty much what I'm sayin'." Sam nodded, a pleased expression on his face.

Violet thought about that, about not even being sixteen yet and being a student at the university. "I had no idea."

"Yeah, well, I guess it's hard to see my enormous brains past . . . all of this." He lifted one of his puny arms and flexed it, wiggling his eyebrows at her. Violet tried to hold back a giggle and then gave in, laughing at him.

Sam grinned back at her, and Violet was sort of amazed by his confidence. She wondered if she'd be so sure of herself if she were the one thrust into such an intimidating environment at such an early age.

"Hey, since you're here, and since I'm done with my classes for the day, you wanna grab a cuppa coffee or something?" he asked.

Violet glanced back at the sign for The Mecca, and

thought about the red-haired girl and her syrupy drink creation. "Sure," she agreed, realizing it solved her dilemma and gave her something to do, at least. "But can we go somewhere with just plain old coffee?"

Violet used the flimsy red plastic stir stick to swirl more of the heavy white creamer into her cup, and then added three more sugar packets. The coffee at The Mecca might've been too sweet, but at Max's Diner they didn't mess around. Here, they served it hot and black.

"So how do you like it so far?" Sam asked, blowing on his cup before bringing it all the way to his lips. He looked like a little kid playing tea party . . . far too young to be taking his coffee black.

"I assume you don't mean the coffee." Violet grinned at him. She thought about it for a minute before answering. "The team? I like it okay. I guess what I really like is not always having to hide what I can do, not always lying to everyone, you know? Plus, if it hadn't been for Sara and Rafe . . ." She hesitated. She didn't think it was a secret, what had happened to her. Especially not one of the cool ones. "I wish I could be useful like that," she said, instead of explaining her situation.

"Are you kidding? You have the coolest . . ." He lowered his voice to a whisper until it felt like they were playing Secret Agents. "You have the coolest gift of all of us," he repeated. "I'd trade you if I could."

Violet laughed. It was hard to take him seriously when

161

he was staring at her with his overeager eyes, pale freckles splattered across his nose, kid genius or not. "You're crazy. Psychometry is way cooler."

Sam scoffed. "Sure it is, if you're Rafe and have all the other stuff that goes with it. Me, I just have the garden-variety version. You know, feel an object and get a vibe. Or not. Mostly not."

"Other stuff?" Violet asked, leaning closer. "What other stuff are you talking about?"

Sam's brows rose, practically disappearing into his hairline. "Um, only the precog stuff!" When Violet didn't respond, he added, "Precognition . . ." He dragged the word out like *he* was the one speaking to a child now. And then he continued in an awed tone, "I might be able to tell something about an object's past, but Rafe can tell the person's future. In fact, I take it back: *He* has the coolest gift of everyone."

Violet was speechless. She'd known, of course, that Rafe had predicted she was in trouble, but she'd never really thought about *how* he'd done it. She'd thought he was like Sam, she supposed, more of your average garden-variety psychic; she didn't realize that knowing things *before* they happened was . . . well, so unusual. "I—I had no idea."

Sam's mouth clamped shut, and he suddenly looked as if he'd been caught with his hand in the cookie jar. His shoulders fell. "Damn," he finally said. "I guess that was one of those cool secrets I was talking about."

"It's okay," Violet assured him, lifting her cup to her

162

lips. "I won't say anything. Your secret's safe with me. Well, I guess *Rafe's* secret's safe with me, but you get the point."

"Good." Sam sighed. "Because he already doesn't like me. I'd hate to make things worse."

"Who doesn't like you? Rafe? Why wouldn't he like you?"

"I don't know," Sam said, as genuinely surprised as Violet was. Honestly, he was a pretty likeable guy. "I don't think he likes anyone, really." And then Sam's gaze lifted to hers, a faint smile lighting his boyish expression. "Except you, of course."

Violet nearly choked on her coffee. "No," she gasped, trying to talk as she struggled around her coughing fit. "You're wrong. He doesn't really like me, either. I think he just puts up with me, maybe because he saved my life and I'm indebted to him or something. Maybe he wants to make sure I pay him back." She smiled wanly at the boy across from her, trying to convince him.

But he shook his head vehemently. "Then you're blind. Or maybe it's just 'cause you didn't know him before you came on the team. He's better now than he was then. Like, he's a kinder, gentler Rafe . . . even though he's still pretty foul most of the time.

"But before you were here, no one could even talk to him. He glared all the time. And God forbid someone tried to make nice and start a conversation." Violet got the feeling Sam was talking about himself now as she listened, dazed. "He'd just bite their head off and storm away. He didn't *want* anyone to like him. Sara was the only one he was actually nice to."

Violet's mind was churning. She thought about the things Krystal had told her, about no one liking Rafe, but it was hard to imagine he'd ever been so . . . so difficult. That wasn't the Rafe she knew. Sure, he was walled off. And sarcastic, and even quick-tempered. But he was also sensitive and considerate. She knew because she'd seen that side of him.

She opened her mouth to say something, but words failed her, and she closed it again. She had no idea what she could possibly say to Sam. She was embarrassed, and she hoped he was wrong. She didn't want to be the reason Rafe was different. She didn't want to be the cause of a kinder, gentler Rafe.

Because that would mean Jay might be right.

That maybe Rafe's feelings were more than just friendly.

FATE

IT FELT GOOD TO GET OUT OF THERE, TO BE AWAY *from her, even if the reprieve was only temporary. At least he could breathe again.*

He walked his usual route, leaving his house and tracing his way around the university. He liked it there, all the old buildings swathed in vines and foliage. All the history and the architecture. All the places he could vanish, becoming whoever he wanted to be.

His frustration uncoiled a bit as he spied the familiar red awning of the café, even as he scolded himself for ending up here again. He stood back, not allowing himself to go any closer, not allowing himself to go inside. He knew it was a bad idea to come here, a place he'd been too many times before. It was breaking the rules.

He'd already broken them once, and look where that had gotten him.

He clenched his fists at his sides, trying to control his mounting rage as he pictured her . . . screaming. He needed to calm down. She needed him to calm down; it wouldn't do either of them any good if he went back home while he was this angry.

But if he hadn't been standing there, counting his breaths and trying to soothe himself, he might have missed her, the girl stepping out onto the sidewalk. She wasn't his usual type; even from where he stood he could see that much. Her hair was wild and curly, not straight and silken. Her eyes, even though he couldn't see the exact shade, were most definitely not dark, not the color of spiced cocoa or burnt mahogany. They didn't warm him. They didn't soothe him.

But there was something about her. Something that struck a chord in him. Something that made his head spin.

He reached for his phone, tucked deep in his pocket. He was careful with it, keeping his hand over the screen as he scrolled through the images he saved there, images meant only for his eyes.

He bit his lip when he found it, when he realized where he'd seen this girl before.

She'd been there, that day at the Pacific Storage warehouse when the police had arrived. He'd seen her in the parking lot as he'd stood in the crowd, making sure they found his ex-girlfriend, making sure his girl didn't have to stay there in the dark . . . alone.

And here she was again, at the café—his café—standing silently, looking lost. Looking . . . lonely.

He didn't know who she was, or why fate had intervened in this way, but when she started walking, he followed her, wondering the

166

entire time what was wrong with him. He had a girlfriend, waiting for him . . . needing him.

He told himself it was nothing, less than nothing. She was just a girl. He was only watching her. It didn't mean anything.

She stopped then at the newspaper machine, and just as she was poised to take her paper, she froze, every muscle in her body going rigid.

That was when he saw it. Fear.

He understood that.

He knew what it was like to be afraid. To be terrified and alone.

And he knew, too, that he needed to find out more about this girl. That he wasn't going home just yet.

CHAPTER 11

VIOLET SAT AT THE KITCHEN TABLE STARING numbly at the paper plate in front of her. Her mom had saved her some pizza and Violet heated it up when she'd gotten home. It wasn't late, but Violet felt like it was, and she was glad she'd told her friends she was staying home. She was too tired to do anything but stay in and feel sorry for herself.

Sighing, she pushed the half-eaten pizza away from her and reached for the newspaper she'd brought home with her. Normally she didn't read the paper, but honestly, she had nothing better to do. It was Friday night and she was at home while everyone else—including Jay—had other plans.

She opened the first page because it seemed like the thing

to do, the logical place to start. It didn't take long, scanning the columns of newsprint, for Violet to realize that the news was generally pretty boring stuff. She skipped the articles on the first few pages about Antonia Cornett, and the continuing search for her killer. Violet knew enough about that case already, images she'd never be able to purge from her mind.

She was about to close the paper when an article at the bottom of an inside page caught her eye. It wasn't so much the article that had captured Violet's interest, however; it was a name: Casey Atkins.

The missing girl.

Violet scanned the all-too-brief article, her heart speeding up as she noted that there was no mention of the serial killer suspected of abducting Casey Atkins. Maybe the story had gone to print before they'd made the connection. Maybe they didn't want to let the public in on the details.

Maybe it was better if the killer didn't realize they were on to him . . . for Casey's sake.

But there was something else about the article that made Violet's breath catch. A photograph.

It was grainy and small, the black-and-white matrix dot style of newsprint pictures, and she lifted it, holding it closer to the light to get a better view. She bit her lip as she stared at it, trying to decide what it was about the image that niggled at her memory, making her brain reel.

Just as she was about to give up, wilting back into her chair in defeat, it came to her and her hand shot up, covering her mouth. She was reaching for her phone before she could solidify her thoughts.

Rafe answered on the first ring, but she cut him off before a single word was out of his mouth.

"What are you doing tomorrow?" The words rushed from her lips. "You wanna meet me downtown?"

"Um, sure. I guess so. What's this all about? I tried to call you all day. Is everything all right?"

At the sound of his voice, Violet gritted her teeth. In her enthusiasm, she'd forgotten what Sam had told her about Rafe being *different* with her. She'd forgotten to worry about what that might mean. And she tried to decide if any of that was even important now. What really mattered was finding a killer, wasn't it? "I . . . uh . . . I'm fine. Much better. And I think I found something . . . about Casey Atkins."

"What? How?"

"I went down to Seattle after school today, to a café called The Mecca. I found the name on a receipt the night we were in Antonia Cornett's house." She smiled, sitting back now. "Well, actually, you found it. It was in the paperback you were holding when the cop came in. I snagged it when no one was looking."

"V . . . ." The warning in his voice was loud and clear, but Violet ignored him. "Why didn't you say something? I would've gone with you."

Using her finger, she dragged the plate closer again and picked off a congealed mushroom. "I didn't have anything better to do, and for all I knew the receipt was a dead end."

"But it wasn't?"

170

She leaned forward once more, balancing on her elbows. "That's the thing. I don't really know yet. Meet me there tomorrow and I'll let you know for sure."

She hung up the phone and stared at it for several long moments, wondering if it was really such a good idea to spend any more time with Rafe than necessary. She was about to call him back, to tell him she'd changed her mind, when there was a soft knock on the back door.

Violet crept across the kitchen floor on bare feet and peeked outside, craning to see out the window in the door. Her pulse leapt when she saw Jay there, standing on the other side, smiling back at her. He held a pizza box in one hand and a grocery bag in the other.

She turned and quickly dropped her paper plate and cold pizza into the trash can before she unlocked the door and let him in.

"What are you doing here? I sorta thought you'd be going to the party after work."

Jay set the box on the counter and kicked the door closed behind him. "Are you kidding? You said you couldn't go out; you didn't say anything about having to stay home alone. I'd way rather be with you than at some stupid party." He lifted the bag as if he were offering her a prize. "I brought ice cream. Chocolate-chip cookie dough."

Violet smiled, taking the plastic bag and setting it by the pizza as she wrapped her arms around him, inhaling deeply and wishing they could have more nights like this. Just the two of them.

"You don't mind that I came, do you? Should I have called first?"

She shook her head, not wanting to let go of him, grateful that he'd decided to come. That he'd rather be with her than with Jacqueline. "No, of course not. I just hope you realize how important you are to me."

He squeezed her back, a silent reassurance that he knew, and that the feeling was mutual. Then he picked her up and carried her fireman-style to the family room. Laughing, they dropped onto the couch and Jay kissed her, at last. Violet forgot all about the pizza and the ice cream. She forgot about Jacqueline, and any crazy notions that Jay should be with someone else.

He was hers, plain and simple.

And no one could change that.

CHAPTER 12

IT HAD BEEN HARD TO SLEEP THAT NIGHT, AND Violet was up way earlier than she needed to be. She was anxious to know if what she suspected was true.

Since she had so much time to spare, she'd decided to swing by the Java Hut on her way out of town to grab a breakfast sandwich and a coffee. She was surprised when she got there and saw Chelsea's car in the lot. It was early for Chelsea, practically ungodly.

It was fairly busy for a Saturday morning, although Violet didn't know if that was true or not, since she hadn't spent a lot of Saturday mornings at the internet-café-turned-restaurant. She found all three of her friends, Chelsea, Claire, and Jules, sitting at one of the booths, plastic menus piled near the edge of the table.

"Hey, what are you guys doing here this early?" Violet asked, sliding into the booth beside Chelsea and giving her a strange look. "And what've you done with the real Chelsea?"

"You're ha-ha-larious, you know that, Vi?" Chelsea retorted, staring back at Violet through the thick lenses of eyeglasses she almost never wore . . . especially in public. "My eyes were killing me this morning. I couldn't get my contacts in."

"Are you sure you don't have pinkeye?" Claire asked, her voice skeptical as she scooted closer to Jules.

Chelsea scowled at her. "I told you, I'm not diseased or anything. Re-*freaking*-lax, Claire. Do you think I'd be here if I was contagious or anything?"

The waitress arrived then, balancing their orders on a black tray. She flashed Chelsea a similarly distrustful look after overhearing what Claire had said, and she apprehensively slid Chelsea's plate in front of her. Chelsea ignored the girl completely.

"Softball tournament," Chelsea said to Violet, answering her earlier question. "Claire's just along for the ride. We tried calling you like a million times this morning, but obviously we don't rate."

"Three," Violet corrected, ignoring the wave of guilt she felt for ditching them yet again. "You called me *three* times. Besides, I have somewhere else I have to go . . . an appointment," she said evasively.

"Yeah, an appointment on a Saturday. Whatever."

Violet flashed an overly bright grin and tried her best to sound breezy. "Well, I'm here now, aren't I?"

"Yeah, I can tell you rushed right over to see us."

Violet perused one of the menus, pretending like it didn't suck to lie to her friends, and then turned to the waitress. "Can I just get a hot tea, and a toasted bagel with cream cheese?"

"Sure, I'll be right back with that," the waitress answered, still eyeing Chelsea suspiciously. She didn't bother asking if anyone needed anything else before turning on her heel and disappearing back into the kitchen.

Making a dubious face of her own, Chelsea glanced down at her plate. She picked up a fork and prodded her runny eggs, making an exaggerated gagging sound. Violet knew it wasn't a *real* gag because Chelsea had the strongest stomach of anyone she'd ever met.

From the other side of the booth, Jules's head snapped up and she glared at Chelsea. Chelsea's eyes flared behind her glasses, making them look about ten sizes too big. She flashed an apologetic grin at Jules before closing her lips tightly, a silent vow to stop making the obnoxious sounds.

But they all knew Chelsea *wanted* to keep going; Chelsea loved that game. When they were in the sixth grade, she used to pretend she was going to puke, making terrible retching sounds until someone would get sick for real. Rachel Lashly was the first person to ever actually throw up from Chelsea's disgusting ruse, but she claimed it was only because she was already coming down with the flu . . . and, as hard as she tried, Chelsea had never been able to make her do it again.

Jules, on the other hand, had proven to be the perfect target for Chelsea. For someone who could beat up nearly every boy on the playground, Jules had a surprisingly sensitive gag reflex, something that Chelsea had found endlessly entertaining. Chelsea would make Jules puke at the most inopportune moments, like when the bus was pulling up to pick them up for school. Or at the mall.

And even once in the middle of class.

But that was the day when Jules had had enough. She'd waited for Chelsea on the playground during recess, giving her friend a bloody nose while everyone stood around watching. Jules had been expelled for a week, but Chelsea had never intentionally made Jules vomit again.

Still, it didn't stop her from pretending her breakfast was making her sick now. "I'm sending it back. This is disgusting." She swirled her plate, showing how the tops of her eggs jiggled.

Claire pursed her lips. "Don't do it, Chels. They'll spit in your food if you send it back. You don't want them spitting in your food, do you?"

Chelsea grimaced as she watched her eggs quiver. "It would be better than eating this slop."

"I hate to be the one to point this out, but that *is* the way you ordered them, Chels." Jules raised her eyebrows as she lifted a hefty bite of pancakes to her full, naturally rosy lips.

"What did you think 'sunny-side up' was, anyway?"

"I didn't think it meant 'half-cooked.' They need to put a warning label on the menu or something." She lifted her hand and waved frantically, trying to get the waitress's attention. Over her shoulder, she declared, "I don't care what you guys say, I'm sending it back."

Violet watched Claire's face fall. "Great," Claire whined. "I guess that means we can't come back here again either."

"You can have my bagel," Violet offered Chelsea, taking pity on Claire. "I'm sure it'll be here any minute."

Chelsea dropped down again, glowering because the waitress had spotted her but was ignoring her, filling coffee for other customers and pretending she hadn't seen Chelsea's frantic gestures. "Bitch," Chelsea muttered. "Wait'll she sees her comment card."

Violet bit her lip. "Have you ever actually filled out a comment card, Chels?"

"You don't know. I might fill one out this time." Chelsea crossed her arms as she slouched back in the booth, daring one of them to argue with her while she waited for Violet's bagel to arrive. "By the way, you dodged a bullet last night. The party was totally lame."

Violet thought about her night, about staying home with Jay, eating pizza and watching movies, and she smiled inwardly. Lame was the last thing her night had been.

"What took you so long? I've been here for half an hour. I'd've gone in without you, but I have no idea what I'm looking for." Rafe scowled as Violet joined him outside The Mecca, his arms crossed impatiently.

The cloudless sky overhead gave the impression that the day should've been brighter, sunnier, but instead it just felt cold and empty. Like a vast gray wasteland.

Violet felt a twinge of satisfaction. She liked that she knew something he didn't, especially since, according to Sam, he was the one who had the cool precognition thing going on. "Sorry," she tried, but she didn't sound nearly as repentant as she should have. "I ran into some friends."

He looked at his watch. "Some of us still value other people's time."

She rolled her eyes, suddenly feeling like she had an idea why he wasn't winning any charm contests. "Whatever. Don't be such a baby. Besides, it's not like you had anyplace better to be, or you wouldn't have jumped at the chance to meet me in the first place."

"Or," Rafe said as he reached out to get the door for her, holding it so she could go in ahead of him, "I want to catch this sicko."

Violet faltered. Of course that was it, she chided herself, embarrassed for thinking otherwise. Why else would he be wasting his Saturday with her?

She felt unsettled as she stepped inside the café and surveyed the art wall and the congested tables and chalk menu. That artsy appeal that Violet had felt just a day earlier was lost on her now, tainted with what she thought she knew, what she hoped to confirm by being here today.

"So? This is it, huh?" Rafe asked, but his eyes were on Violet, not on the café.

"Why?" Violet stepped closer to him, her voice dropping. "Do you sense something?"

He shot her an amused look. "Do I *sense* something? Really? That's the best you can do? Do you want me to check for evil spirits while I'm at it?" He smirked. "I was only asking because *you* said this was the place."

"Whatever. You don't have to be such a jerk," Violet told him, her cheeks burning. "I was just thinking that maybe . . . you could," she stammered. "Maybe you might *feel* something?"

Rafe tipped his head closer, until it was right next to hers, and suddenly she was far too aware of him. Of his lips and the blazing blue of his eyes. He quirked an eyebrow at her, just one. "I have to actually touch something to feel something. Just FYI."

"Oh?" Violet said, nodding.

"Yeah. That's pretty much how it works."

"Do you want to?" she breathed. "I mean touch something?" Her heart was racing, slamming so violently it felt like a sledgehammer, and she worried it might actually crack a rib.

He inched the tiniest bit closer, his breath mingling with hers. "I do," he said softly, his voice barely a whisper as his daring blue eyes held hers . . . longer than they should have. "But I think we should order a coffee so you can tell me what this is all about. Don't you?"

Violet wanted to nod, but she was too afraid to. Their lips were far too close. Dangerously close. "Sure."

She blinked when he pulled back and strode toward the counter, his heavy boots thudding along the floor, and she followed him, feeling bemused. She was relieved that the red-haired girl wasn't working today.

"What can I get you?" the boy behind the counter asked.

Rafe ordered quickly, just a black coffee, the same way Sam had ordered his. He reached for his black leather wallet, which was strung to the hip of his jeans by a steel chain, and pulled out a twenty. And then the two of them stood there, waiting for Violet to decide as she searched the corkboard for a recommendation.

For one recommendation in particular.

Finally she said, "I'll have that one." She pointed to the snapshot of a dark-haired girl with shiny hair and big brown eyes. "A green-tea soy latte."

The boy didn't even turn to look at the corkboard, but Violet could see his jaw tense and he blinked hard several times. "That's Casey's drink."

Violet nodded. It was all the confirmation she'd needed.

"How did you know?" Rafe asked as they took a table in the back. He dropped into the chair and stretched his legs out in front of him.

Violet's drink was too hot, and she took a small, careful sip before setting it on the table. "I saw her photo . . . well, a really grainy photo in yesterday's paper after I was here. She looked familiar, but I couldn't be sure it was her until I came back to look at the corkboard." She frowned. "I'm almost sorry it *was* her. Did you see his face? I hate knowing them. I hate knowing who they were. I mean, are," she corrected quickly. Casey Atkins wasn't dead. Not yet anyway. "But you know what this means, don't you?"

"That you were right?"

"No," she said uncertainly. "Well, yeah, I guess so. But that's not what I'm talking about."

Rafe took a swig of his coffee, hiding his grin behind his cup. "I thought that's what girls liked to hear . . . that they're right."

Violet threw her napkin at him. "You're ridiculous, you know that? No, it means that Antonia Cornett and Casey Atkins might have known each other. At the very least, they have this place in common." Suspiciously, she glanced at everyone in the café around them. There was a couple, their heads bent together over the table until they were practically touching as they whispered quietly to each other. At another table was a group of girls that reminded Violet of her friends. They were animated and loud and they talked over one another, and then laughed even louder at their own jokes. "He might have found both of them here."

Violet half-expected Rafe to make fun of her, to tease her about going all Nancy Drew on him, but when she looked back at him, she saw that he was thinking the same thing she was, his gaze appraising everyone.

"We have to tell Sara," Violet whispered.

Rafe gave a sharp, determined nod, and then he downed the rest of his coffee and slammed his cup on the table. "You're right. She needs to know this. It could be something. I'll tell her when I get back to the Center." He stood quickly.

Violet jumped up too. "No way, I'm coming with you," she insisted, reaching out to stop him. She was the one who'd figured it out; she didn't want to be left out.

She'd gotten used to the quick burst of static that erupted between them whenever they touched, but this time, when her fingers clasped around his wrist, the sensation jolted her, both physically and emotionally. She felt the ground shift, not literally, but the effect was just as unsteadying. She jerked her hand back, squeezing her fist into a tight ball.

Rafe must have felt it too, because his eyes flashed, finding hers and holding them with dark warning.

Neither of them spoke; they just watched each other warily for several long moments.

Finally a slow grin spread over his face. "Well, that was awkward."

Violet flexed her fingers, still awed by the strange sensation rippling through her. "Do you mind explaining what the hell that is?" she asked. "You feel it too . . . *don't you*?" Her thoughtful green eyes lifted to his.

"Yeah," he grudgingly admitted. "I felt it. And you should really keep your hands to yourself, V. That shit freaks a guy out." But his voice had dropped and his tone had grown serious. His gaze clouded over.

"What? You think it was me? You think *I* did that?" Violet scrutinized him. "Have you ever felt anything like that before?"

And then she watched as his defenses dropped back into place, the wall that insulated him from everything. From everyone. His expression smoothed and his voice turned cool, emotionless. "Yeah, V, you're not the first girl I've ever touched." He turned away from her and marched toward the door. "Come on, we have a job to do. Why don't we concentrate on that?"

Violet glared at his back, and the word *jerk* rose to the surface, but she managed to swallow it. He was right; they'd come here for a reason, and that reason had nothing to do with either of them. "Fine," she managed. "I'm right behind you."

Standing beneath the red awning, Violet watched Rafe for longer than she should have. She doubted she'd ever understand him; he confused her like no one she'd ever met before. And, for some godforsaken reason, he also intrigued her. She wanted to know why he kept everyone at such a distance. And why Sam had said that she was different, because right now, she was pretty sure that wasn't the case. She sort of thought what everyone else did, that Rafe was an ass.

She turned away from him, heading in the opposite direction, back toward the parking lot where her car was parked. It was then that she noticed it, that same strange sensation she'd felt the day before. That same stinging sensation that prickled more than just the hairs of her nose.

That found its way all the way down inside of her.

Stronger today, even, than it had been before. Stronger and more enticing.

And she thought she knew why.

Because today the sleeping pills were finally wearing off. Today her head was clearer, her senses were more alert. Her ability was unhindered.

And this sensation was an echo of some sort.

She glanced around, searching for some hint as to where it might be coming from . . . *who* it might be coming from. But no one person looked any different from anyone else. No one seemed unusually interested in her. Everyone kept moving, shifting and pushing along the sidewalks.

From somewhere behind her, Violet recognized the noisy rumble of Rafe's motorcycle revving, and then she heard the steady drone of his engine as he pulled into traffic. She had the vague realization that he was leaving without her, that he was going to beat her to the Center, but she stayed where she was, rooted to her spot as foot traffic continued around her.

Just when she thought it might be getting closer—the irritating sensation growing more intense—Violet heard the cutting blare of a horn coming from down the street. Coming from the direction Rafe had been headed. The sound was too long and was followed immediately by a distinctly abrasive metallic scraping that sent icy prickles racing up Violet's spine.

She went completely and utterly rigid. And then she was

running, her feet pounding viciously against the pavement beneath her. She shoved her way through the crowds that were already starting to form, already trying to bear witness to someone else's tragedy.

Around her, Violet heard sharp gasps and the frantic rise of murmurs melding together into a buzzing cacophony. All the while, she fervently prayed that it wasn't what she thought it was. That it wasn't *who* she thought it was.

But when she burst through the crowd, she saw it: Rafe's motorcycle lay completely still at the center of the intersection. A green sedan that had been coming from the opposite direction was also sitting in the intersection, stopped almost directly on top of the bike. Violet watched as its driver emerged dazedly from her vehicle, blinking furiously as she reached up and gingerly touched her face. Angry red abrasions tore across the skin of her cheeks, chin, forehead, and nose. Inside the woman's car, her air bag had deployed.

Violet scanned the asphalt—the chaos of the scene—searching for any sign of Rafe. When she didn't see him right away, she felt a moment of relief, a lightening in the center of her chest as she figured he must have been okay after all. Maybe he'd walked away, he'd somehow come away from the crash completely unscathed, and was standing somewhere in the throng of people . . . that derisive smirk on his face.

It wasn't until she spotted the cluster of people congregating on the other side of the woman's sedan, when she recognized the all too familiar toe of Rafe's scuffed black boot, that she realized just how far he'd been thrown during impact. Panic nearly choked her as she began shoving people out of her way, clawing past strangers who stood blocking her path. She ignored the sharp looks and indignant mutters as she hurtled forward, desperate to reach him.

She slowed when she got close, numbly finding her way to the center of the crowd now. Her hands shook at her sides, and when she saw him sprawled in front of her, *lifeless*, she fell to her knees. Above her, she could hear at least two people talking into their cell phones, reporting the incident and relaying the events of Rafe's accident—and his injuries—to the authorities.

She tried not to listen as words like *unresponsive* and *labored breathing* infiltrated her consciousness. She dazedly watched as a woman expertly lifted his slack arm and pressed her fingers to his wrist. After a moment, the woman glanced up at a man on his cell phone and said the words *thready pulse*.

"Rafe." Violet was now shaking all over, but she ignored the others, her voice tearing out of her in strident shreds. "Rafe, can you hear me?" She wanted to reach for him, to wrap him in her arms and rock him, to promise him that everything would be all right. But seeing him there, his arms and legs splayed limply around him, his eyes unblinking—he looked too damaged to touch. So instead, she ran her fingertip along the brim of his helmet, grateful he'd been wearing it. "Rafe," she uttered on a tortured sob.

A hand gripped her shoulder. "Young lady." The man on the cell phone stared down at her, the handset of his phone gripped firmly against his jaw. "Do you know him? Do you know who he is?" he repeated.

Violet nodded, unable to tear her gaze away from the boy lying in front of her.

"What's his name?" the man asked again, his fingers digging in harder this time.

"It's Rafe," Violet answered absently, a tear slipping down her cheek and falling onto Rafe's leather jacket as she bent over him, silently begging him to wake up, to open his eyes and tell her he was okay. "His name is Rafe."

"And his last name?"

Violet blinked, frowning as she willed herself to concentrate, willed herself to remember. What *was* his last name? Had she ever even heard it before? Finally, she tore her eyes away from Rafe's limp form and stared up at the man as she wiped her chin with her sleeve. "I don't know," she confessed hollowly.

CHAPTER 13

THE EMERGENCY ROOM WAS CHAOTIC, EVEN ON a Saturday afternoon, practically combusting with echoes. Violet huddled farther into her chair, trying her best to block out the rush of sensory inputs that were both real—those that everyone around her could sense, moans and the sounds of crying babies, howls of both laughter and of pain—and those that only she could distinguish.

She hugged herself tighter, wishing once more that someone would just come out and tell her how Rafe was. It had been hours already, and she just wanted to know he was going to be okay.

She glanced at the clock on the wall above the admissions

desk only to realize that barely five minutes had passed since the last time she'd checked it. She hated being here alone.

The whoosh of the automatic doors drew her notice, as they had every time they opened to let someone in or out, but this time she jolted to her feet when she saw who stepped inside. She left the isolation of her seat in the corner to meet Sara halfway.

"I've left you a dozen messages." Violet fumbled over her words. "It's Rafe. We were at The Mecca . . . it's the café where the girl worked . . . Casey Atkins . . . and when we were leaving . . ." Violet hesitated, not quite sure how to continue or how much information to give. "I didn't see it happen," she finally said, her vision blurring as she glanced at Sara. Sara's own eyes were ringed with dark shadows and her hair was rumpled as if she'd just awakened, even though it was well past noon.

"The woman thought she had the right of way . . . she came right at him . . ." Violet explained, reaching for Sara's hand, not sure what she expected from her.

She was surprised when Sara's cold fingers clutched hers in a viselike grip. "Where is he now? Have you talked to anyone? How's he doing?" Sara assaulted Violet with her trademark no-nonsense, rapid-fire questions.

"Last I heard, they were taking him up for an MRI. But they won't tell me anything else. They'll only talk to his family."

Sara released Violet's hand. She opened her small hand-bag and began scouring through it, searching for something.

Violet realized she'd never seen Sara in anything other than her work clothes before—suits, skirts, heels, starched shirts. She took a moment to examine this casual, off-hours Sara who wore black yoga pants and a gray pullover sweatshirt that was easily two sizes too big for her. Sara found her wallet and pulled it from her purse as she strode toward the admissions desk, to the same stern-faced woman who'd denied Violet access just minutes earlier.

"Do you know how to reach his parents?" Violet asked hopefully, following right on Sara's heels. Maybe now they could finally get some answers.

Sara spoke in a clipped voice over her shoulder. "Violet, you'll have to wait out here." And then she dropped her driver's license on the counter in front of the desk clerk. "I need to speak to someone about a patient who was brought in." Violet wondered why she didn't flash a badge or something . . . anything to try to get some information out of the unsmiling woman. And then Sara spoke again, no longer paying attention to Violet. "His name is Rafe Priest," she said. "He's my brother."

Violet was still letting everything sink in, feeling more than a little blindsided by what Sara had told the admissions lady about being Rafe's sister. Low voices around her buzzed of car accidents and heart attacks and sick children and broken limbs. She tried her best to tune out their words—along with everything else she could sense.

And then there was that other thing . . . Sara was Rafe's

sister? How was that possible? How had she not known that? But it all made sense now. Why they seemed to understand each other so well.

Violet couldn't stop thinking about it. Or him.

She'd settled back into her spot in the corner, leaning her head back and drawing her knees up to her chest, doing her best to get comfortable. She didn't look up until she heard a familiar voice. Unfriendly and cold, but familiar nonetheless.

"Great," the girl muttered venomously as Violet jerked her head up. "Figures you'd be here."

Unlike Sara, who'd walked in looking harried and rumpled, Gemma dazzled beneath the glare of the emergency room lights, right down to her shimmery silver top and matching handbag. Violet glanced down at her own small purse with its pink bejeweled skull and crossbones. She'd never really cared before that it was outdated, even when her friends had made fun of it. Her grandmother had given it to her, one of the last gifts she'd given Violet before she died. The skull and crossbones were an inside joke about their shared ability.

Gemma quickly closed the distance between them, the heels of her ankle-length boots clicking on the white tiles in clipped, angry bursts. She perched delicately on the edge of one of the few open seats in the waiting room, next to Violet.

"How did you know we were here?" Violet asked, mystified by the other girl's presence.

Impatiently Gemma stared at her. "Sara told me. So?"

She scowled at Violet, her voice razor-sharp. "What happened?"

The vehemence in her voice made Violet wince, as if she'd just been slapped. Whatever she'd done to Gemma, the other girl had no intention of forgiving her anytime soon. But that so wasn't the point, Violet thought, her own anger starting to simmer now. Here they were, sitting in the emergency room with no idea how Rafe was. She still had no word from Sara or the doctors who'd been working on him, and the longer they were gone, the more worried Violet became. "I don't know what your problem is, Gemma, or what I ever did to you, but if you have something to say to me, then spit it out."

Gemma glowered at Violet for a long, hate-filled moment; then finally, she shrugged. "It's not really you," she said at last, but her voice was no less caustic. She sighed as she crossed her long legs, cocking her head as her eyes narrowed to dark, perfectly lined slits. "I mean, technically it is, I suppose, but I doubt it's your fault, really."

"What is that supposed to mean, Gemma?"

Lowering her voice, Gemma's lips curled into something between a snarl and a smile. "In case you didn't know, I'm empathic," she explained, her tone haughty, practically demeaning. And even though Violet wasn't sure what the other girl was getting at, her hackles were up now. "Which means I can sense things from other people."

Violet tried to mimic Gemma's glare as she narrowed her eyes. "And your point is . . . ?"

"It means I absorb what others around me are feeling. And because of that, more than anyone else I've ever met, it's hard to be around you." She wrinkled her perky little nose, and Violet wanted to punch her in it, right then and there. "To put it frankly, Violet, you reek of death . . . and it's revolting."

Violet had no idea what to make of that. She'd been called a lot of things, been teased as a little girl for having curly hair and gangly legs, but she'd never thought about the implications of her own ability tainting her in that way. She was still gaping when Gemma suddenly jumped up from her seat and shot across the waiting room. At first Violet didn't even realize what was happening; she thought she was the one who'd chased the other girl away. Her and her creepy ability.

I reek of death. Not exactly the words every girl dreamed of hearing.

When she glanced in Gemma's direction, she realized Sara was back, talking to Gemma. Violet stood on legs that felt far too unsteady and crossed the space between them. But she froze, her heart slamming against the walls of her chest, the moment she saw the stricken expression on Gemma's face, and the streaks of mascara now tracing their way down her cheeks.

Lead pulled at Violet's feet, weighing them down and pinning her to the ground. "What—what happened?" Violet stammered. "Is he . . . ?" She struggled for the right words, her voice causing Gemma to look up at her. The other girl swiped at her eyes, her expression turning suddenly fierce as she smeared her makeup even more. "Is he worse?" Violet asked at last.

Gemma shot Violet an angry look. "He's fine." The words sliced through the air. "He's an asshole, but he's fine."

Sara put her hand on Gemma's shoulder, her expression pained. "Gemma," she warned before turning to Violet. Her brow creased. "He's okay," she explained to Violet, her voice patient. "He's beaten up pretty bad, and they've got him somewhat sedated, but he's going to be fine. He's asking for you."

Violet glanced uncomfortably at Gemma.

"Happy?" Gemma snapped. "You're still the only one he wants to see."

Sara headed toward the admissions desk, and Gemma reached for Violet's arm, her fingers digging in viciously. "You'd better not hurt him," she hissed under her breath. "I mean it. He doesn't need anyone else hurting him."

Violet stared blankly at Gemma's formidable expression as Gemma's grip finally loosened. She wondered where, exactly, the threat had come from. She had no intention of hurting Rafe; why would Gemma even say something like that?

She felt weird leaving the other girl behind as she followed Sara to the counter, where her ID was scanned and printed onto a sticker that she had to wear on her shirt.

Sara led her in back, and they stopped outside a sliding glass door with a huge number 33 on it. Violet had expected they'd both be going inside, but Sara smiled feebly. "Go ahead. I get to take him home later; I'll spend time with him then." It was strange to be reminded that she was his sister. Then Sara touched Violet's arm, her face screwed into a mask of . . . something. Apprehension. Concern. Both, maybe. "Don't upset him, okay, Violet? He's been through a lot today, and he's worn out. Just let him say what he needs to say so he can get some rest." *In other words,* Violet thought, *don't ask a lot of questions. Not yet, anyway.*

Violet just nodded and left Sara standing outside as she entered the darkened room.

She wasn't sure what she'd expected: tubes down his throat, wires attached to noisy machines, full-body traction with casts and splints. But it wasn't like that.

The room was quiet and the lights had been dimmed; there was just a small box light above his bed that cast a faint glow like an oversized night-light. Violet settled silently onto a rolling chair beside the metal-framed bed as she waited for Rafe to notice she was there.

His eyes were closed and his breathing was deep and even. She'd watched Jay sleep before, and he was always restless, his breathing irregular. Sometimes he muttered in his sleep, sometimes he twitched, but always he looked disheveled, messy.

Not Rafe, though. Rafe looked peaceful. His hand lay across his chest, and Violet could see the tubes from his IV protruding from the back of it. Two clear bags of fluid hung from the tall silver stand looming beside his bed.

She jumped when a machine at her side beeped softly and the blood pressure cuff strapped around his upper arm inflated automatically, registering his vital signs. She wondered if there were nurses watching from monitors at their station.

"You came." Rafe's voice was gravelly and sluggish. There was a quality buried within it that Violet had never heard before from Rafe. Something raw and hopeful. He smiled lethargically, as if his facial muscles were heavy, leaden. Violet watched as he lifted his hand—the one with the IV tubes sticking into it—and his bleary eyes struggled to maintain focus on her face. His hand only made it halfway to her face before dropping back to the crisp white sheets again as if the effort had been too much for him. "I was hoping I'd see you again, Sophie."

The slur of his words was almost charming, in a drunken sort of way, but Violet frowned over the last word he'd spoken, the name he'd called her. She leaned forward, afraid to touch him or even to jostle his bed as she carefully leaned her elbows against the firm hospital mattress. "Who's Sophie, Rafe?"

Rafe startled then, his muscles tensing and the endearing smile melting from his lips, giving way to a perplexed scowl as his eyes swam into focus. His voice, when he finally spoke again, was still laced with fatigue. "What are you talking about?"

"You called me Sophie."

Rafe shook his head, wincing as he did. "No, I didn't," he groaned. "You must have misheard."

Had she? She was pretty sure she didn't. But what difference did it make what he'd called her? She was relieved to see him awake. Alive, for that matter.

"I was so worried about you. I'm so sorry about what happened, Rafe."

His expression softened, his brows drawing together. "It wasn't your fault. Sara said it was the other driver—" He scowled again, but this time he seemed to be struggling to remember.

"It was," Violet assured him. "She was making an illegal turn, and . . ." She hesitated. "She didn't see you."

Rafe nodded, and Violet wondered how much of the accident he recalled, if anything. She hoped he'd conveniently stricken it from his memory.

"I'm glad you're okay," she said at last, a pained frown making its way over her face.

"Pshh." He tried to wave his hand to dismiss her concerns, but it fell again before he could make any real statement. "I'm fine. Look at me. I've never been better."

Violet studied him—scrutinized every inch she could see. Scrapes covered his hands, his cheek, and his chin—at least where she could see them around the bandages. Even his elbows had been wrapped up, from where the asphalt had ripped through his leather jacket, she assumed. Bruises were forming too, even ones that she could see through the transparent IV tape across his knuckles. She didn't think she wanted to know what might be hidden beneath the covers. "Yeah, you look great," she quipped. "Seriously, how bad is it?"

"I got some stitches," he said, pointing at the gauze on his forehead. "And some bruised ribs, but it must not be too bad; they're just waiting for the doc to sign off and then I get to go. Besides—" He grinned, tapping the place where the IV tube disappeared beneath his skin. "I gotta say, if you're gonna get hurt, this is the place to be. The drugs here aren't half-bad." His head sagged heavily against the pillow.

Violet got to her feet, worried over the weariness she saw on his face and recalling the warning from Sara about letting him rest. "You look tired."

He shook his head slowly. "No. Don't go. Stay." But his words were slower now. "Just a little longer."

Violet hesitated, then settled down again. She looked at her hand, so close to his on the sheet. She imagined closing the distance, running her fingertips across the top of his battered knuckles, covering his hand with hers.

She could; it wouldn't mean anything. They were just friends, she and Rafe, and she was worried for him. Friends could touch each other. Friends could hold hands.

Her heart hammered at the thought as she considered doing that very thing. And then she drew her hand away, dropping it into her lap, and balled her fingers into a determined fist.

She glanced at his face, watching as his eyelids drooped. He blinked, struggling against their weight and finally succumbing to it. She waited until she thought he was probably sleeping again, and wondered how long she should sit there. How long until it was weird that she was staring at him while he slept.

His eyes didn't even flutter when the nurse paced

soundlessly to the other side of the bed, lifting his wrist and deftly finding his pulse as her gaze dropped to her watch. Violet turned in her seat, surprised that she hadn't even heard the ninjalike nurse come in. She ignored Violet as she counted, and Violet watched her, wondering if she felt the same thing Violet did when she touched him. If she felt that spark, that prickly connection, whenever their skin met. But watching her, Violet doubted that was the case. She was sure the nurse felt nothing except for the flickering of his pulse when she touched him.

When she set his hand down, the nurse scribbled on his chart and shoved her pen into the front pocket of her lollipop-emblazoned scrubs. She punched a couple of buttons on the IV pump, checked each of the fluid-filled sacks hanging from the metal stand, and crept silently from the room again, leaving Violet alone with Rafe in the dark.

Violet got up now, slowly, quietly.

Rafe didn't open his eyes, but she heard his voice, whisper-soft. "Will you come visit me tomorrow?"

"I don't know where you live," Violet answered just as softly.

"My sis—" He stopped himself, but not in time, and it was all the confirmation Violet needed. "Sara will tell you," he managed at last, reforming the words over his thick tongue before collapsing into sleep.

Violet squinted as she stood in front of the strip mall. It wasn't exactly what she'd expected; more like the kind of place you'd find greeting cards than tarot cards. Even the neon sign—The Crystal Palace—made Violet think of those prisms that people dangled from their rearview mirrors, the ones that sent out dappled rays of multicolored lights whenever the sunlight hit them just so.

Inside the store, however, was an entirely different story.

The first thing Violet noticed was the burning smell of incense—clove-scented and nearly cloying—and the soft sounds of a sitar stirring lyrically in the background. She reached out to part the curtain of brightly colored plastic beads that was suspended just beyond the doorway. The beads were fashioned after multifaceted jewels in varying sizes, and they clattered together as she slipped between them.

"Violet? What are you doing here?" She glanced up to see Krystal sitting behind an old wooden cash register that looked as if it belonged in an antique store. Krystal came around to the front of the counter, vivid strips of blue hair sticking out from the spiky knot on her head, her expression switching from surprise to worry in a heartbeat. "I heard what happened to Rafe. Gemma said his bike's totaled."

Violet wanted to disagree with Krystal's blunt assessment, to say that it wasn't that bad. But she couldn't manage it. The truth was, his bike probably *was* totaled. "Yeah, I guess so. He's gonna be okay, though. He gets to go home tonight." She held up the business card, the one she'd taken from Krystal's car. "I hope it's okay that I just showed up like this. I don't want to get you in trouble or anything."

"Yeah, we're super busy today," Krystal drawled

sarcastically, glancing around at the empty store.

Violet looked around too, taking in shelf upon shelf filled with bottles of lotions and candles and incense, the odd assortment of books and tarot cards, and the miscellaneous jewelry displays strung with all manner of stones and crystals and feathers. In one corner, there were silk cushions scattered about on an intricately woven rug surrounding a short, round table.

"That's where we do readings," Krystal said, her gaze following Violet's.

"Do you do them?" Violet asked. "The readings, I mean? I thought you just talked to ghosts."

"I do." She grinned, reaching for a stack of cards on the counter behind her. The deck looked old, its edges worn, but the intricate designs on the backs of the cards looked hand-painted, each bearing the depiction of a woman draped in a diaphanous white gown and wearing a butterfly crown. There were swans at her feet. "Anyone can learn to read the cards, Violet. Sometimes my readings are just a little more . . . accurate. You wanna give it a shot?"

Violet thought about that and shook her head. "Nah, I don't think so. I'm not sure I wanna know what happens next. I think I'd rather be surprised."

"Suit yourself." Krystal set the cards back down. "So what *did* you come for?"

Violet shrugged. "I don't know." She wandered to a shelf of pretty brown bottles, each with matching labels from a company called Organic Alchemy. She picked up a jar of patchouli oil with a black rubber stopper and uncorked it, taking a sniff. "I guess I wanted to make sure you knew. About Rafe." And then she realized what a lame excuse that was, knowing she could just as easily have called to give Krystal the news. "I guess . . ." Her voice trailed off, trying to decide. "I guess I wasn't really ready to go home yet. Can I ask you a question?"

Krystal wandered over to the pile of pillows and dropped down, crossing her legs in front of her. She leaned back on her arms, staring up at Violet. "Shoot."

Violet sat too, so that she was across the table from the other girl, staring at her wide, dark eyes, envying the way Krystal looked so open, so willing to share her innermost thoughts and feelings. "Do they scare you? The ghosts? When they talk to you, are you ever afraid?"

"Afraid? Nah." Krystal's lips curled downward as she shook her head. "They've been coming to visit me since I was a baby. My mom talked to them, and probably her mom too. I never knew it was weird to have *real* imaginary friends, to have conversations with people no one else could see. It wasn't until Missy Bigsby made fun of me in kindergarten, calling me Crazy Krystal, that I realized I was the only one doing it. Everyone else thought I was just . . . talking to myself." She shrugged. "Whatever. Missy can suck it, if you know what I mean. Some girls deserve to end up divorced and alone at twenty-one."

Violet couldn't help laughing, even though she felt bad for the kindergarten version of Krystal. She would have been mortified if the other kids had known about her secret. "So you and this Missy girl, you stayed in touch?"

Krystal smiled deviously. "Let's just say that one of my invisible 'friends' didn't appreciate Missy flippin' me crap, and gave me a heads-up about what her future held." She looked satisfied with herself, a smug smile curving her full lips.

"Wow," Violet breathed. "Remind me never to get on your bad side."

"Please, I was five. I've got better things to do now than worry about whether people think I'm crazy or not." Krystal toyed with a small rip in her fuchsia tights, reminding Violet that she was more sensitive than she let on.

"Well, if *you're* crazy then I guess we all are," Violet said. "I mean, think about it, you might talk to dead people, but I go out of my way to find them."

Krystal snorted, glancing up from the hole she was picking at. "You got that right. I guess crazy isn't all bad. Sometimes crazy saves lives."

Violet thought about Antonia Cornett—about her ghost—coming to visit Krystal and telling her that Casey Atkins was missing, that she'd been taken by the collector. She stopped watching Krystal's hot pink fingernails tugging at her frayed tights and watched her eyes instead. "Do you think we'll find Casey, Krystal? Alive, I mean?"

Letting out a heavy breath, Krystal looked up at Violet. "I hope so, Vi. Goddammit, I really, *really* hope so."

DENIAL

HE WATCHED HER FROM THE DOORWAY, HIS
*heart aching. "I'm sorry," he whispered, gently setting the tray on
the dresser by the door. "You know it's not your fault, don't you?"*

*Her wide eyes stared back at him, and he thought maybe—
maybe—he should uncover her mouth so she could answer him.
Maybe she was ready to be quiet now.*

*He stepped closer, slowly, so as not to startle her. She had a deli-
cate nature, he'd learned. Like a butterfly. Or a flower. In the end,
it was probably the reason they never really clicked, why she couldn't
be the one. There was nothing delicate about him; his mother had
always told him so.*

That didn't mean she should be frightened of him now, though.

He slipped the rag away from her lips and frowned when he saw how dry they were.

"Here." He reached for the tube of ointment on the bed stand. "Let me . . ." Again he was cautious, ever aware of her constitution. He didn't want her to cry again. And he certainly didn't want her to scream. "Better?" he asked after applying a generous layer of the cream to her parched lips.

She didn't answer right away, just kept that frightened-as-a-lamb gaze trained on him until he felt his cheeks growing hot with embarrassment.

"Stop it." His voice quavered, even though he told himself he had nothing to be ashamed of. "I don't want you to be scared of me. I've done my best to treat you kindly. I've fed you and cared for you when you were all alone. You remember that, don't you?" He reached out and caressed her cheek. It was fine skin, soft like silk. He closed his eyes, pretending that the two of them could stay like this forever.

When he opened them again, all traces of fear were gone from her eyes. She felt it too, he realized. She wasn't ready for it to end.

"Can I?" he asked as he lifted the sheet. He climbed in without waiting for an answer. He knew from her expression that she wanted it as much as he did.

His mouth went dry, just as it always did when he got this close to a girl, even the ones he knew this well. It was a thrilling feeling, and he felt bolder . . . he wanted more. His hand traced the soft curve of her belly and he pulled her close, hugging her tightly until they were one body. One mind.

He nuzzled the side of her neck and breathed in the scent of her,

205

*hoping he'd never forget this moment as he slipped his hand down
the length of her arm, his fingers intertwining with hers.*

Already they were stiff and cold.

*It was too bad she was so fragile, he thought, as he drew back
and glanced into her wide, glassy, unblinking eyes. She could have
been perfect. She could have been the one.*

CHAPTER 14

VIOLET HATED THAT SHE'D SPENT SO MUCH TIME standing in front of the mirror the next morning. She'd thrown on jeans and a T-shirt and then, second-guessing her choice, had changed out of the worn athletic T-shirt and slipped on a fitted top with tiny white buttons over a lace-trimmed tank top. She wondered why it mattered. Why she even cared what she looked like all of a sudden. She was only visiting Rafe, after all.

When she caught herself daubing gloss on her lips, she changed her mind again, berating herself as she ripped at the buttons on her shirt. "Stupid Rafe . . . always messing with my head . . ." Tossing the top on the floor, she snagged a zip-front hoodie off a hanger in the closet, causing it to swing violently on the wooden dowel. "I shouldn't even go see him. If he hadn't been riding that stupid bike in the first place . . ." She slipped her jacket on and yanked the zipper all the way up to her chin before checking herself in the mirror. She'd left her hair loose, letting it fall in curling cascades around her shoulders. It looked wild and tempestuous, matching the fevered expression in her emerald eyes. "Perfect," she announced to her reflection as she picked up a piece of tissue and wiped her lips clean once more.

At the last minute, she slipped a long chain around her neck and rubbed the stone, the way she'd seen Krystal do with her own necklaces. Black onyx, Krystal had told her, that's what the stone was called. It was a meditative stone, used for protection, sort of like an energy shield.

Violet didn't feel any different, didn't feel "shielded," but she liked having the stone, even if it was only because her friend had given it to her.

Her mom had stopped her before she'd made it out the front door. "He's going to be okay?" Her voice sounded weary, and Violet knew she shouldn't have been surprised that Sara had already called.

Violet kept her fingers on the doorknob, unsure why she was suddenly uncomfortable. "That's what they said. They did an MRI and took some X-rays, but when I left they were releasing him to go home. He'll probably have to take it easy for a while."

"He's lucky," she said. "Ask your uncle Stephen, those

things are dangerous." The way she said "those things" made it sound more like Rafe had been trying to ride a rabid bull than a legal motor vehicle.

But Violet had been hearing the same speech since she was a little girl. Ever since she'd made the mistake of telling her mom she wanted to join a biker gang. She was seven at the time, and didn't have the guts to tell her parents that the real reason had nothing at all to do with riding motorcycles; she just wanted to be able to say she was a "Hell's Angel."

"I know, I know," Violet insisted, lifting her hands in surrender. "I think that video Uncle Stephen made me watch—what was it called, *Death on the Highway*?—was enough to scare any kid into driving like a grandmother."

The sliver of a smile found her mother's lips. "Tell him I hope he feels better, 'kay, Vi?"

Violet smiled back before ducking out the door, anxious to get out of there, to not be talking about traffic safety with her mother. To not be talking about Rafe.

She hadn't planned on stopping at the Center, but since it was on her way, and because she was feeling uncertain about going to Rafe's, she found herself pulling into the small lot despite herself.

Most of the businesses in the warehouse district were closed, lending it a strange, remote feel that it didn't have during the busy workweek. Since it was a Sunday, Violet hadn't expected to see any cars in the lot, least of all Sara's, so she was surprised to find the imposing SUV parked in front.

She turned off the ignition of her battered old Honda as she dug her keycard out of her purse and hurried up the steps of the building.

Inside everything was quiet and dark. All the hallway lights leading to the inner door of the Center had been turned off and there was a disquieting sort of calm to it. There were no sounds, nothing to indicate that anyone else was inside the building, and Violet hesitated at the second secured entrance, her keycard poised above the black magnetic pad. When she'd been issued the security card, Sara had insisted that the Center was available to her any time she needed it, that she was free to come and go as she pleased.

Violet swiped the plastic card in front of the reader and when the green light flashed, she leaned against the door, shoving through it.

"Sara?" Violet called out, but no one answered, and Violet wondered if Sara was actually around after all.

The phone in her pocket vibrated and Violet ignored it. It was probably just her friends again, wondering where she was and why she was avoiding them. Guilt stabbed at her.

She slipped over to the refrigerator and pulled out a soda before wandering to Sara's workspace, the only place that could actually be considered a real office in the Center, even though there wasn't a real door to keep anyone out. Sara's computer was on, and the screen saver changed, a slideshow of landscape images that looked like framed photographs. There was nothing personal about the photos; Violet had seen these snapshots before. They were preprogrammed and had come with the operating system.

Violet tried again, letting her fingers graze over the top of the polished desktop, as smooth and unmarred as Sara herself—everything in its place. She bumped the mouse and the screen saver vanished, and Violet found herself staring at the desktop of Sara's computer.

But it wasn't the neatly arranged icons on the screen that she noticed; it was the background image. Not standard. Not preprogrammed.

An actual photograph of Sara with a woman who looked like an older version of herself. A little more worn and weary, but so familiar that Violet was certain they were related. They had the same sharply focused blue eyes.

The same ones that Rafe had.

"Violet? What are you doing here?"

Violet gasped, her hand flying to her chest—away from the mouse—and she hoped Sara didn't think she'd been snooping on purpose.

She turned, her eyes wide and her heart pounding. "Nothing. I wasn't doing anything."

Sara's eyebrow quirked. She still looked tired, her face drawn, with purple shadows smudged beneath her eyes, but she was definitely more pulled together today than she had been at the hospital the day before. Somehow she managed to make even jeans and a sweater look formal. "I just meant, what are you doing here on a Sunday?" And then concern clouded her face and her brows drew together. "Is everything okay?"

Violet offered a hasty nod. "Yeah, I'm fine. I didn't hear you come in."

Sara smiled. "I came in the back way."

"I didn't know there was a back way."

The corner of Sara's mouth ticked up, as if she had a secret she was dying to share. "There are lots of things you don't know yet."

But even as she said the words, they both recognized the truth in them. There were things that she and Rafe hadn't meant for Violet to know. Yet now she did.

She exhaled. "I guess you have some questions for me. Come on, let's have a seat."

Sara led Violet to a seating area and settled onto one of the oversized chairs. She slipped off her shoes, tucking her feet beneath her. Violet sat on the sofa, fidgeting as she tried to get comfortable.

Sara sighed wearily as she leaned against the armrest. "I'm sorry you had to find out that way. I certainly hadn't planned to blindside you like that."

Violet's lips twitched at Sara's choice of words. "How had you planned to blindside me?"

Wistfully, Sara smiled back at her, and she looked down at her lap for a moment. "It's just . . . you're the first person Rafe has even come close to opening up to since . . ." She hesitated again. "You're the first friend he's made since he's been here."

"That's kind of what I've heard, but I don't really get it."

Sara frowned, lifting her blue eyes as she tried to explain.

"You're different, Violet. He's different when he's around you." Violet recoiled against Sara's words.

She supposed she hadn't really believed Sam when he'd told her, but hearing it from Sara . . . she could no longer deny it was true, even to herself.

"What about you?" Violet asked. "He has you, and you're his . . . *sister.*" The word sounded strange on her tongue, unfamiliar in the context of the two of them.

Sara grinned slowly, knowingly. "Yes, he has me. And I'll always be there for him. He's the reason I formed the team in the first place. When he first told me . . . well, you know, what he could do, it caused . . . problems for him." She winced, and Violet wondered if she'd even realized she'd done it. "He got into some trouble—it wasn't his fault—but he needed someplace to go. I offered to take him in."

"Does everyone else . . . I mean, do the others on the team . . . do they all know about you and Rafe?"

Sara shrugged, reminding Violet so much of Rafe in that moment it was almost eerie. "I imagine they know, or at least suspect. They *are* psychics, after all. But Rafe prefers it this way, with no one talking about it. He doesn't want anyone to think he gets special treatment. And I think he feels like the less they know about him, the less they'll think he's one of them."

"But he *is* one of them."

Grinning, Sara answered, "Just don't tell him that. He likes to think of himself as a loner. He doesn't like to think he needs anyone." She leaned back. "He's wrong, though.

He needs us, he just won't admit it."

"What about your parents? Where are they?" Violet asked, wondering if she was prying.

But Sara didn't seem to mind. "My dad's fine and living in Boise. Rafe's dad—" She sighed. "He's never been around. He took off after he found out our mom was pregnant. No one's heard from him since. My parents were divorced when I was four, and Rafe wasn't born until I was already a teenager. Honestly, I barely noticed him, even though he did everything he could think of to get my attention." She squeezed her eyes shut, as if the memory were painful. "I wish I would have let him tag along all those times he asked me if he could. I wish I'd been a better sister."

Violet felt bad for her. She didn't have siblings, but she knew what it was like to have her little cousins following her around, wanting her attention. She couldn't imagine turning her back on them. "And your mother? Does she live around here?"

Sara frowned. "Our mom died from lung cancer, almost two years ago. The tragedy is, she wasn't even a smoker. The doctors have no idea how she got it." Her voice cracked, and Violet felt guilty for asking such personal questions. But Sara continued, blinking against unseen tears. "Rafe went to live with my mom's sister—our aunt Jenny—after that. I came back for the funeral, but even then, I was so busy . . . overworked . . . and I didn't realize how . . ." She shrugged, struggling for the right word. ". . . how *lonely* Rafe was. I mean, I knew he was sad; we both were. But now when I look back, Rafe had completely withdrawn." She choked on a bitter laugh. "I chalked it up to his age. Aren't all teens withdrawn and mopey . . . especially the ones who just lost their mother?"

Violet didn't know what to say. But she wanted to hear more . . . about Rafe. About his past.

"A few months after the funeral, he called me in the middle of the night . . . asking for my help. I already knew he'd run away; my aunt had called in a panic when she'd found his note, so I wasn't surprised to hear his voice on the other end of the line. In fact, I'd been waiting for it." Again, that wistful smile touched her lips, and her eyes shimmered a deep, brilliant sapphire. "But boy oh boy, did he surprise me when he started talking, telling me what he could do, telling me where he was and what had happened. I traced the call, and had the local police on their way before we'd even hung up."

"What . . ." Violet hesitated, not sure she was supposed to ask. "What was it? What did he find?"

Biting her lip, Sara's eyes grew distant as she recalled that night. "That's the thing, it wasn't *what* he'd found, Violet. It was *who* he'd found. And Rafe hasn't been the same since." Her eyes sharpened again. "At least until he met you."

Violet shook her head, a deep frown furrowing her expression. Her eyes were wide and her heart beat painfully within her chest. She couldn't find her voice, but she could see from the uncertainty on Sara's face that she wasn't sure if she should continue.

215

Sara's lips curved into a tight smile, but her eyes remained sad and faraway. "Rafe had a dream about his girlfriend, a girl whose family—her mother and her little brother— had been on the run from her abusive father. At the time I didn't know anything about his dreams, that sometimes they were more than just dreams. I mean, really, dreams are just dreams, right? But not Rafe's. Did you know that about him? That he gets *flashes*, he calls them, of the future? That he dreams things that haven't happened yet?"

Violet shook her head, not really sure how to answer. Sam had explained a little, but not about the dreams.

Sara's hand smoothed her hair. "He understood what the dream really meant. He knew that his girlfriend was in danger, that her father had found them, and he decided to go after her . . . to try to save her, I guess." Her face crumpled. "But when he got there, it was already too late. The girl's father had slaughtered them all and had already taken off."

"Kind of like what James Nua had done to his family," Violet whispered.

"Precisely. That's why I was so worried about Rafe when we went to the station that day. Seeing James Nua, and knowing what he'd done, was harder on him than he'd ever admit."

Violet understood in a way she hadn't before.

"Anyway, that night, when the police arrived and found Rafe there, he was the only one still alive. He was taken into custody and questioned, but never formally accused. He didn't tell them that because of his flashes, he knew where the father was hiding out. He waited until I got there and told me instead.

"And he was right. The bastard was exactly where Rafe said he'd be, drunk out of his mind in a cheap motel room off the interstate. He never even bothered cleaning up . . . he was still covered in their blood."

Violet shifted nervously, trying to tell herself it didn't matter but unable to stop the question from bubbling up in her throat nonetheless. "What was her name?" she asked. "His girlfriend . . . what was her name?"

Sara hesitated, her face screwing into a mask of uncertainty. "I've already told you too much. I doubt Rafe would want me talking about any of this."

But Violet already knew. "It was Sophie, wasn't it?"

"How did you . . . ?" But Sara just shook her head, her voice distant. "He hasn't been the same since."

No wonder Rafe had sounded so hopeful when he'd called her Sophie at the hospital. Violet's heart ached for him as she blinked back her own tears now.

First his mother. And then Sophie.

Sara sighed heavily. "After all that, I decided it was time for Rafe to come live with me so I could make up for being such a crappy big sister. At the time, I'd been working sixteen-hour days and practically sleeping at the office. With Rafe there, I started bringing my work files home so I could be there . . . with him. That was when I discovered how useful his ability could be." She sighed as she recounted the details. "I woke up one night when I couldn't sleep and caught Rafe going through my folders. At first I was pissed. Those were confidential FBI files, he had no business looking at them." Her bemused smile was at odds with her words. "When I yelled at him, Rafe just gave me that look of his—the one that says: *Relax, I've got this under control.*"

Violet smiled too. She knew the look, Rafe's signature expression.

"And then, just like that, he told me who did it. He knew who exactly the killer was and how he'd done it." She chuckled derisively. "I'd spent the past four months of my life poring over the evidence and questioning witnesses again and again and again. And there he was, my baby brother, looking me right in the eye and telling me where to find the murder weapon."

Violet let out her breath; her chest ached from holding it. "He had another dream?"

Sara shook her head. "No. That's the thing; it wasn't a dream this time. He knew from just thumbing through the personal photos we'd collected from the victim's home. From just . . . *touching* them. That was when I started to dig deeper, investigating what he could do. I realized that his dreams or waking visions—or whatever you want to call them—are triggered by touch. It was the first time I'd ever heard the word *psychometry.* With his girlfriend, she'd left him one of those plastic troll dolls, the ones with the fuzzy hair—kind of a memento, I suppose. And because he'd been holding it and because it had been hers, Rafe dreamed about her. But he doesn't have to be sleeping to have a premonition. I'm still learning the ins and outs, but it seems like everyone's gifts work differently."

Violet thought about what Sam had told her, about *his* ability being different from Rafe's, the garden-variety sort of psychometry.

Sara kept talking, not needing to be prompted now. "The more research I did, the more fascinated I became. I tested Rafe, giving him more files, letting him handle more evidence and items from the cases—mostly old ones that had already been solved—so I could gauge his accuracy. Sometimes it would take days, even weeks, but he was pretty good. He got about seventy-five percent of them right. The others . . ." She shrugged, her lips curving downward. ". . . he just came up 'blank.' He said he didn't sense anything at all.

"In the meantime, I was trying to find out if there were others with gifts like his. I started putting out feelers and kept coming up empty. People at work were starting to look at me like I was crazy, and maybe I was. And then, one day, I heard about a girl.

"She was in foster care, and was being bumped from house to house. She was only fifteen and had already been in twenty-four foster homes. No one wanted her. She got in trouble at every school she attended. She was truant on a regular basis, fell asleep in class, and was being bullied by other kids. Yet somehow she managed to maintain a three-point-eight-three GPA, despite move after move. The school administrators accused her of cheating on more than one occasion.

"A police officer actually brought her to my attention after she called them about her foster dad, a family man everyone in the community admired. Turns out he was a serial rapist they'd been trying to find for years . . . and somehow she knew."

Violet was intrigued. Was the girl Krystal? It wasn't hard to imagine Krystal having difficulty getting along in foster care with her outspoken personality and her unusual looks. Most foster parents probably hoped for kids who slipped a little more under the radar than Krystal did.

"When I met her," Sara continued, "she was angry and withdrawn and reluctant to even talk to me. I thought that maybe introducing her to Rafe would help, but he refused— he was still dealing with his own issues—so I was on my own with her. It took nearly two months to get her to open up to me, but when she finally did, she revealed everything.

"She explained the myriad of ways she'd alienated her foster parents. At first, she didn't know she had an *ability* at all, but she'd understood that she was different because she recognized things that the other kids didn't. She knew when her fifth foster mother was defrauding the system by collecting checks for a child who'd run away. She knew too when her third and eighth foster fathers were abusing other girls in the home. And she would tell everyone who would listen: caseworkers, teachers, babysitters, even the foster parents themselves. But she found out quickly that no one believes a six-year-old, especially one with a history of making unsubstantiated claims. All she had were her 'feelings,' and feelings weren't enough to file charges, only enough to get a little girl moved to the next home.

"In the end, though, she'd just stopped communicating

at all, deciding it was best if she remained silent at all times. Most of the foster homes got tired of all the calls from the school because she was 'unresponsive.' But she couldn't keep silent about her feelings at the last house even if it meant she had go back in the system again. And by the time I met her, she felt like she was some sort of freak."

Something Sara said was bothering Violet. "Wait, when you say 'feelings,' do you mean she was empathic? As in Gemma?"

"Right. Gemma. Who did you think I meant?" Sara asked.

"I don't know, I guess I thought you were talking about . . . someone else." Violet tried to imagine Gemma as the lonely foster kid that Sara described, withdrawn and uncommunicative. Definitely not the Gemma *she* knew. "So what happened? Where did she end up?"

"Let's just say it wasn't hard for me to get approval to be a foster parent, and by the time I broached the subject with Gemma about coming to live with us, I'd already earned her trust. She couldn't wait to get out of the system." Sara scowled, her brows creasing. "I think Rafe's still mad that I never consulted him."

Violet's head was spinning now. "Wait a sec." She held up her hand; it was almost too much. "So you're saying Gemma *lives* with you and Rafe?"

Violet took the coffee Sara handed her, even though the smell of it did nothing to soothe the churning in her stomach. They were in the kitchen now, and Violet was sitting at the same table where she'd watched Gemma reading Jay's

221

palm. She reached for the sugar.

"And she *still* lives with you?" Violet finally asked, trying to wrap her head around what she'd just heard. It was almost weirder than the fact that Sara was Rafe's sister.

Sara nodded, taking the seat across from Violet. "She does. And it works out rather well for us. Well, for Gemma and me," she corrected. "Rafe and Gemma . . ." She hesitated. "They're like oil and water. Rafe can be . . . stubborn." She shook her head exasperatedly. "And Gemma's not much better. It's like having two toddlers living under the same roof sometimes." And then her expression morphed into a wide grin. "Or two teenagers, I guess."

Violet didn't know why it bothered her so much that no one had told her this before.

She just frowned into her coffee, disappointment weighing on her. Sara reached across the table to lay her hand over Violet's. Her touch was firm but reassuring, and nothing like her brother's. "I'm sorry, Violet. It's hard for kids like Gemma and Rafe to open up, I suppose. They've considered themselves outsiders for so long, they have a hard time trusting anyone."

Violet wasn't sure what to think. She pulled her hand away from Sara's and traced her fingertip around the rim of her coffee cup. Part of her wanted to walk away, to leave the team and all its secrets. She didn't know if she wanted to be part of a group that couldn't be honest with one another about the simplest things, like relationships and living arrangements. How could she trust them with her secrets if they didn't trust her with theirs?

But she knew she was being dramatic. She knew she could trust them because she already had. They'd already saved her life once.

"So, how'd you guys end up here?" she asked at last, wanting to hear the rest of the story.

"At the Center?" When Violet nodded, Sara pursed her lips. "Shortly after Gemma came to live with us, I went to my superiors and asked about creating a new unit." She grinned at Violet. "Kind of a psychic detective division."

Despite herself, Violet grinned back at her. Out loud, it sounded ludicrous, even though that was exactly what the team was.

"I was denied, of course," Sara went on. "At least officially. But, later, I was approached by a director—someone much higher than me—about working on my own, outside the restrictions of the FBI. He knew of an organization that was interested in what we could do, and they were willing to give me the freedom I needed to run my own team. They even provided the financial backing for the Center. In return, they occasionally send us cases that require the utmost discretion. Sometimes it's something as simple as a background check on an employee or a colleague. Sometimes it's working with law firms or the district attorney. And sometimes, they ask us to investigate something more . . . serious. As long as they don't ask us to do anything illegal, I don't mind the arrangement; it frees us up to work on the cases we choose to work, the ones where I feel all of your skills are used best."

Violet had speculated about the high-tech facility and how a team of psychics who helped solve crimes for law enforcement agencies could afford such a luxurious space.

She'd even felt strange taking money from Sara, even though Sara had insisted it was her job now and she should be compensated. Still, it was weird collecting a paycheck for something she had no real control over.

But now it made sense to her. There was someone else, some outside entity—an entity with a lot of money, apparently—backing them. In exchange for sharing their abilities.

Violet was suddenly grateful that her ability didn't involve reading people's thoughts or emotions, the way Gemma's did. The idea of *spying* on someone's most private feelings was sort of repulsive.

Then again, she chided herself, she was the girl who was drawn to the dead. *Repulsive* was relative, she supposed.

But it made her feel better knowing she'd probably never have to answer to the people with the big checkbooks. She was more comfortable with bodies.

Sara's phone rang and she pulled it out to check it. She frowned at the display. "Sorry, Violet, it's one of the detectives working the collector case; I need to take this." She scooted back from the table and left Violet alone in the kitchen.

Violet decided this was as good a time as any to go. She dumped her coffee in the sink, offering a quick wave to Sara, who was sitting at her desk now, listening intently to the detective on the other end, before she slipped out the door.

CHAPTER 15

SHE KNEW THE MOMENT SHE REACHED THE BOT-
tom of the steps outside the outer door that something was
wrong.

But it wasn't what Sara told her that bothered Violet, she
realized as her heart began to beat too hard—too fast. It felt
like she was trying to breathe through sand, the air was suddenly dry and coarse. This was something else altogether.

She wasn't alone.

She took a step backward, the heels of her shoes bumping against the bottom step. She felt trapped. She wanted to
race back up the stairs, to see if—by some miracle—the door
hadn't locked behind her. But she knew that it had; she'd

heard the telltale click. And her keycard would do her no good; it was already lost in the cluttered depths of her skull-and-crossbones purse.

She scanned the parking lot, searching the road and every crevice, nook, and alleyway she could see between the buildings around her. Everything appeared to be deserted.

Yet the hair standing up on the back of her neck told her otherwise. And it wasn't just the hairs that warned her; it was the presence of an echo—or rather, echoes—that confirmed her suspicions. The haunting imprints that raked every inch of her skin, piercing her outward calm as she stood there, trying to decide what to do next.

She clutched her cell phone in one hand and gauged the distance to her car. Those keys, at least, were already in her other hand. She held them tightly, not wanting to lose track of them. But even as she squeezed them, allowing them to give her a false sense of comfort, she worried she was too far away. Or rather, that the person carrying the imprints was too close.

Still, she had to do something. She couldn't just stand there, waiting for something to happen.

In the distance, she heard the loud bass of music bumping, and she thought maybe a car was coming. But after a moment, the sound faded, and she realized it was heading in the opposite direction.

She had one chance, she finally decided, one chance to make it to safety. If only she could make it there in time.

She turned quickly, not wanting to second-guess her

plan as she raced back up the steps. Time seemed to slow to a blur and from somewhere behind her, she felt, and heard, the rush of echoes moving closer . . . closer . . . closer.

They were coming fast now, and above a haunting sound she'd heard once before, she recognized the pounding of footsteps and the swish of fabric.

He was running right for her.

She pressed the button on the intercom with a sharp sense of satisfaction. Blood rushed past her ears, deafening her and making it impossible to tell if she'd pushed it hard enough, signaling that she was out there . . . calling for help.

Before she could blink, she felt a muscled arm snake around her throat, and a hand close viciously over her mouth. She was dragged backward, violently hauled down the stairs and away from the intercom that might have connected her to Sara. The cell phone fell from her hand, skittering across the ground.

Violet struggled—or tried to—but the arms that held her bore down with brutal force, squeezing her so tightly that she was already suffocating within them. She thrashed, trying to break free from the callused hand that covered her mouth and nose. Her eyes bulged and her throat burned as her windpipe threatened to collapse on itself.

He whisked her away from the entrance, carrying her as if she weighed less than nothing. It took her a moment to realize they were in the alleyway between the Center and the next building. It was dark in the space between the massive warehouses, darker than it had been out in the open.

And when he released Violet, throwing her to the ground, she landed hard on her hands and knees, coughing and gasping for air. She didn't bother to look up. She didn't need to see his face to know who he was. Or what he was capable of.

James Nua. She would have recognized those imprints anywhere.

"Look what we have here." His words came out like a growl, mingling with the choral voices of the echo he carried. "Bet you didn't expect to see me again." He squatted down in front of her, forcing Violet to look directly at him. She cringed, unable to tear her gaze away from the slithering black marks that wriggled beneath his skin, shifting around the permanent ink on his face and neck. He'd shaved his head since she'd seen him at the jail just three days ago. It was smooth now, clean, and the swirling echo snaked over his skull now too.

Unsteadily, Violet struggled to her feet. "Why are you here?" she squeaked out, her throat barely making room for her words. "What do you want from me?"

He rose too, matching her movements so that his mouth remained just inches from hers. So close that Violet could feel his sticky breath. So close she was certain he could taste her fear. "I came here to find you." One of his black brows slashed upward. "And you made it so easy," he sneered. "Not that many White Rivers around. My boys and I, we were able to track you down like . . . *that*." He snapped his fingers in front of her face, and Violet flinched.

Her heart hammered recklessly as she struggled to think of a way out of this. Tried to decide *if* there was a way out.

"Why m–me? Wh–what did I do?"

"I think you know why. I think you should stop asking stupid questions." His jaw flexed and Violet could see him gritting his teeth, could feel the unrestrained fury oozing from him in viscous waves. "I think you should stop pissing me off by lying." His fist shot out without warning, and Violet was thrown backward by the powerful blow. Her cheek just below her left eye exploded with shattering pain, and her vision blurred as she crashed to the ground behind her. "I don't know what you told them, or what you think you saw, but you don't know shit." Violet barely had time to catch her breath before he'd taken a long stride and his foot was flying toward her. Instinctively, she rolled away from him, but he was fast, and she felt the toe of his shoe graze her hip.

"S–stop . . . *please*," she begged, her face in her hand, her cheek throbbing savagely. "I didn't see anything! I swear." It wasn't a lie, not really.

"Then what? Did you hear her? Did you hear that dumb bitch screaming for her life?" A sadistic grin broke over his face. A depraved and sinister grin. Violet felt sick as his voice dropped. "Did you hear her screaming for the lives of her babies?" Violet tried to shake her head, to tell him no, she hadn't heard anything, but he was already reaching for her, grabbing a fistful of her hair. He yanked her so hard that her neck felt like it had snapped as he lifted her so her face was even with his. "Do you know how much trouble you caused me? You should've kept your fucking mouth shut!" Spittle sprayed from his lips as he cursed her, his face red with rage. "I'm'a gonna kill you, bitch."

And then he was dragging her by her hair, away from the mouth of the alleyway into the shadows beyond, where no one would see them. Violet struggled, her fingernails digging into the pavement, trying to find something, anything, to grab on to.

She believed what he'd said about killing her, and she was desperate to find a way to stop him. When he threw her down behind a pile of wooden pallets covered with broken-down cardboard boxes, her entire body was shaking, her fingertips bloodied and raw. She desperately hoped that the haunting chorus of echoes he carried wasn't about to become the eerie backdrop to her death.

He loomed over her, wearing an expression that made her blood freeze.

She was no longer thinking when she kicked out at him, operating in pure survival mode now. She put every ounce of strength she had into her legs, and she was rewarded when she felt his kneecap grind beneath her foot. When she heard him gasp sharply, practically a scream, Violet scrambled to her hands and knees, realizing she still had a chance.

"Help!" she shrieked, running—stumbling, really—away from James Nua. "*Please* . . . someone help me!" But her voice was splintered, too soft and too frail.

And then the other sound was back, the thumping resonance of bass.

But she couldn't run fast enough, and she shrieked as she was jerked from behind, caught by her own hood when James Nua snagged it, hauling her backward.

Violet fell, squeezing her eyes shut so she wouldn't have to watch the creeping black vines that crawled beneath James Nua's skin as he stood above her.

It was then that she heard the soft click in front of her face, and felt the whoosh of air just beneath her nose.

And she did look. Unable to stop herself.

Nua held up a knife, a switchblade with a polished steel blade for her to see. His lips twisted into a menacing snarl as he touched the tip of it to Violet's neck, just below her left ear, and traced a fiery path along her jawline. She could feel the drag of the blade, the smooth metal sliding over her skin. If she moved—if she breathed—he might very well cut her.

"You fuck with me . . . *I . . . fuck . . . with . . . you.*" His voice was low and he dragged out each word, each syllable, as his narrowed eyes held hers. She felt his muscles tense and she knew that this was it. "Dumb bitch," he whispered.

A gunshot rent the air, making Violet jump, and she felt the point of the knife prick her skin. Above her, James Nua went rigid, his eyes widening as he released her jacket and she fell back. He stood there for moment, confusion contorting his features as he struggled to sort through what had just happened. And then his mouth opened and he released a gut-wrenching, ear-shattering howl of half pain, half rage.

Like Nua, Violet's brain moved too slowly. But she seized her opportunity to escape. She was on her back, and she scooted away from him, stumbling awkwardly over her own hands and feet as she crawled as far from him as she could manage. As she did, as she pressed herself against the

231

concrete wall, she started to make sense of everything in front of her.

Fresh blood bloomed at James Nua's side, the stark crimson stain spreading against the white of his T-shirt. He let go of the knife as he clutched his wound with both hands, his eyes incredulous, his face contorting with pain.

"Stay where you are!" Sara ordered from the alley that opened onto the street, and Violet could see that her gun was aimed directly at James Nua now.

Violet watched recognition dawn on his face as pain contorted into undisguised fury. With effort, he staggered to his feet.

"I said *stay where you are!*" Sara yelled again, taking a cautious step closer.

Nua just grinned at her, but even from where she stood, Violet could see the beads of sweat prickling across his forehead.

Violet remained still, watching Sara's approach. Relief unfurled within her, but she was shaking all over and her teeth chattered violently.

Behind Sara, the music drew closer, and Violet's stomach tightened. It came upon them slowly, and Violet blinked as she turned to the street beyond the alleyway. It was moving far too deliberately.

As the nose of the car came into view, the resonating bass pounded so loudly that Violet could feel it beneath her feet. Sara was watching it too, positioning herself so she could keep Nua in her sights while never losing sight of the big red car. She kept her gun aimed at Nua's grinning face.

It was like a scene out of a movie. Violet saw the boys, both with the same tribal-like tattoos as James Nua's. Neither looked old enough to be driving. One kept his hand on the steering wheel while pointing his gun down the alleyway. The other boy sat higher, perched in the passenger-side window frame, leaning over the roof of the car, his gun directed right at them. As if on cue, both boys began firing at once.

Sara's training was evident, and she moved like lightning. She dropped to the ground and was firing back before Violet could even breathe. Violet pressed herself as close to the ground as she could, covering the back of her head with her hands. She didn't need police training to know that lifting her head was a bad idea.

The rapid bursts of gunfire lasted mere seconds before Violet heard the peal of tires. And then there was silence.

Violet knew, even without looking, that James Nua had gone. She knew she was safe, at least for now. His imprints were nowhere near her.

But he could still come back, Violet thought, shuddering.

Yet that wasn't why she stayed where she was, her face pressed against the filthy blacktop beneath her, breathing in dirt and oil, and letting pebbles grind into the swelling flesh of her cheek. She stayed there straining, trying to feel for new echoes . . .

. . . not yet ready to know if Sara had survived.

Because if she hadn't, that meant Rafe had just lost his sister too.

CHAPTER 16

"VIOLET! VIOLET, ARE YOU HURT?" SARA'S HAND
was at her shoulder, but it was her voice, so dynamic, so . . .
alive, that made Violet tremble with relief.

She pushed herself off the ground, sitting up on her knees
while she collected herself.

Sara gave her the once-over, then glanced back toward
the street, her weapon still clutched in her hand as she
watched for signs that James Nua might reappear.

"Don't worry." Violet smiled weakly. "He's gone."

"You sure?"

Violet nodded and Sara visibly relaxed, letting her hand—
and her gun—drop to her side. "Just stay put for a sec," she

said, pulling out her cell phone. "You don't look so good."

Violet didn't feel very good either, but mostly she just felt shaken. Well, aside from her bloodied fingers and a throbbing eye. She listened as Sara dialed someone at the police department directly, rather than calling 9-1-1.

When she hung up, Sara squatted beside her. "What about you?" She reached out and prodded Violet's cheek, her intrusive fingers probing the base of Violet's eye socket. It took every ounce of willpower Violet had not to cry out, but the last thing she wanted was to let on how badly she was injured. All she really wanted was to go home, take a long, hot bath, and crawl into bed.

Scratch that, just the bed. And maybe some extra-strength Tylenol.

"I don't feel anything moving," Sara said almost absently as her fingers explored the injury, and Violet had to bite down on the inside of her lip to keep it from quivering. "How's this?" Without warning, Sara applied pressure.

Violet jolted and squeezed her eyes shut, waiting until the stars behind her eyelids disappeared. She reopened them slowly, her hands fisted at her sides, somehow managing not to cry. "It's—*it's fine*," she hissed from between clenched teeth. "Great, in fact. I think it probably looks worse than it is, you know?"

She definitely didn't want Sara calling an ambulance. She already didn't know how she was going to explain this to her parents.

Her parents. Her stomach dropped and her head reeled.

There was no way she wanted to explain that she'd just been attacked outside the Center. They were worried enough about what she was doing with her new team. If they knew she'd been assaulted . . .

Violet couldn't let herself think what that might mean. Still, she should call someone, she supposed; she definitely didn't think she could drive herself home. Maybe Jay would come get her.

Of course he would, she silently corrected herself. He was Jay; he was always there for her.

She glanced around, her eyes darting back and forth nervously.

"What's wrong?" Sara asked, following Violet's gaze.

"My purse. I must've dropped it when . . . when he grabbed me. Maybe it's by my car."

"It's okay, we'll look for it after the police get here. They're on their way now."

Violet nodded. Of course. The police would find it, probably in the same place she'd dropped her phone.

Sara knelt down beside Violet while they waited. "I'm so sorry about this." She patted Violet's knee, doing her best to comfort her. "No one should have to go through what you just did."

"I'm just glad you heard me."

Sara frowned, looking intensely at Violet. "What are you talking about?"

"The call button. I couldn't get to my keycard so I pushed the call button. I was hoping you'd know I needed help when you heard the buzzer." Wasn't that why Sara had come looking for her? "Didn't you hear it?"

Sara shook her head, slowly, hesitantly. "No. I didn't." And then she stood up, brushing off her knees as the sound of sirens approached. She looked down at Violet, who was confused now. "It was Rafe. He called me and said something was wrong. He said he was sure you were in trouble."

For the second time in her life Rafe had saved her, something she was more than just grateful for.

She knew she didn't need to go to the hospital by the time she'd finished answering questions and recounting her statement over and over again. She was scraped, especially on her hands, and bleeding from some small gashes on her hands and elbows. But once she'd cleaned them up, she realized they weren't serious. A little peroxide and some Band-Aids and she'd be good as new, she was sure of it.

It was the shivering that was making her crazy, since she couldn't seem to make it stop. It was the kind that had nothing to do with cold and everything to do with the fact that she'd just gotten the crap kicked out of her.

Violet sat in the passenger seat of Sara's SUV, hugging herself and glancing nervously up and down the street, watching as police cars, both marked and unmarked, came and went. From down in the alley, there were constant flashes from a camera as crime-scene investigators recorded evidence. Sara finished up with one of the female officers who had taken Violet's statement. They chatted in a way that made Violet suspect they knew each other outside of this situation, which she realized wasn't that far off, since Sara seemed to know everyone in law enforcement.

Violet's questioning hadn't taken all that long, and she'd been surprised when someone told her she'd only been outside the Center less than five minutes. The attack felt as if it had lasted hours.

She kept the window down, and could hear snippets of Sara's conversation with the officer she spoke to: ". . . he'd been following her," Violet heard Sara explaining to the woman who took notes. ". . . he knew what school she went to . . ." Sara looked up, glancing past the officer's shoulder, to where Violet was sitting. ". . . thought she'd seen what he'd done . . ." She continued, and Violet wondered if Sara knew she could hear them. "I wish someone would've told me the charges didn't stick . . ."

Violet wanted to hear the rest, but that was when she saw the black Acura pull up. Jay's car.

She climbed out of Sara's car on shaky legs as Jay was stopped by one of the uniformed officers. She saw Jay reach for his ID and hand it to the cop. She waited where she was, still shivering, until Jay was allowed through.

Jay stood motionless when he reached her, and Violet moved first, stepping toward him, closing the gap between them, and laying her hand over the thin fabric of his worn Led Zeppelin T-shirt. She needed to feel him. He reacted then, gently cupping Violet's chin as he inspected the damage to her face. His fingers traced her injuries, his frown deepening. "Are you okay?" His eyes traveling the length of her as his hands moved down her arms and then up again, settling gently on each side of her face, pinning her so he could inspect her more closely.

Mutely, Violet nodded, not caring that people, Sara and the police officers around them, had stopped what they were doing to watch the two of them. "And Sara shot him?"

She nodded again, her cheeks brushing his hands as they framed her face. His grip was so soft, so tender.

Violet could see the fear in his eyes. "I have to tell you, the idea of losing you scares the hell out of me, Vi. You know that, don't you?" He sighed heavily, still holding on to her as he stared back at her. "Promise me, no more gang fights."

Violet half-laughed and half-grimaced. "I swear it." She reached up and gripped one of his hands, turning into his palm. He squeezed back, lacing his fingers through hers as he dropped his other hand and pulled her to him.

It was Sara's voice that interrupted them, making Violet jump. "They found your cell phone . . ." She handed it to Violet. "And your keys." Sara dangled the familiar surfboard keychain Jay had gotten her when he and his mom had gone to Hawaii. It said *Maui* on one side and *Victoria* on the other, the closest he could find to *Violet*. "It's nice to see you again, Jay." Violet had nearly forgotten that they'd met before, that night at the mountain cabin. "Are you driving her home?"

"Is that okay? Is she almost done here?"

"I think that's a great idea. She shouldn't drive herself."

Then she turned to Violet. "We'll have someone bring your car to your house by tomorrow. And I'll call your parents as soon as I can." Sara tucked the keys in her pocket and then turned to Jay.

Violet gripped Jay's hand; she wasn't ready to explain this to her parents, but she knew she had no choice. They *were* parents, after all.

"What about my purse?"

Sara shook her head. "It wasn't there. Are you sure you had it with you? Could you have left it somewhere else?"

Violet's head whirled. It had to be there; she wasn't wrong about this. There were only two places it could have been: in front of the Center, or in the alley.

"Don't worry, they'll keep looking," Sara assured her, patting her arm.

There was a quiet moment as Sara thoughtfully surveyed the scene before them.

Violet glanced toward the woman who Sara had been talking to. "Why didn't you tell her? Officer Durden? You know, about me. That I knew James Nua killed his family?"

Sara glanced reluctantly at Jay, but didn't hesitate. "Not everyone needs to know what you kids are capable of. Sometimes it's better to keep what you can do . . . *quiet.* Even the DA never really knows where I get my information. We have an understanding, I tell him he needs to dig deeper, and he doesn't question how I know." She glanced down regretfully at Violet. "I really am sorry, Violet. It was dumb luck you even ran into Nua in the first place, and that you happened to be wearing your school sweatshirt at the time." She shook her head. "I mean, really, what are the odds?" Her voice took on a pensive quality. "We should never have gone back there that next day. I should never have taken the chance he'd see you again. It's my fault. I'm supposed to keep you kids safe, and I let you down. I'd do anything to protect you."

"I know," Violet said, and meant it. Sara emphasized safety in everything she did, every decision she made. There was no way she would have intentionally put Violet—or any of her team, for that matter—in danger.

They stayed there like that for a long, quiet moment.

Finally, Violet asked the question she was hesitant to broach. She was trembling as the words left her lips. "What about James Nua? What happens now?"

Sara gave a cursory nod. "Every agency in town is looking for him. I got a partial plate, but I imagine he and his buddies have already ditched the car somewhere. Either way, he's going to have to go for help eventually—that wasn't a flesh wound. And the second he walks into any emergency room, clinic, or doctor's office, we'll be notified and he'll be arrested. I'd say he has three . . . maybe four hours tops." She rested her hand on Violet's shoulder.

But that wasn't what Violet noticed, the gentle, reassuring gesture. It was something else altogether that made Violet freeze. Literally.

Sara's fingers were frigid. Not cold, but arctic, like they'd been turned into solid ice. And her skin was equally hard and unyielding.

Violet turned toward Sara. Everything moving slower now, as if time too had frozen. Sara smiled at her, her face the same as it always was. Her lips, her nose, her cheeks, her chin, everything formed as they should be. Even her eyes, that same brilliant blue as Rafe's, remained the same.

Everything but her pallor, which was now far too white. There was a thin veneer of frost that coated every surface of her skin and dusted her perfectly tweezed brows and the thick fringe of her lashes, making them look brittle but beautiful.

"Is everything all right?" Sara asked, her breath coming out in a plume of steam that only Violet could see. Sara's eyebrows furrowed and Violet knew she was staring, but she couldn't stop herself.

It was the most striking imprint she'd ever witnessed.

"You're wrong," Violet breathed, her voice filled with wonder. "He's already dead." She blinked slowly. "James Nua. He just died."

Sara thought about that. "You . . . you can *feel* it?"

Violet stared at the woman in front of her. "*See it*, actually."

Blinking, Sara glanced down at her hands, the only part of herself she could really look at. "And you're sure?"

"Positive."

BONDING

HE CHECKED HIS REFLECTION AS HE PASSED THE
oversized gilded mirror in the lobby of the upscale boutique hotel.
Typical, *he thought.* This is exactly the type of place she
would want to meet. *Someplace where she could remind him that
she was better than him.*

*But he couldn't help grinning at the image that stared back at
him. He wondered if she'd be surprised. He was no longer the gawky
child he once was. No longer bashful and afraid. No longer ordinary.*

*A woman draped in a designer dress and glittering jewels turned
her head. She practically tripped in her expensive heels, so she could
watch him as she walked by despite the fact that she was clutching her
date's—or possibly her husband's—arm. He was aware of the image*

he presented to the world. He was tall and handsome and charming.

But, of course, he could appear serious and shy too, when the need arose.

He'd become something of a chameleon. It was how he found so many of his girlfriends.

Right now, however, in this instance, the look he was going for was refined, and he smoothed his hands over the front of his jacket one last time before entering the main dining room.

He spotted her immediately; very little had changed in the past years. His stomach roiled nervously, despite his constant internal reiterations: I am good enough. She can't hurt me unless I let her. Words are only words.

He hated that she still held this much power over him, and as he approached he felt his steps grow clumsier and his shoulders hunching. He concentrated, not wanting to trip in front of her, and as he reached the table he straightened to his full, impressive height.

"Mother," he said, his voice not sounding nearly as pathetic as he felt.

She glanced up, as if she'd only just realized it was him, even though he'd felt her ruthless gaze on him the entire time. "Well, don't just stand there. You're making a spectacle of yourself."

His jaw clenched, but he took a seat without a word.

A pretty, brown-eyed waitress brought their menus. She was exactly the type of girl he'd normally notice. But not tonight. Tonight another woman demanded his attention.

The waitress smiled warmly as she took his drink order—nothing stronger than tonic water. He needed to keep a clear head. He couldn't afford to give his mother any advantage. She took far too much pleasure in cutting him down.

"Forget it. You don't have a chance," his mother announced in an all-too-familiar tone, bringing back painful childhood memories.

She can't hurt me unless I let her. The mantra repeated in his head as he glanced up at her, pretending he had no idea she was referring to the waitress. She was wrong, though; he'd seen it in the girl's eyes.

He took a breath. "You look . . . rested." And she did. Four years abroad had been good to her. She'd shopped and spa'd her way across most of Europe. Her skin looked youthful and refreshed, and her eyes sparkled as maliciously as ever.

The years had been better for him, though, he silently congratulated himself. Four years away from her dictatorial rule. Four years rebuilding the boy she'd spent twenty years tearing down. Four years of deciding who he really wanted to be.

He grinned inwardly over his accomplishments—over all of the girls his mother thought he'd never be able to get.

The waitress came back with their drinks and he flashed his most devastating smile at her as he thanked her, his practiced voice the perfect blend of confidence and boyish charm. He felt a surge of smug satisfaction when she giggled nervously, and nearly spilled the white wine spritzer his mother had ordered.

"I brought you something," he said once they were alone again, pulling a small package from his pocket. He'd wrapped it in tissue and tied it with ribbon himself, hating that, even after all these years, he still wanted to please her so badly.

When she just stared at it, her eyes filled with rancor as if it would be beneath her to open the handmade package with her own

245

hands, he leaned forward. "Here," he said, trying to hide the disappointment from his voice. "Let me."

His fingers trembled as he untied the bow, and then tore through the insubstantial paper, revealing an antique filigree locket with a tiny luminous pearl at its center . . . a gift from one of his girls.

He thought it was perfect. He thought it would be beautiful on his mother, accenting her lovely throat.

He waited for her to say something, but there was silence. Virulent silence.

She glared at him as she reached for her drink, and he noticed her hands for the first time since meeting her here tonight.

Some things never changed, he realized belatedly, as he gazed at her impeccably manicured, lilac-polished fingernails.

CHAPTER 17

HER PARENTS HAD MET THEM AT THE FRONT door, and as much as Jay might have wanted to bolt, Violet was grateful that he'd stayed by her side. If she thought the police were thorough, it was nothing compared to the barrage of questions she'd faced at home.

And in the end, when all was said and done, Violet couldn't stop her mom from blaming Sara and her team for what had happened to Violet.

"Mom," Violet interrupted again, not wanting to have this conversation now—or ever, really—as she tried, once more, to explain. "It wasn't Sara's fault." She collapsed onto the couch, too tired to do anything else as she glanced up at her mother. "It could've happened to anyone," she said, still trying to convince herself it was partly true since she still didn't know where her purse was.

"Mugged? Are you honestly going to sit there and tell me this had nothing to do with one of the cases you're working on? That this was some sort of *coincidence*?"

Violet thought about that, sagging deeper into the cushion. Technically, James Nua was never her case. Or Sara's. She'd just run into him at the police station after she'd been caught in Antonia Cornett's apartment. "That's exactly what I'm saying," Violet answered, trying not to choke on her own words. "The case we're working on had nothing at all to do with this."

Jay frowned at Violet over the top of her mom's head, but Violet ignored him.

"Sara came as soon as she knew there was trouble," Violet added.

Maggie Ambrose sighed, her shoulders drooping as she knelt down in front of her daughter. "Mugged, Violet? Come on. I don't have to be 'special' to know you're keeping something from me. Both of you." And then she took both of Violet's hands in her own. "You can't blame us for being worried—or even upset. You've asked us to trust you and we have . . ." She met Violet's gaze, but even though Violet didn't want to hear what her mother had to say, it didn't stop her from continuing. "At some point you have to trust us."

"What . . . what are you trying to say?"

"I'm not saying anything yet. I'm just saying your dad

and I need to talk things out. We need to think about what happened and what it means."

Jerking her hands from her mother's grip, Violet folded them tightly in her lap as she stubbornly blinked back tears. Her cheek ached, as did almost everything now. But nothing as much as the ache in her chest.

There was no way she could stop working with her team . . . not now that she'd finally found them.

Having Jay there with her was the best kind of medicine. Once they were alone, he was both sweet and attentive, and more gentle than Violet would have thought possible.

"I can't believe this happened to you. When are you going to stop putting yourself in danger?" His voice was laced with outrage. He was furious that someone—anyone—had laid hands on her, had hurt her in that way. He sighed heavily. "I wish I'd've been there, Vi. I would've never let him hurt you like this."

Violet didn't tease him about his threats to stand up to a gang member; he was too serious, and she was still too dazed to make jokes about it. The only thing that made either of them feel better was that Violet was certain James Nua was dead.

Jay brought her a hand mirror from the bathroom, and together they curled up on her bed and began exploring her injuries, each of them running their fingers carefully over the bruise beneath her eye, testing the feel of her swollen skin, and examining each scraped finger.

When he was finished, he climbed down from the bed and sat on his knees, leaning over her. He gently unclasped the necklace Krystal had given her, and Violet was glad he didn't ask her what it was or where she'd gotten it. She didn't want to talk about her team right now.

She watched as he lifted the hem of her shirt so he could look for bruises beneath, and she smiled, doubting he wouldn't find any, but was awed by the reverence she saw on his face. By the time his eyes lifted to hers, his expression was calm again, reassuring.

He flattened his hand lightly over the surface of her stomach, softly letting his palm glide over her skin in a feather-soft caress. He brushed lightly across a scrape along the side of her rib cage, from where Nua had dragged her while she'd struggled against him. Jay's fingers just barely grazed it. And then he bent forward, letting lips touch the tender abrasions. He took his time, his mouth—and his warm breath—giving her goose bumps. Violet sifted her fingers through his soft hair, tugging him closer until she was torn between two very different kinds of agony—the kind just below her skin's surface, and the one that came from deep within her.

When she realized she was only torturing herself, she released the soft waves of his hair. "Are you almost done?" she breathed raggedly.

Jay grinned, raising only his eyes to hers. His lips moved lower, until at last he found the faintest bruise at her hip. It was where James Nua's foot had clipped her.

She felt his lips then, tenderly—so, *so* tenderly—press

against it. His tongue flickered lightly over her skin's surface. Heat surged through her, making her nearly forget there was any pain at all. Then he moved all the way up and kissed her lips, more firmly than she would have imagined she could bear, one final time.

"Now I'm done," he retorted, one brow raised as he scrutinized her glazed expression with complacent satisfaction.

He stood and Violet felt a stab of panic. "You're not leaving, are you? It's barely five o'clock."

"Is that your way of asking me to stay?" He was grinning again, and his hair was a wild, tangled mess. She hated how desperate she sounded.

"No. If you have to go . . ." She sulked, wrapping her arms defensively over her chest, pretending it wouldn't bother her to see him walk out the door.

Jay half-frowned, half-smiled, a look that only he could manage and still be disarmingly handsome. "Of course I'm staying, Vi. I'm not sure I'm ever leaving you alone again."

Violet sighed, a relieved sound that came from deep in the back of her throat. "Whatever. I'm pretty sure this is a one-time thing you've got goin' on here. The only reason my parents gave you an all-access pass to my bedroom is because they're pretty sure we can't mess around. I mean . . . look at me. After tonight, it turns back into an isolation chamber."

It was almost hard to believe that they'd once been given free rein to her bedroom, with closed-door privileges and all . . . especially considering they'd now been relegated to the public areas of the house only. Not that she blamed her parents, really. Back then, before Violet and Jay had been a couple, the worst her parents had had to worry about was how much junk food they were sneaking before dinner. Or whether they were actually doing their homework or just playing around on the internet.

Now there were other things they could be doing when no one was watching.

Either because of Violet's injuries, or because they felt guilty about trying to force her off the team, tonight was different. Not only was Jay in her bedroom, but the door was closed.

And Violet was too hurt to make it count.

Jay crossed the room to her dresser and pulled the top drawer open. "I don't know if anyone's told you this, but you're kind of a mess," he teased, pulling a T-shirt out and tossing it onto the foot of her bed. "Besides, you should probably put something more comfortable on." He was just pushing the drawer closed again when he paused.

Violet saw the bottle in his hand when he turned back around to face her, the transparent brown pill container he held. "What's this?" he asked, his tone serious now.

She shrugged. "Dr. Lee gave them to me. I was having trouble sleeping."

"Maybe you should take one now," he said, glancing pensively at the bottle.

She thought about how fuzzy she'd felt when she'd taken them before. "I don't think so. I'm fine . . . really."

"Come on, Vi," he implored as he drew her curtains closed, his brows raised. "Stop trying to be so tough. I mean, look at you. You've been shivering ever since I picked you up. It seems like sleep might be exactly what you need." He read the handwritten label and shook one of the white caplets into his palm.

Violet didn't argue when he offered it to her. She knew he was right. Her body ached and she was exhausted. And the doctor *had* prescribed them for just that reason. She reached for the water on her nightstand and swallowed it. Then she climbed beneath the covers, grimacing as she rolled onto her side, trying to get comfortable.

Jay turned off the overhead light, leaving just the light coming in from between her curtains as he crossed back to her bed. He tucked the covers around her before climbing on top of them, curling his body around her.

As his heavy arm draped over her gently, she heard herself ask, "Why not under the blankets?"

His arm tightened, just the barest of squeezes, and she felt his breath in her hair. "Because there's no way I'd ever be invited back if your dad caught me *in* the bed with you." And then his lips brushed the back of her head. "Now, go to sleep, Violet."

At some point Violet was aware Jay was no longer in the bed with her, even though she'd never actually heard him telling her good-bye or felt the shift of the bed as he'd gotten up to leave.

But, now, hours later, as morning approached, she became distinctly aware of the fact that someone else was in her room with her.

Shuffling footsteps found their way through the blackness of her bedroom, and she forced her eyes to stay shut. There was the soft clink of glass on her bedside table and then the sound of pills clattering inside a plastic bottle. Violet thought of the pills tucked away in her dresser drawer, the ones Jay had given her earlier, and realized she still felt hazy. But the effects were beginning to wear off, if only slightly. "I brought you some more Tylenol," her mother's voice said softly. "In case you need them . . ." There was a heavy sigh, and then her bed dipped.

Her mom's hand reached out and gently brushed her cheek, so lightly that Violet almost didn't feel it at first. "You understand *why* we're worried, don't you, Vi?" she asked softly.

It didn't matter why, Violet thought, bracing herself against her mother's explanations. Their reasons didn't change anything; they were talking about forcing her to give up the one place she felt . . . normal.

"I know you do." Her mother went on, not seeming to care—or even notice—that this was a one-sided conversation. "I can't let anything else happen to you. I've been second-guessing my decision to let you do this . . . with them . . . since the very first day. And every time you walked out that door. Do you know how many nights I've lain awake, waiting until I heard you come in again? Do you think I ever slept until I knew—for sure—that you were safe?" There was another pause, but it was brief. *"This,"* she said, her thumb moving gently to the bruise beneath Violet's eye, "is nothing. *This* isn't my biggest fear and you know it."

There was a long pause, a weighted, expectant pause. Violet held her breath, waiting for what was coming.

"Sara called to say they found Casey Atkins. They got a call that she was in a warehouse downtown, just like the other girl."

Her mom didn't have to say that Casey was dead. Violet understood. She lay there, silently mourning for the girl, wishing she'd been able to do something for her. Wishing she'd been able to find a way to stop her killer.

Wishing her parents weren't thinking of pulling her from her team.

"I can't lose you." Her mom's voice sounded steely. Determined. "I won't." She stood then, and again Violet forced herself not to groan against the discomfort of her bed shifting.

When she thought she was alone again, Violet opened her eyes, but her mother was propped against the doorframe, light filtering in from the hallway behind her, outlining her like an apparition. "I knew you were listening."

Violet's expression was wooden as she answered. "Just because I understand your reasons doesn't mean I have to accept them."

CHAPTER 18

VIOLET WASN'T SURPRISED THAT NO ONE HAD come in to wake her. She'd assumed her parents were letting her take a sick day.

But it was worth it. The last thing she wanted to do was to explain her black eye each time she changed classes. And what was she supposed to say, anyway? That she got beat up by a gang member? One who'd been killed by a former FBI agent, the lady who ran the team of psychic investigators Violet worked for?

Maybe she'd just say she ran into a door; that seemed infinitely more plausible than the truth.

She came downstairs to an empty house. Her mom had been working more now that summer was approaching—her busy season, when the seasonable weather brought shoppers out to the local farmers' markets in droves. She was already out in the converted shed she used as an art studio. Violet worried about trying to eat anything, her stomach still churning in the same way it had after the first time she'd taken Dr. Lee's sleeping pills. Eventually she settled on some dry toast, choking it down with hot tea.

She took a sip and thought about Casey Atkins. Ever since her mom had told her about the girl, Violet couldn't stop thinking about her. She felt terrible, both helpless and useless. What good was her ability if she couldn't help anyone with it?

Her phone alerted her to a text, and as she checked it she realized she'd missed several messages. She felt her stomach knotting tighter and tighter as she scrolled through them. She didn't know if it was good or bad that she was getting used to the pangs she felt whenever she avoided Chelsea and her other friends, but reading the texts inquiring as to why she wasn't at school sent a fresh surge of regret coursing through her.

But there was also one from Rafe:

I hope you're okay.

It was just that single message, but it reminded Violet that she wasn't the only one who'd been hurt. With everything that had happened yesterday, she'd nearly forgotten about Rafe.

She punched out a quick response:

Don't worry about me. I'll come see you as soon as I can.

Closing her phone, she poured a glass of milk and tried

to swallow the guilt that burned more than the stomach acids reaching up her throat. And then she grabbed her mom's car keys and rushed out the front door.

Violet felt strange sitting in Dr. Lee's office without an appointment, like she was breaking some sort of grown-up protocol. Fortunately for her, no one really considered her a grown-up yet.

Nervously tapping her foot, she listened to the music coming through the speakers overhead. She recognized it as the same looped CD that always played in Dr. Lee's waiting room. *Dull* was the operative word for his musical selection, Violet thought, but she assumed that was sort of the point. It was meant to be background noise . . . probably meant to be calming and unremarkable.

When Dr. Lee opened the door to his office, Violet jumped to her feet. "Um, hi, Dr. Lee."

His bushy brows gathered at the bridge of his nose. "Violet? What are you doing here? We didn't have an appointment, did we?"

"No. I, uh . . . I was hoping I could, um, talk to you for a few minutes."

He examined her face, the way everyone did now, and she tried not to bristle beneath the scrutiny. It was natural, she supposed, that kind of curiosity. "I'm sure I could spare some time for you." He stepped aside, his professional voice ushering her inside. But once the door closed behind them, that tone changed. Instead of taking his usual seat, he moved to stand in front of her, frowning sympathetically. "I heard about what happened, but this is . . ." He took a breath, screwing on his shrink face again. "Well, it's hard to look at."

"It's better than it looks." The words had become like a running mantra for Violet, her way of telling everyone she was okay. But then she shook her head as she dropped onto the leather couch, a spot she'd always purposely avoided, deciding this wasn't the time for false assurances. And the truth was, pretty much everything sucked right now. When she opened her mouth, her voice came out sounding tearful and pathetic. "I got my butt kicked by a gang member. And I think my parents are making me quit the team . . ." Tears stung her eyes as her words tumbled over one another. Dr. Lee passed her a tissue. "I don't blame them, really. Look at me. If I were them, I'd probably blame Sara too. But it wasn't her fault." She blew her nose.

Dr. Lee waited, crossing his legs.

"But the thing is, I'm not sure I can listen this time. I've always been so good . . . or at least I try to be. But this time . . . this is different. I mean, sure, I'm a little banged up." She let out a watery laugh. "Okay, a *lot* banged up. But I just don't think I can *quit* the team."

Dr. Lee uncrossed his legs but remained silent.

Violet didn't pause. "I need them. When I'm with them . . . it's the only time I don't feel like some sort of . . . freak."

"Freak." He repeated the word—her word—letting it linger between them.

"Yeah." She nodded, letting her hands fall into her lap, her fingers clutching the tissue. "When I'm with them, I feel like . . . I'm not alone. That someone . . ." She shrugged. "Gets me."

Dr. Lee nodded, slowly and noncommittally, not giving Violet any indication of what he was thinking. Of whether he was on her side or not.

His next question didn't clear her confusion any. "Do you think that's enough of a reason to disobey your parents? To feel like someone *gets you*?"

Violet frowned. There was more to her connection with them than that, wasn't there? She owed them, she supposed, for saving her life. She understood them, sort of. And she was comfortable there. But was that really enough to say she belonged there? "Can I ask *you* a question?" Violet crumpled the tissue into a ball, wadding it tightly as her eyes met his. "Who do *you* work for? I mean, I never filled out any paperwork and you never asked for my parents' insurance cards or anything. I know you see most of us on the team, for one reason or another, so does that mean you work for Sara? Do you tell them what I tell you? And if you do work for her, shouldn't you be trying to talk me into staying with the team?"

Dr. Lee smiled. It was the most composed smile Violet had ever seen. More so even than her dad's, and that was saying something. He handed her another tissue, and Violet took it, wiping her nose. "This might be hard for you to believe, Violet, but just because you want something doesn't always mean it's the best decision."

Violet sat there quietly, considering Dr. Lee's words. She wasn't sure if he was talking about himself—and the team—and wanting her to remain part of their group. Or if he was talking about her threats to defy her parents.

Somehow, she felt like he meant both.

After a long moment, she spoke again, her voice faint. "You didn't answer my question."

His patient smile never faltered. "Which question was that, Violet?"

"Who do you work for?"

Dr. Lee exhaled. "I work for the same people you work for. The people who run the Center."

MELANCHOLY

HE SAT IN THE RESTAURANT, WATCHING THE girl. The corner booth that gave him the advantage of a full view while keeping him mostly hidden from view. It was a good place to be. A good place to watch.

Last night had been good for him. Seeing his mother after all these years. Facing his fears. Confronting childhood demons. Confronting her.

He felt stronger. Surer of himself and who he'd become.

Even when she'd berated him, even after they'd gone back to his place and she'd criticized his housekeeping, his décor, his taste in wine, he'd simply tuned her out, ignored her forked tongue. Ignored her blistering words and her venomous rants.

She could never appreciate the kind of man he was. She wasn't the kind of woman who could understand a gentle soul like his.

It didn't matter, though. He wouldn't be seeing her again. After last night, he'd decided he was done with her.

Sitting back, he tried to erase the memories of his mother from his mind. He didn't want to think about her right now, not while he was here. Watching her.

He studied the girl as she moved from table to table. She smiled and laughed, joking with those she spoke to. She was confident in ways that none of his other girlfriends ever had been.

Maybe that had been his problem. Maybe that was the reason none of his other relationships had worked out. He'd been choosing the wrong kind of girls.

Maybe now he had the opportunity to change all that.

So what was wrong with him, then? Why couldn't he concentrate? Why couldn't he stop thinking about the other girl, the young one?

The one who'd needed him.

He was just tired, he told himself. Two nights without sleep . . . two long nights without someone he could come to, someone to soothe him and make him feel . . . better. It was starting to wear on him.

That was why he didn't see her approaching, why she'd caught him unawares.

"Refill?" she asked, her big brown eyes watching him with vibrant intensity. The very same eyes that had brought him back here in the first place. And then he saw a spark of awareness. "You were here last night, weren't you? With an older woman." She reached across the table to fill his cup, leaning just a little too low and revealing a glimpse into the opening at the top of her blouse. "Your mother?"

It took only a moment to recover, to find his voice again. "Good memory." His face slipped into the perfect mask of appreciation. "I couldn't stay away, I guess."

She paused, timing every move brilliantly. Her tongue flicked over her lips just before she dazzled him with a smile that, on anyone else, would've stolen their very breath. But not him. He knew the moment she'd become the aggressor, the moment she'd started calculating her moves that she wasn't the one. She was different today than the night before . . . bolder, more aggressive. Wrong.

They were never supposed to seek him out.

He was the man in this relationship.

"Well, let me know if I can bring you anything else." She smiled suggestively. And when he smiled back at her, an intentionally bland smile, she shrugged. "Enjoy your meal."

He watched her short black skirt swish from side to side as she moved to the next table. It was better to know now, he silently assured himself, already erasing images of the waitress from his mind. Better that he hadn't let himself get attached.

It didn't matter anyway. There were plenty of other girls out there. Girls that would die to have a man like him. A true gentleman.

He waited until he was sure no one was looking and he reached into his front pocket, pulling out his cell phone. He scrolled through the photos he'd taken, ones he'd looked at a thousand times already. Ones he'd practically memorized.

He paused when he saw the ones he'd taken yesterday in front of *the run-down warehouse he'd followed her to. His stomach clenched as he recalled hearing her cries for help, and he hated himself for not answering them. For hiding, and waiting.*

Something had stirred in him. Something primal and possessive.

He glanced down at one of the images, recalling the way her eyes—the wrong color for him—had looked the day he'd spotted her, outside The Mecca.

At that moment, he realized it. He knew then that she needed him.

Suddenly it didn't matter that she wasn't his usual type. He ran his finger over her riotous curls, wondering what it would be like to have her vivid green eyes gazing into his.

There was definitely something about her.

Violet, he thought, repeating the name he'd overheard the boy on the street calling her that first day. Before he'd followed her. Before he'd known even more about her. Violet Ambrose.

Soon, he would sleep again.

Soon, he'd have a new girlfriend.

CHAPTER 19

VIOLET SIGHED WHEN SHE SAW THE MINIVAN IN her driveway, the one her aunt was always trying to convince her was cooler than a normal minivan. Violet insisted that a built-in DVD system and Bluetooth wireless didn't change the fact that it was still a minivan.

It didn't hurt her mood, though, to see that her car was back. The tan Honda was parked beside her aunt's car, and despite her black mood, she plastered on her best fake smile, preparing herself to be smothered in well-meaning concern.

"Oh my!" Her aunt Kat pounced on her before she was even through the door, her hand flying up to cover her mouth as she got a look at Violet's face. "Geez, Vi, I . . . are you . . ." Her face scrunched up. "Oh my goodness, I'm so glad you're safe," she breathed at last, pulling Violet into a fierce hug.

"It's not as bad as it looks." Violet recited the words, trying to make her aunt feel better.

"She's lying." Her uncle Stephen winked at her as he sauntered into the front room, joining them. The taste of dandelions flickered across Violet's tongue, the imprint he'd forever carry on him.

"Hi, Uncle Stephen." He hugged her too, tighter even than her aunt had. "Hey, baby. How're ya doin'? Had a rough time of it, huh?"

There was no point denying the truth. "I've been better. Kinda sucks getting your ass kicked."

Her uncle laughed against her ear, giving her one last squeeze. "Yeah, it kinda does, doesn't it? Maybe you need some karate lessons or something. Next time *you* can be the kicker."

"Next time I'll try to run faster," Violet said, hoping they'd bypassed the awkwardness of the situation.

But then her uncle's expression changed, growing serious. "I think you should reconsider what you're doing, Vi. With Sara Priest and her group. It's dangerous. Just look at you."

"You've been talking to my mother," Violet accused, knowing it wouldn't have mattered; her uncle would have felt the same way, with or without her mother's interference. "Really, Uncle Stephen, it wasn't Sara's fault. She didn't—"

"I doubt anyone thinks it *was* her fault. But sometimes

267

when you're involved in dangerous situations, even if you're not *directly* involved, things can happen. This is just one of those times. No one's blaming Sara, exactly, but you have to admit, if you hadn't been working with her this probably wouldn't have happened in the first place."

Violet wasn't sure what to say. She didn't want to admit anything, even if he was technically right. In her heart she knew Sara never meant for her to get hurt, that she'd have done anything to protect Violet. But Violet also knew she bore her share of the burden. If she hadn't gone behind Sara's back in the first place, breaking into Antonia Cornett's house with Rafe and Krystal, she would never have met James Nua. He would never have tried to kill her.

And he'd still be alive today.

She shuddered at the thought of him, of what he'd done to his girlfriend and their two small children. She couldn't help thinking he deserved what he got.

"Look," her uncle said, his tone solicitous. Violet saw her mother leaning against the doorway to the kitchen, listening, and she forced herself to focus on her uncle instead, not wanting to see that judgmental look in her mom's eyes. "Just think about it, Vi. Think about what you're doing and who you're doing it with." He smiled at her, naked concern etched throughout every line of his face. "Believe me, if we didn't love you, we wouldn't nag."

He draped his arm around his wife then, a broad grin parting his lips as he gazed down at her adoringly. "Unfortunately, you come from long line of stubborn women." Violet didn't bother pointing out that she and Kat weren't actually related by blood; she had a feeling it wouldn't have made a difference.

"Speaking of stubborn . . ." Maggie Ambrose said from her spot at the doorway. "The kids are begging to go to the park." Two blonde heads poked out from behind her legs.

"You promised, Dad," Joshua complained as Cassidy clumsily pushed him out of the way.

Cassidy stopped abruptly in front of Violet. "Owie!" the three-year-old frowned, pointing to the bruise on Violet's face.

Violet half-laughed, half-scowled at the little girl. "Thanks, Cass. Just what I wanted to hear." She held her hands out to her little cousin. "Come here, you." When Cassidy jumped into her arms, Violet lifted her up. "So, you wanna go to the park, huh?"

"Wanna go to da park, Daddy!" Her tiny voice pealed throughout the room and Violet found herself envying her cousin's exuberance.

Glancing at her uncle Stephen, Violet offered, "I'll take them." She looked at Kat. "Really, I don't mind."

Kat nudged Joshy. "What do you think, guys? You wanna go to the park with Vi?" And then she turned to Stephen, her face expectant. "I might even be able to fit a quick Starbucks run after I drop you at the station."

Uncle Stephen kissed his wife on the forehead. "Seriously, Kat, you gotta get out more. You need to dream a little bigger than Starbucks."

***

Violet waved as Jay crossed the field. Not that he hadn't already seen her, or rather Cassidy. The moment the little girl had spotted him, she'd started squealing his name and running in lopsided circles.

Clearly Violet had some competition.

After all the safety checks and double-safety checks—her aunt making sure the car seats were properly secured in the backseat of her Honda—Violet had texted Jay and told him to meet her at the park as soon as school got out.

She whistled when she checked the time on her phone. "You made record time, my friend. What'd you do, ditch class early to get here?"

He winked at her as he dropped to his knees to let Cassidy come barreling into his arms. "Jay! You're here!" She shrieked when he caught her, and then he tossed her in the air, catching her before she came all the way back down. She was still laughing when she shouted breathlessly, "Wanna push me?"

She clutched his fingers and dragged him to the swing set. He waited patiently as the little girl wiggled back and forth, adjusting and readjusting her position. When she finally stopped squirming, Jay asked, "Ready, Cass?"

She just nodded up at him, her expression intent as her fingers clutched the chain.

"I have to admit, Ambrose, this was a pretty good idea."

Violet took the swing next to Cassidy's and pushed herself with her feet, leaning backward as the swing glided

270

upward. She felt Jay's hand at the small of her back, and he pushed her, propelling her forward.

"Higher!" Cassidy squealed from the swing beside Violet's. Even at three, the little firecracker wanted to do what everyone else did as she tried to keep up with her older cousin.

Violet dropped her feet, letting them drag through the gravel to slow herself down. "No, Cass. That's as high as you can go. Maybe when you're older."

"I'm older," the little girl pouted. But her argument was forgotten when Jay pushed her again, jolting her just the tiniest bit higher. Her small fingers tightened around the metal links, and she shrieked with unconcealed delight.

Violet wrapped her elbows around the chains of her swing. "It *was* a good idea, wasn't it?" Without waiting for an answer, she went on. "I just didn't want to sit around the house anymore. I didn't want to hear my mom talk about me and the team and Sara. I hate the way she looks at me, like she can't decide whether she should hug me or scold me."

Kat brought the kids to this park all the time, and Violet glanced over to watch Joshua play with a little girl he seemed to know. The two of them made their way up the ladder to the top of the slide; then they sat one in front of the other—forming a very short train—and slid down together, falling in a heap in the gravel at the bottom. The little girl's mother watched from the bench she sat on, glancing up occasionally with mild interest to make sure neither of the kids got hurt.

To Violet, watching the kids play was like glimpsing into the past. She could see herself in the girl, and Jay in her little cousin. They had once been like that. They had been those carefree kids.

And then she giggled as she thought about where they were now, on the swing set, in the park, and she realized they still were like that.

"What?" Jay asked slyly, taking Cassidy's place on the swing as she hopped off to go join her brother and his little girl friend.

"Don't climb the ladder, Cass," Violet called after her. "It's too high!" And then, shrugging, she mused, "I was just thinking about us." She leaned her cheek against her hand as it clutched the chain.

Jay nudged his swing sideways, so it nearly brushed Violet's. "What about us?"

"I was just thinking how cute we must have been, when we were their age." She glanced toward the kids, who were racing up the ladder again.

His arm snaked out, capturing her before the momentum of his swing could drag him away again. When the swing did pull, they both moved in that direction. "We're still cute," he said, but his voice was low and filled with unspoken longing.

She lifted her chin, their faces just inches apart now, and Jay's grip around her waist kept them together. "Yeah?" she breathed. "You think so?"

His other hand moved to rest on the side of her face,

covering her bruise . . . not concealing it but cradling it. His thumb shifted, stroking the tender path of skin. "I do, Vi. I think we're perfect."

She felt vibrations throughout her entire body. Even her lips tingled. She couldn't imagine being loved more. Didn't think there was anyone she'd rather be loved by.

His mouth grazed hers, intensifying the tingling sensation until she felt like every nerve in her body was alive . . . alert. "Jay," she whispered.

"Vi, I'm glad your parents are making you quit the team. I just . . ."

"Jay!" the little girl's voice squealed, interrupting them. "Catch me!"

Looking up, Violet saw Cassidy perched atop the tall slide, her arms waving to them. "I'm bigger!" she announced proudly.

As if their actions were synchronized, they both jumped off the swings at the same moment, Jay racing toward the laddered steps as Violet rushed to reach the bottom of the slide.

"Come on down, Cassie. I'll catch you," Violet coaxed.

The girl's eyes narrowed obstinately, her voice so determined, yet so tiny, reminding Violet how little she really was. "No. Jay can catch me."

"Jay's right behind you. Stay there, he'll help you get down."

Cassidy turned to see Jay, who was almost to the top of the ladder, and then she turned back to Violet, her expression changing dramatically. "He's gonna get me . . ." The sing-song quality of her voice was frantically enthusiastic. This was definitely a game to her.

Just as Jay was in arm's reach, Cassidy giggled and leaned forward, launching herself down the slide. She went fast . . . faster than Violet had expected the tiny three-year-old to go, almost as if the slide had been greased.

By the time she reached Violet's outstretched arms, she was moving like some sort of missile bent on a path of destruction. And when she collided against Violet's chest, Violet gasped sharply from the impact. Yet even as she wrapped her arms tightly around her cousin, she heard her-self scolding her. "You can't do that, Cass . . . you scared me . . . you could've gotten hurt. . . ."

And as she said the words, she heard them in her own head, repeated back to her . . . in her mother's voice.

Violet grimaced, dragging herself awake as she realized she'd fallen asleep on the couch. The television flickered through the dark room. Her dad must've turned the volume all the way down before he'd gone up to bed because there was no sound coming from it.

She had to admit, she was glad he'd stayed up with her. Even though she didn't always agree with her parents, she could count on her dad to be the voice of reason.

"Do you hate us?" her dad had asked when he'd joined her on the couch while she'd absently flipped through the channels.

Still trying to ignore him, Violet shook her head. "Nope. Not hate," she'd answered. "Just . . ." She shrugged. *What?* she wondered. *Frustrated? Irritated? Sad?* "I don't know, pissed, I guess."

Her dad made a tsking sound, a warning to watch her language, but he'd asked, "At us?"

Violet turned to look at him, considering his question. "Well, yeah. But not just at you. At everything, I guess. I really don't wanna talk about it, if that's okay."

He'd patted her knee but stayed where he was, quietly staring at the screen. After a moment, he said, "You can be mad, Vi. At me, and your mom . . . at whatever you want. Just don't stay that way. Hate and anger are tough emotions to hang on to. They'll eat you up."

Violet had sighed. It was so hard to stay mad at her dad, and after a few moments, she'd leaned her head against his shoulder. "I wish you'd trust me to decide if I should stay on Sara's team or not."

He'd tipped his head so it was leaning on top of hers. "I know you don't understand this now, but sometimes you need to trust us to make the best decisions for you."

They'd stayed there like that, the silence stretching, until finally he patted her knee, calling a truce and changing the subject. "Are you sure you don't want to come to Uncle Stephen's with us tomorrow night? Aunt Kat's making tacos. I know you like tacos."

Violet shook her head. "No thanks. I'm not feeling up for it. I'm gonna see if Jay wants to come over and hang out."

His brows had drawn together. "Are you sure you're okay, Vi? Anything I should be worried about?"

Violet exhaled noisily and stretched her legs. "Nope. I really don't feel like being social." She squeezed her hands, making fists with both of them and opening them again. "But mostly I'm just exhausted."

CHAPTER 20

VIOLET GLANCED DOWN AT THE PIECE OF PAPER Sara had ripped from her notebook just before she'd left the hospital, just a scrap . . . with an address scribbled on it. Sara's address. Rafe's address.

The huge brick-and-steel building she stood in front of was just blocks from Chinatown and definitely wasn't the kind of place she'd expected to find when she got there. She chewed on the side of her finger, rethinking her decision to come here at all. Maybe it would've been better if she stayed away from Rafe. She couldn't help remembering the way she'd itched to reach across the sheets that day at the hospital, and she wondered if it hadn't been more than just concern over an injured friend.

Her thumb was hovering over the buzzer as she tried to decide, part of her wanting to stay, part of her wanting to flee, when she saw Rafe pushing open the entrance to the building, an imposing outer door with bars across the paned glass.

"Hey," she said, suddenly feeling self-conscious about showing up without calling first. "How did you know I was here?"

Rafe studied her, and a part of her expected him to say he'd predicted her visit, but what she got was far less interesting. "I had to get up and stretch my legs. I don't care what Sara says, it can't be good for anyone to stay in bed that long. I saw your car when I was looking out the window."

"Is she here?" Violet asked.

"Sara? No." Rafe's eyes narrowed. "What about you? Do your parents know you're here?"

Violet shook her head. If her parents had their way, she didn't know when she'd have the chance to see him—or anyone on the team—again. "I just . . . I just wanted to make sure you were . . . okay."

He shoved away from the door as he took a long stride toward her, letting the door slam behind him. "I should be asking you the same thing," he said, cringing, his voice filled with concern.

Violet knew how she looked. The bruise on her cheek had turned a strange combination of green, yellow, and purple. The swelling had gone down, but not enough for anyone else to notice. "I'm fine." She hedged and then tried to shrug it off. "If you like bar-fight chic."

His face darkened. "I wasn't really talking about what's on the outside."

"You mean, like, it's what's on the inside that counts?"

Rafe grimaced, the ghost of a smile finding his lips. "Well, when you put it that way, it sounds sort of . . ."

"Sweet?"

"I was gonna say lame. But, yeah, I guess that works too."

"Yeah? Well, you look . . ." She was going to say *better*, but she practically stumbled over the word. He looked anything but better. If she looked beat-up, he looked downright thrashed. Even behind the bandages, Violet could see scrapes and mottled skin. "Terrible. You look terrible." She moved closer to him on the landing as he unlocked the closed door. "But better than the last time I saw you, I guess."

Rafe tried to laugh, but winced and grabbed his ribs. "Damn, V, I wouldn't plan on a career in nursing if I were you; your bedside manner stinks." His eyes clouded over when he saw her stroking the black onyx hanging from around her neck. "Krystal?" he asked.

"For protection," Violet clarified.

"Um, yeah, I got one too. Mine's for healing." He tugged at the silver chain around his neck. He held up an irregular-looking stone that had been tucked beneath his shirt. It was cloudy—opaque—and Violet wondered at the mystical qualities Krystal believed it possessed. "I meant it's *from* Krystal. Right?"

"Oh, yeah . . . right." She nodded, realizing she'd

misunderstood his question.

He let her inside and she followed him into the vestibule as he pressed the button in front of an ancient-looking elevator.

Grinding and shuddering, the elevator sputtered to a stop at the ground floor, the door opening loudly. Violet hesitated. "Are you sure that thing's safe? Looks sorta sketchy."

Rafe winked at her, holding his hand out mockingly. "After you."

She wasn't wrong; the elevator *was* sketchy. The thing just *felt* old, unstable beneath her feet. It was smaller than the more modern elevators in the high-rises around the city. Cramped and dark, like being trapped inside a coffin.

She shifted nervously. "You know, a little exercise never hurt anyone."

Rafe pressed the button and then leaned casually against the railing, shoving his hands in his pockets as he studied her. "It's five floors up. You can walk if you want, but I'll take my chances."

The elevator started upward, jerking unsteadily and making screeching and grating sounds that couldn't possibly mean anything good. "If this thing goes down, I'm totally blaming you," Violet insisted, gripping the worn brass handrail on her side.

"Are you gonna freak out every time you come over? It's just an elevator, V," Rafe criticized.

"What makes you think I'm coming over again?" she

shot back, leaving him behind in the elevator the moment the doors slid open.

Once inside the hallway, Violet could only see one door on the entire floor: a large, arched door that was coated in layers of peeling black paint. Without inviting her to follow, Rafe brushed past her to open it, leading the way inside.

Again, Violet was taken aback by what she saw, wondering what it was exactly that she'd expected.

The place he shared with Sara practically oozed urban charm. It was the kind of high-ceilinged loft Violet had always imagined in places like New York or San Francisco, yet somehow never imagined so close to home in Seattle. There were visible rafters and ductwork, tall exposed brick walls, and dark wood floors that practically gleamed. It was spacious in the same way the Center was spacious, but that was where the similarities between the two ended.

Unlike the Center, with its modern, high-tech, officey feel, Sara and Rafe's loft was definitely a home. The kitchen had been remodeled—or more likely had been built from scratch—and looked like something out of a kitchen design magazine. There were granite countertops, stainless steel appliances, and low-hanging pendant lights enclosed in amber-colored glass that gave off a soft, inviting glow. Even the furniture, although modern, with low backs and squared corners, was warm and inviting, upholstered in shades of rich red and gold and brown.

"Wow," Violet breathed. "I can't believe you live here." This was a far cry from her Buckley farmhouse.

"Wait'll you see the view." He started to reach for her hand, and then drew back quickly. "C'mon, it's sort of incredible," he explained, leading her toward the giant windows that overlooked the city below.

Joining him, Violet could see buildings and bridges, and train tracks and traffic, stretching all the way down to the waterfront. She wanted to stay there until the sun went down. To watch as the sky darkened and lights all over Seattle flickered on, taking on a life of their own.

"Pretty cool, huh?" Rafe swayed, bumping her shoulder so lightly she almost didn't feel it.

Except that it was all she felt . . . and her cheeks burned as her breath caught in the back of her throat.

I shouldn't be doing this, she warned herself silently. *Rafe shouldn't make me feel like this.*

But it was nothing. Less than nothing, she insisted, feeling foolish for arguing with herself. Rafe was just her friend. He wasn't Jay. He could never be Jay.

"I heard about Casey," Violet said, unable to stop the words. "I wish we could've saved her. I wish I could've been more . . . useful."

Rafe glanced down at her. "You were useful, V. You were the one who found the connection to the café. Who knows, that could be the key. Sara says killers have 'hunting grounds' and maybe that's his. At least they have a place to start."

Violet thought about that. It wasn't nothing, she supposed. "So, you and Sara, huh?"

Rafe shifted on his feet, stuffing his hands deep in his pockets as he gazed back outside. "You mean that she's my sister? Kinda no big deal, V. We've been related pretty much our entire lives."

"So why not tell everyone?"

Rafe flinched, almost as if the words had been tangible, painful. He stood there for a moment, an uneasy silence engulfing them, and then stalked away, leaving her standing alone at the window. He went to the kitchen and started going through cupboards, searching for nothing in particular. "*Everyone* knew," he said quietly. "You were the only one who seemed surprised by the news."

"Because you never told me. *No one* ever told me."

His back was still to her as he opened the fridge. "You never asked."

But now she was the one who felt hurt. She glowered at him, wishing she could shoot daggers with her eyes. "Are you kidding? I have to ask or you won't tell me anything? How was I supposed to know what to ask? You and Sara, that's kind of a big deal. Seems like something one of you could've mentioned."

Rafe slammed the door but didn't turn around. Violet waited, wondering why he couldn't just admit he'd made a mistake by not telling her sooner.

When at last he faced her, his cheeks were flushed, hot and red, and his eyes glittered brightly. "Not everyone has what you have," he bit out, his voice cold, like an arctic whisper. "Not everyone has parents and a home and people

283

who care about them. After what happened with Mike and Megan . . . with their dad—" The mention of that night in the mountain cabin made Violet recoil. "You should understand that some of us have gone through *things* that we don't want to share with everyone."

She took an uncertain step forward, not willing to let it go. "All I wanted to know was why you didn't tell me Sara was your sister."

"Because. I don't want you to know me, Violet."

Violet stopped dead in her tracks and stared at him with unblinking eyes.

He'd called her *Violet*. Rafe didn't call her that; he called her "V," his own personal nickname for her. She'd never minded, always thinking it was kind of endearing.

It hadn't dawned on her before what it really was: his way of keeping her away.

Violet wanted to close the distance, to reach out to him.

Instead, she said, "I won't hurt you, Rafe."

His lashes looked impossibly black and thick against his pale skin, and suddenly he looked more boyish than Violet could have imagined possible.

Her chest ached and she blinked hard. She tried to find her voice, tried to think of something else to say, but there was nothing. Just silence. And need.

"Am I interrupting some sort of moment here?" Gemma's voice sliced through the still that hung between them, and Violet couldn't believe that neither of them had heard the front door open.

She turned to see Gemma gaping at them in open-mouthed disgust, as if she were eyeballing a horrific car wreck. "I can come back later if you two lovebirds need some time alone."

Violet blinked as she remembered what Gemma had said about her, about her stinking of death, and she wondered if Gemma smelled it now. Or if there was something else she sensed on her. Something infinitely more private.

Rafe managed to collect himself before Violet did, and he rubbed the back of his neck. "What are you doing here, Gemma?" He left the kitchen and went to stand next to Violet.

"Um, believe it or not, Rafe, I still live here. And last I heard, you haven't had any luck getting me evicted, so deal with it."

Rafe grabbed Violet's hand, ignoring the static charge that jolted their skin the moment they touched. "Come on, I'll show you my room," he mumbled as he dragged Violet away from Gemma.

Gemma said something behind them, but he just slammed his door, blocking out her words. The bitter tone, however, was unmistakable.

"What is it with her?" Violet asked, peeling her hand from Rafe's.

But before she could say anything else, she'd looked past him, and she covered her mouth in surprise. And instead of feeling uncomfortable about being alone with him in his bedroom, she suddenly felt laughter bubbling up in her throat. The last thing she'd expected was this kind of neat-freak orderliness. Not from Rafe, with his unkempt hair, ripped jeans, and threadbare T-shirts. It was almost stark it was so tidy.

But it was his bookshelves that really captured Violet's interest. They were tall, every shelf overflowing, with books stacked in front of books. There were knickknacks too, all perfectly arranged, an old metal lunch box, mismatched picture frames . . . a troll doll with bright pink hair.

Violet wondered if that was the doll Sara had told her about. Sophie's doll.

"She's always like that," Rafe answered, but Violet was ignoring him now as she wandered toward the shelves. She ran fingers along the spines as she read the titles in her head: *On the Road, The Catcher in the Rye, 1984, The Giver, Fahrenheit 451.* There were classics sitting alongside books by Stephen King, Michael Crichton, and Anne Rule. There was no rhyme or reason to his hodgepodge reading collection. "She's mad because I'm not the brother she always dreamed of."

"You think she's bitchy to me because *you're* not nice to her?" Violet stopped, her finger poised over a tattered copy of *To Kill a Mockingbird.*

Rafe shrugged. "I don't know, kind of."

"That's ridiculous." Violet's lips quirked, her eyes widening. "Maybe you should teach her to use her big-girl words, and then we'll know for sure."

His eyes dropped, but his mouth curved into a shy smile.

"I just meant she's kinda pissed that I haven't been nicer to her since she moved in. It's not that I don't like her or anything . . ." His voice trailed off.

"It's just that you don't want to get to know her." Violet finished his sentence.

He looked up, his eyes meeting hers, and shrugged again. "I guess so."

Hesitating, Violet spied a photograph sticking out from between two of the books. It was ragged around the edges, but even from her vantage point, Violet could see that Rafe was in the photo beside a blonde girl. Not pale blonde, like Gemma's—perfectly styled and fashionable. This girl's hair was darker blonde, more natural-looking.

Without thinking, Violet pulled the picture free and examined the frail-looking girl with black-lined eyes and a pierced lower lip. In the photo, Rafe's arm was slung possessively around the girl's neck. He looked . . . happy. "Is this . . . Sophie?"

Something flashed behind Rafe's eyes—hurt or misery—worse than the physical damage to his body, but gone much more quickly. "Man, she told you everything, didn't she?"

She recalled her conversation with Sara, the way Sara had opened up about their mother but had been reluctant about discussing Sophie. "She didn't want to. I asked."

"I guess it's my fault. If I hadn't said her name . . ." He took the picture from Violet's fingers and slid it back between the books without even glancing at it. "You know, she had it too," he explained quietly, mournfully. "That thing that happens whenever we touch, that shock between us. I felt it when I touched her too. You two are the only ones I've ever had that with." His gaze flicked nervously to hers.

"So . . . what is it?"

He shrugged, as always. "I don't know. I didn't know then and I don't know now. All I know is . . ." His voice lowered. "I don't hate it."

Violet's cheeks burned. "Do you think it's because you're . . . that you can . . ."

Rafe stepped toward her and instinctively she backed away. "What? Do I think it's what?"

It was her turn to shrug. "Because you're psychic? That we have some sort of weird . . . connection?" Violet turned away from him, her gaze flicking nervously over the titles on the bookshelf again to avoid the intensity of his gaze. "Sam says you're different with me. Is that true?" And when he didn't answer, when the silence went on too long and Violet wasn't sure he understood, she tried again. "Are you? Different, I mean?"

When she heard him speak, his voice was right at her back. She could practically feel his breath against her neck. He was close. Too close, and Violet felt her stomach tighten. "I am," he whispered, even quieter than usual. "I don't want to be, but I am."

Violet shook her head, wanting to deny his words and giving the only answer she could. She didn't know if she could even breathe.

His hands, both of them, touched her arms while he stood there, behind her. The shock of his touch was overshadowed by the pounding of her heart and the blood beating through her veins.

She heard him swallow, and his fingertips tightened just the barest amount.

Violet squeezed her eyes shut. She didn't know what to say, but everything seemed wrong. "Rafe . . ." was all she managed.

His hands fell away. "I know." His voice sounded like it was being ripped from his throat. "I already know, you don't have to say it. I've known all along, it's what I do. It's one of my *gifts*." He practically spat the word, making it sound vile, dirty. "But it doesn't mean I have to feel the same way. And that's why I don't want you around."

Violet turned to face him, tears stinging her eyes as she blinked furiously, angrily. Why had he said all of this? Why couldn't he have left things the way they were?

But he wasn't finished with her yet. "It's also why I can't leave you alone."

CHAPTER 21

VIOLET FELT LIKE AN IDIOT AFTER SHE LEFT Rafe's, and she replayed the conversation in her head all the way home. How had she not seen that coming? How had she not known that Rafe's feelings were more than just . . . *friendly*?

But the more she thought about it, the more she realized she *had* known. Why else would Rafe have gone out of his way to spend so much time with her, especially when both Krystal and Sam had told her that Rafe avoided everyone else?

Yet somehow she'd deluded herself into thinking that none of that mattered. That if *she* didn't feel anything more, then he would never act on his feelings.

Except, maybe she did feel something more.

That's crazy, Violet insisted, biting down on her lips and tasting blood. *I don't feel anything.* Rafe was her friend, nothing more.

She belonged with Jay.

She glanced at the sky and wondered when it had started getting dark, and how she hadn't noticed the gradual shift from daylight to dusk as she'd left the city. But she knew why. She felt numb. Worn-down and numb.

Relief trickled through her when she pulled into her driveway and realized her parents weren't home yet, that they were still at her aunt and uncle's. She texted Jay, asking him to come over when he got off work.

She had no intention of telling him what had happened at Rafe's house; there was no point giving him any more reason to be suspicious of Rafe. Besides, Violet assured herself, she had no intention of giving Rafe another chance to share his feelings. At least not *those* feelings.

For now, she decided, the best thing she could do was to keep her distance from Rafe and hope he got the message.

Violet stretched out on the couch as she wiggled her toes, curling and uncurling them, trying to shake off the irritating prickling sensation she had from sitting too long. She picked up the half-empty Gatorade bottle in front of her and carried it to the kitchen.

Watching the blue liquid slosh down the sink, she squinted at the blinking light coming from the answering machine. She dropped the empty bottle into the recycling bin and pressed the button.

Her eyes widened when she heard Sara's voice and she leaned closer, not wanting to miss a word.

". . . I just wanted to let you know that I received a threatening phone call from one of the kids involved in the shooting on Sunday. We're pretty sure he was the brother of the boy who attacked Violet, the one who was . . . killed." She cleared her throat. "Anyway, he made some vague threats about retaliation, all of which were directed against me, but I figured you should know about it. I didn't call Violet. I'll let you decide what to tell her, but I'm going to talk to the local police department to see if they can get someone to keep an eye on her . . . just in case. If you have any questions—" Violet stopped the message and listened again, her skin dusting with goose bumps.

She tried to remember the faces of the other two boys, the ones who'd been in the car, but all she could remember were their tattoos . . . their guns . . . and the music.

Then she remembered her missing purse and she trembled. The last time she'd seen it was right before James Nua had attacked her. What if this boy, James's brother, had picked it up? What if he had her ID, and knew where she lived?

What if revenge on Sara wasn't all he wanted?

She leaned forward on the counter, biting her thumb as she stared at the light on the machine. When her parents got home they were going to hear that message, and if she thought it was bad now, it was about to get a million

292

times worse. She'd never be able to leave the house again. She wouldn't be able to go to the bathroom without an escort.

She'd been so worried about her parents' decision to keep her from her team—from Sara and Rafe—that she hadn't really considered the possibility that they might actually be right. That she wasn't safe working with them.

Her finger moved to the Play button so she could listen to the message one more time, but then she changed her mind and watched as she hit Delete instead.

"Message erased," the electronic voice announced in the dimly lit kitchen.

What had she done? Did she really intend to keep something like this from her parents?

Of course not, she told herself, shaking her head with conviction. Of course she'd tell them. Just not tonight.

Tomorrow. She would definitely tell them tomorrow.

When the phone rang, Violet jumped, her heart leaping into her throat. She hesitated, taking a steadying breath, relieved when she saw it was only Rafe. Part of her wanted to ignore talking to him altogether, to bury her head in the sand and pretend he no longer existed. But she knew she couldn't do that. It was probably best if she just faced him and got it over with.

On the third ring, she picked it up. "Hello?"

"V, I'm so glad you answered."

"Um, yeah, that's what happens when you call someone." She hoped her voice wasn't as shaky as she felt.

"I have news," he breathed enthusiastically. "We've got him!"

"What do you mean *we've got him*?" Violet asked, taking a step back.

"*Him*. The collector."

Violet fell limply onto one of the kitchen stools and watched as rain outside beaded and drizzled down the windows. And then, because she couldn't manage anything else, she asked, "How?"

She could hear the unchecked emotion in his voice as his words rushed out. "I saw him, V. They found a woman this morning in a cold storage warehouse, wrapped in a blanket. She was much older than the others, but her nails were painted and her makeup was done, exactly the same as the girls he's killed before. And she was wearing a locket. Sara managed to get it and bring it home to me." There was a pause, a silence that Violet strained toward, her eyes expectant as she listened for his voice. "Once I touched it . . . oh my God, I saw everything. *Everything*."

Violet had never heard Rafe talk about his ability before, about how it really worked. She tried to imagine how he got all that from simply touching a locket. She was amazed. She wanted to hear everything. "What was it like? What did you see, exactly?"

"I saw him, and I know his name: *Caine*. He looks so . . . so normal. So sane. Like any other college guy at the campus. I can see why the girls wouldn't have been afraid of him. But he's so fucking dark, V. He's so twisted and messed up inside. He steals them away and keeps them locked up. He wants them to love him. That's what he's been searching for all along. *Love*."

Violet cringed, imagining what it must've been like for those girls, held hostage while he tried to convince them to love him. And she realized he wasn't just a collector.

He was a girlfriend collector.

"I saw where he lives too. A nice place in the city with a basement that he converted into a dungeon." He hesitated, letting out a loud breath. "Sara's on her way there now with the cops. They're gonna stop him."

Violet shook her head, blinking, her hands trembling. "I can't believe it, Rafe . . ." She whispered, her words filled with reverence. "You did it." A tear slipped down her cheek. "Thank you. Thank you for calling me."

"I knew you'd want to know." Rafe answered as if nothing had changed between them . . . even though everything had.

Violet hung up the phone, realizing a huge burden had been lifted, one she hadn't even known she'd been carrying.

Caine wouldn't be able to hurt anyone else.

Thanks to Rafe.

She wished her gift worked like that, that she could help the way he just had. But even if she couldn't, she was glad to know there were people like Rafe out there. Like her team.

She squeezed her fists again as she paced restlessly, wishing Jay would hurry up and get there, and wanting her hands and feet to stop tingling. She was seriously starting to worry that she was having some sort of delayed neurological reaction to her attack, that maybe she'd been more injured than anyone had realized. Not only could she not shake the tingling sensation, but it seemed to be getting worse.

She finally decided that her blood sugar must be low and she needed food, a sandwich or something. She hadn't eaten anything all afternoon, and on the drive back from Rafe's, her stomach had been grumbling noisily.

She pulled some bread, sliced ham, mustard, cheese, and lettuce from the fridge, and was searching for a tomato when she heard the clattering sound coming from the front porch. Closing the refrigerator door, she listened for it again. It was hard to hear anything above the heavy raindrops that pummeled the house, but she concentrated anyway, waiting.

There, she thought when she heard it again. A rustling noise. *Someone's definitely out there.*

She checked the clock. Jay was still at work for another half hour, but she picked up her phone anyway, making sure she hadn't missed a call from him while she'd been on the other line.

There was nothing on the caller ID. Nothing since she'd talked to Rafe.

She knew it was probably just the wind, but she couldn't shake the feeling that something was off. She blamed the stupid prickling that set her hairs on end, that and the message from Sara, for making her so jumpy. Either way, she couldn't just stand there, waiting to see if an intruder was trying to break into her house, could she?

She wrapped her fingers around the handle of the knife she'd been planning to use on her tomato, and with the phone in the other hand, she tiptoed toward the front door.

Her pulse was racing as she stopped in front of it, pressing her ear against its cool surface as she tried to see out the peephole.

As far as she could tell, there was no one out there. But she waited anyway, straining to hear something . . . anything besides the rain, her fingers tightening around the knife's grip.

She concentrated on each breath she took, trying to calm herself, to convince herself that everything was fine, that she was just overreacting. It had been a rough week, and her imagination was working overtime.

And then she heard the sound again, a soft scratching on the other side of the door. Like nails . . . or claws, to be precise.

Her shoulders sagged. *Carl!* It was just the cat, trying to let someone know he was out there.

She laughed out loud as she crept to the window, peering out just to be certain. She saw him sitting there, impatiently flicking his tail back and forth as he waited for someone to let him in. Violet tapped the inside of the window and his head snapped her way, their eyes locking.

"I'm coming." She grinned, letting the curtain fall back in place as she unbolted the door and stepped aside. "Man, you're—" She froze, covering her nose with the back of her hand, trying not to drop the phone as the harsh odor of burning rubber assaulted her, making her eyes burn.

Carl had been hunting.

"Oh my God, cat, you reek. I'm sorry, but you can't stay in here tonight—" she complained, setting the phone down as she tried to scoop the cat up. But he recognized her tone—he'd heard it too many times before—and he slipped past her, racing up the stairs before she could catch him.

"Great," she muttered, blinking her watering eyes as she waited for the acrid stench to fade. She turned and bolted the door. She'd have to find him and put him out eventually; there was no way she could sleep under the same roof as him until that particular imprint lost some of its . . . impact.

This is just perfect. Violet sighed, rolling her aching shoulders as she shuffled back toward the kitchen, the knife hanging loosely at her side now. On top of everything else, she either felt a draft or she was on the verge of a fever. She wondered if her mom had forgotten to shut a window again. Her timing sucked since they were in the middle of a rainstorm.

But when she reached the kitchen, her back stiffened and her grip around the knife's handle tightened reflexively. She stood motionless as her eyes, still irritated from the imprint of burnt rubber, scanned the room.

She didn't see anyone, but that didn't matter. Violet knew she wasn't alone.

The back door stood wide open, and she tried to imagine a scenario when it had ever blown open before, even during a windstorm. She knew it had never happened.

She opened her mouth, meaning to call out, to see if maybe her parents had come home. But her instincts told her to be still. Silent. So she waited.

And then she saw it, and her throat tightened to the size of a needle, making her breath come out on a painful wheeze.

It was her purse, with its familiar jeweled skull and crossbones, sitting in the center of the kitchen table as if it had never been missing at all. As if she'd never dropped it in the first place.

She thought of James Nua's brother, and the threatening calls Sara had received, but she knew now that he had nothing to do with this.

Each beat of her heart was palpable. Each breath excruciating as she stood there, wondering where he was, suddenly understanding the prickling sensations. Suddenly understanding why her hands and feet stung so violently, and wondering how she hadn't caught on sooner. She knew too why her eyes burned. And she recognized another imprint, one she'd dismissed because it was overshadowed by the smell of charred rubber . . . it was the bitter taste of rubbing alcohol.

These weren't Carl's imprints; they were Caine's. These were the echoes of the dead girls he'd wanted to love.

What happened next was so sudden Violet barely had time to blink. From behind the kitchen counter there was a flash of movement, and then he was there, out in the open and descending on her. It was both lightning-fast and molasses-slow. She was just clearheaded enough to get a good look at his face, to recognize what Rafe had meant when he'd said he understood why the girls wouldn't be afraid of him.

He was handsome. *So very, very handsome,* she thought just as he collided with her, knocking her flat on her back. And before she could even breathe again, his knee jammed in her stomach and her eyes went wide as she exhaled loudly, noisily, painfully.

He didn't speak to her. In fact, he remained awkwardly silent as he gazed down at her, his expression less than predatory. If Violet hadn't known better, she would have sworn she saw regret in his eyes.

"Please. Don't . . . do . . . this . . ." Violet panted, gasping for breath beneath his weight.

He didn't respond to her, just continued to watch her with that same remorse-filled gaze.

If she could just make it to the door, she told herself. These were her woods. Even in the dark, she was sure she could lose him.

With a sudden burst, Violet rolled swiftly and unexpectedly to her side. She still had the knife in her hand, and even though her fingers shook, she knew she could use it if she had to. And she was almost certain she would have to.

Caine was pitched off balance by the sudden movement and she slipped out from beneath him as her survival instincts kicked in. She heard him topple behind her and she jumped to her feet, staggering dizzily for a moment before gaining her balance.

It wasn't until she felt his hand close around her ankle,

his fingers gripping her firmly, that she turned, and without thinking swung the knife. She watched as it arced through the air and her heart stopped.

But what she didn't count on was losing her balance.

He jerked her foot, the one he was clutching, and Violet reeled, falling out of control. She careened forward, toward him, and even as she flailed, she still hoped she might cut him with the knife she clutched in her fist.

She heard his sharp gasp just as she felt the knife, and its sharp point, slide uselessly across the floor beneath her. And then she hit the ground too, all the way this time, landing in a panting heap on her stomach, her hands splayed clumsily around her. She scrambled, moving as quickly as she could, struggling to get up. But her right hand slipped in something wet and slick on the hardwood, and she slid back down, banging her cheek against the floor once more.

She heard him above her. "Shh . . . it's okay," he assured her, his voice as beautiful as his face. Quiet and soothing. The voice of a devil. "I've got you. I've got you now."

Violet turned her head, tears filling her eyes as she looked at him again, wondering why he'd chosen her. Wondering what she'd done to deserve this.

She saw the blood then. On the floor and on him, and realized that she *had* cut him. Just not badly enough.

She watched as his hand came toward her, grasping a cloth that was once white, but was now stained red with blood from his hand.

"No," she whimpered. "Pl—" But the cloth was already covering her face now, and she could no longer smell the stench of burning rubber. All she could smell was a cloying sweetness that seemed to seep into every part of her.

She felt dizzy, and her limbs went limp . . .

. . . and then there was nothing.

CHAPTER 22

THE FIRST THING SHE WAS AWARE OF WAS HER breathing. She was still breathing. She knew because each breath took far too much effort and wasted far too much energy. Yet she couldn't stop them from coming, the breaths. One, and then another, and then another. Each one was slow and shallow and difficult.

No matter how hard she tried, she couldn't pry her eyelids open. They were heavy, as if they'd been weighted down. With rocks or maybe bricks. Something immovable.

But it was her mouth that was the worst. So parched. So dry. Her tongue felt withered, like desiccated old leather. And there wasn't enough saliva to keep it from shriveling further.

She was dying. Not dead yet, maybe, but dying for sure. She didn't want to believe that, but she knew it was true.

Somewhere . . . somewhere very, very far away . . . a sound.

Grinding. No, rumbling.

She knew the sound, recognized it.

A chain saw.

But it was so far away. So very, very far away . . .

Time passed. She counted not by days, but by dreams. She never awoke. Never stopped dreaming.

Sometimes while she slept there was a voice, a soft, gentle voice, reassuring her that she was okay. That she was still "his girl."

An image of a boy flashed. A boy with laughing eyes and sandy-colored hair.

But the voice was all wrong. It wasn't the boy's voice she heard.

Still, the voice was there. And he lifted her head and cradled it gently, giving her water. She drank until she choked. Until she gagged. She felt the water trickle down her chin to her neck. And then he'd lay her back down again, and he'd wipe her dry, holding her hand and waiting until her body stopped convulsing.

Then she was alone again.

The moment she felt the skin of her eyelids parting, she nearly whimpered out loud. But somehow she held it back.

She didn't want to draw attention to herself; she didn't want the voice to know she was awake again.

She rolled her eyeballs one more time, using them to pry her lids apart, to unstick them, and the opening grew . . . first on her right side, and eventually, on the left one too.

She didn't mean to, but she let out a soft sigh.

"I was wondering when you'd wake," the voice said from somewhere nearby. From right beside her, she realized.

She blinked, glad that she could, and let her head follow the sound, trying to locate him.

He wasn't hard to find; he sat beside her on a bed. In a room she didn't recognize. It was dark outside, no light coming in from behind the curtain, but there was a light fixture overhead, and it was bright enough to let her see her immediate surroundings.

She saw varnished pine walls, a checkered quilt, a ruffled canopy overhead. It was a little girl's room.

"You've slept almost the entire day. I thought you'd miss dinner."

A day? She struggled to remember the last time she'd been awake, but she was certain it had been far longer than just one day.

She tried to focus on his face, but her vision blurred. She blinked again, this time squeezing her eyes shut and reopening them.

His features were vaguely familiar, in a strange and elusive way. She couldn't quite put her finger on where she'd seen him before, but that didn't dispel the unease she felt in his presence. The prickling sensation warned her that he was not to be trusted.

Somehow, she knew he was the reason she was here.

"Whe—" She tried to talk, but it was too difficult. Her voice didn't even register; it was just an arid breath. Dry, like dust.

"Shh." He pressed his finger to her lips, and that was when she smelled it.

The blistering stench of burnt rubber.

And everything came back to her in a rush.

It was him.

Caine.

And she was Violet.

She understood the feeling of needles that stabbed at her skin. The way her eyes burned from the acrid stench. And the hint of rubbing alcohol on her tongue—not an antiseptic at all—but an echo.

They were all coming from *him*. He was the carrier of these imprints.

He stored them—wore them—completely unaware that she knew about them. But Violet knew who—and what—he was. A killer.

She turned away, unable to bear the onslaught of emotions that overwhelmed her, knowing that she too might end up part of his collection.

"If you're good," he explained, ignoring her rebuff and holding a bottle of nail polish in front of her face, "I've brought you a treat for after dinner."

The sound was back, the chain-saw noise she'd heard before. It seemed like forever ago, but after what he—Caine—had told her about sleeping all day, she was fairly certain it had only been yesterday.

This sound, she knew, wasn't an echo. It didn't come closer when he was near. Unlike the other things: the astringent taste of alcohol, the tingling, the burning rubber that made her eyes sting.

The chain saw was just a chain saw. But why?

She glanced around the room again, at the rustic feel, and several things struck her at once. It was morning. She'd slept all the way through the night, yet there was a cloudiness that clung to her, a haze that muffled her clarity, and she realized he must have drugged her. Again.

The soup.

She'd wondered at its taste, if it was only the strange echo he carried lingering on her tongue or whether there really was an underlying flavor of something almost . . . medicinal.

She remembered, after eating it, the way her eyelids had fluttered while he'd held her hand, painstakingly working on her fingernails. She remembered wanting to draw her hands away from him, to make him stop, but she'd been unable to. She'd been too weary and weak, too disoriented to put up any kind of fight.

Instead she'd watched him, blinking sleepily as she wrestled with the grogginess while he meticulously painted each nail.

But now she was awake . . . and alone. Now was her chance.

She tried to sit up, but panic welled up from her gut as she realized she was going nowhere.

She couldn't see her feet, but she knew it wasn't their weight—or her inability to summon her muscles into compliance—that kept them from responding. They were bound beneath the blankets that covered her—the too-charming, pink-and-white checkered comforter—one tied to each post at the end of the bed. Her shoulders ached, her back too, as her hands were stretched up and to her sides. She could see that he'd fashioned strips of torn bedsheets as makeshift ropes to secure her wrists to the canopy bed she lay upon. Several strenuous tugs made it clear that the bindings were sturdy.

Still, she kicked and thrashed anyway. Not caring that it was pointless. Not caring that she was alone and trapped and wearing out her precious reserve of energy.

If she could have, she would've screamed too. But the gag across her mouth muffled her voice, making it feel like a hoarse murmur. The anemic sound was lost in the uneven grumbling and humming of the chain saw outside.

The exertion exhausted Violet, and she collapsed, spent, her heart racing out of control as she tried to forget who he was . . . Caine. Tried to forget the things he'd done and the girls he'd killed.

And then she remembered what Rafe had told her about those girls—about Caine himself.

That he wanted them to love him.

Violet settled back, trying to allay her fears. Trying to calculate and plan.

She needed to get out of here. She needed to find a way to make him trust her.

To make him believe she could love him.

It was the only way.

He didn't visit during the day, she noted. It wasn't until the sun fell that he ventured into her room, creeping silently.

She knew now that this wasn't the house Rafe had told her about, the house in the city with a dungeon in its basement. She knew he was keeping her some other place.

She silently thanked her father for teaching her to use the sun as an indicator of time during their treks through the woods. She knew how to mark the passage of hours in the day, and even through the thin gingham curtains, she'd been able to track the shift from morning to afternoon to dusk.

Dusk had been easy, though. That's when he came.

He carried another tray of dinner, another bowl of pharmaceutical-grade soup. The last thing Violet wanted to do was to eat the soup, though. Not *that* soup. Yet her stomach growled in protest. She needed the food, she knew. Eventually she'd have to give in; it would do her no good to starve to death. Then she'd never be able to escape.

But it would do her even less good to sleep if this was the only chance she had to gain his trust.

She kept her gaze on him as he switched the overhead

light on. Just as she had the night he'd come into her home and attacked her, she couldn't help noting his golden looks, and she wondered what had made him so dark and sadistic on the inside. She wondered if he even realized that's what he was, or if he somehow deluded himself into thinking this was okay. That everything he did was okay.

He smiled sheepishly as he came to her side of the bed, and she struggled not to recoil from the imprints that clung to him. "Are you thirsty?"

Against her better judgment, Violet nodded eagerly. The water could easily be drugged too; she wasn't stupid. But she was so, *so* thirsty. More so, even, than she was hungry.

"No screaming," he warned, his eyes narrowing, his hands poised at either side of the gag. She noticed it then, the bandage on his right hand, much smaller than she'd imagined he would need after seeing all the blood at her house. She'd barely nicked him, it seemed.

Her heart beat an erratic rhythm and her chest constricted, but Violet nodded again, this time forcing herself to keep eye contact with him. She needed to make him believe she could love him.

When the rag fell from her lips, she sighed. "Thank you," she croaked aridly. She tried to smile, but her lips were cracked—the skin too dry, too brittle—making her wince instead.

He frowned as he reached behind him, searching the bedside table. He turned to look, and then balled his fist. Violet could read frustration in every tensed muscle of his body. "I'm sorry," he ground out. "I should've had something for your lips. It's just . . . this isn't the right place . . ." He banged his fist on the table and the dishes rattled noisily.

Beside him, Violet jumped too. "It's . . . okay . . ." She didn't want to cry, but she was so vulnerable, trapped here with a madman.

He nodded, accepting her acquiescence, and he settled down again, smiling once more. His mood shifts were erratic, not at all subtle, and Violet worried she wasn't sharp enough to keep up with them.

"Here," he offered, lifting a glass of water to her lips.

Like the night before, she gulped at it, desperate for as much water as she could get. But he held back, drizzling it slowly, doling out a little at a time.

When he pulled it away, she strained to follow, but the strip of sheet wound around her neck tethered her. Her head snapped, a brutal reminder that she had only so much leeway.

She bit back the desperation that threatened to overwhelm her. "Wh-what's . . . your name?" Her pulse pounded in the base of her throat and her skin tingled all over. She had no idea what she was doing, if she was saying the wrong things or not. It felt like a dangerous game.

His sharp intake of breath was jarring, and she held her own, worried she'd played him wrong. He glanced down at his hands, a frown on his face as he studied the fists lying in his lap. *He's been quiet for too long,* she thought. *I pushed him too soon.*

The bed shifted, and panic shot through her. He was

leaving. He was going to leave her all alone again. No food. No more water.

And then he whispered, his voice softer, and much more hesitant, than hers had been. "It's C-Caine."

Violet's eyes widened. She didn't know what to say. She wasn't like Sara. She wasn't a trained profiler with years of experience behind her. She was a seventeen-year-old girl being held hostage by a killer. And she was terrified, afraid that any misstep might be her last.

She swallowed, telling herself she could do this. "Th—" Her voice shook. "Thank you, Caine."

His gaze flew to hers, searching, she knew, for the truth in her statement. Or probing, more likely, for the lie. This was it. This was her chance to show him.

She inhaled and let the corner of her mouth move up. Ever so slightly. Just the barest hint of a smile.

But she had to be careful.

Too much and he'd see it; he'd know it wasn't real. That none of it was real.

She felt dizzy, and her lip quivered . . . a tiny, hopefully imperceptible twitch. There was nothing false about the uncertain expression in her eyes. There was no part of her that wasn't afraid.

When the bed shifted again, this time sinking from his weight, she knew she'd done it.

He settled down once more. Somehow Violet had convinced him to stay.

ACCEPTANCE

CAINE. HIS NAME WAS CAINE.

And she knew that.

It was a step he'd never taken before.

A new beginning. He didn't fight his smile as he crept across the creaking floorboards, and then it faded from his lips. He hated the way everything here made noise, squeaking and groaning like complaints. He hated the outdated furniture and the musty-smelling pillows and the big, wide-open windows that overlooked the lake. Picturesque, his mother used to call the windows on their summer visits, but he disagreed. To him it was like being in a fishbowl. Especially at night, when the darkness outside was so complete, so impenetrable, that even the palest light inside put him on display. Neighbors or not.

That was why there were sheets hanging over each and every window now. So that no one could see inside. So that no one could look in and watch him. Spy on him. Judge him.

So that he and his girl could be alone.

The grin came back as he glanced down at the clean nightgown he carried . . . a gift. It was pretty, the nightgown. White cotton with just a hint of starched lace along the scooped collar. Pristine, just like her.

He stopped when he reached her door. It wasn't locked, another thing he hated about this house . . . he hadn't had time to outfit it properly. Still, he was good with his hands, and he'd managed to put a decent room together using the things he had at his disposal . . . sheets, wire, duct tape.

Plus, the isolation was good.

And now that they were getting to know each other, he doubted she'd want to leave. She hadn't even screamed, and they always screamed at first.

Not her, though. Not his girl. She was special.

Thank God, because he needed her. He needed to sleep. It was dark and it had been too long since he'd really slept. Good sleep. Deep sleep.

But with her here, all that would change. Now he could rest.

Because now he wasn't alone.

CHAPTER 23

HE WAS IN THE BED WITH HER.

Even if Violet hadn't felt the slant of the mattress and the steady rhythm of breathing coming from beside her, she'd have recognized the imprints on him from anywhere.

She released a shaky breath, struggling against that same fog she'd felt before . . . after eating the soup. Too many hours spent lying prone made her back ache like it had never ached before. Even the prickling sensation that Caine brought with him couldn't overshadow this kind of pain. The noxious rubber smell he bore only made it easier for her to remain alert. His imprints kept her lucid.

She flexed her toes, moving as fluidly as she could. She

didn't want to disturb him. She didn't want him to know she was awake.

But her foot didn't just flex . . . it shifted. And her eyes widened as she lay there for several long, unblinking moments, trying to decide what that meant. Trying to decide what to do next.

She mimicked his breathing pattern. If he woke, she wanted him to believe she was still asleep. And then slowly, carefully, she tried her hand—the one farthest from Caine's side.

It moved too.

Relief blossomed and she drew it down as steadily as she could. She clutched it against her own chest, against her heart. Curling her wrist, she wanted to sob with relief as the pain in her shoulder subsided at long last.

When, after endless moments, she was sure she hadn't disturbed him, that he was oblivious to her stirrings, she let her hand drift upward until it found her throat.

She gasped as she realized the bindings at her neck were missing too, and then she bit her lips, silencing her own cry of relief.

She stiffened, waiting. Until she was certain Caine still slept.

He'd untied her. She was free. But why? Why would he take a chance like this?

A low, muffled groan escaped his lips. To Violet, it sounded like a growl or a bellow, not like a comforting sound of sleep. He shifted too, and she nearly forgot how to breathe, her chest collapsing in on itself.

She stayed where she was, unmoving, unblinking. After what felt like an eternity, she closed her eyes and tried again, moving ever so slightly, rolling as gently as she could onto her side. When he didn't react to that, either, she moved farther still, edging breath by breath toward the side of the mattress.

She had no plan after that. She had no idea where she was or what she would do if he awoke. All she knew was that she had to try. There was no choice.

His smell—the harsh scent of scorched rubber—filled the room around her, and the volatile flavor of alcohol assailed her tongue. She ignored it all.

Still lying down, she dropped her leg over the edge of the bed. Every muscle in her body tensed as she waited for him to realize what she was doing.

The consequences wouldn't be pretty, that much she knew. That much she'd witnessed.

She had to be cautious, steady, silent.

The inside of her lip bled from where she bit down, shushing herself. Her foot brushed the solid floor beneath her and her heart skipped. But she couldn't be too optimistic. There was still a long ways to go.

She eased up, using her arm to lift herself from the mattress.

He slept so soundly—so peacefully—beside her that she half-wondered if he'd drugged himself as well. It was a ridiculous notion, of course. A hope-filled delusion.

As soon as she was sitting, dizziness swept over her. She

blinked and struggled not to sway . . . not to collapse back onto the bed again. She fisted the sheets at her sides, waiting for her vision to clear.

After a moment, once her head cleared, she made some quick mental notes. The room was dark, but she knew the basic layout. Bed. Chest of drawers. Door.

That was the important thing: She knew where the door was.

Her bare toes settled on the cold floor beneath her and she tipped forward, gripping one of the canopy posts for support. A post that just hours earlier had held her immobile.

She swallowed, her parched throat aching and raw. Her heart beat so hard in her chest, she feared it might explode.

And then . . . she stood.

She took a tentative step.

And then another. And another.

She crouched now, feeling her way in the dark. Her fingers grazed the mattress as she used it as a guide. Each step was carefully plotted, her toes testing the ground ahead of her.

As she reached the bedpost closest to the door, she released it, suddenly lost in a sea of darkness. Yet she didn't slow. She couldn't slow.

She reached out, her breath catching as her fingertips brushed the wall and she feathered them along until she felt the frame, and then—with a silent sigh of relief—the door-knob.

When it turned, she nearly cried.

It wasn't until the door was closed behind her that she felt her heart start again. It was less dark out here, in the hallway. Somewhere ahead of her, in one of the rooms beyond, a light was on.

It was faint, but unmistakable.

Violet crept forward on careful, noiseless feet. It was only then that she realized she wasn't wearing her own clothes . . . that she was dressed in what looked like a child's nightgown. It was old-fashioned and stiff, and the lace at her neck itched. She reached up to scratch it, freezing as she caught a glimpse of her hand.

Her fingernails were painted a familiar shade of pale purple.

Her stomach tightened and she forgot about the lace, her feet moving faster now, her thoughts crystal clear. She had to escape.

Like a moth, Violet flitted toward the light and found herself standing in a cave of sorts. Every window had been sealed, covered with mismatched sheets that had been cut apart and taped back together with long strips of silver duct tape. There was no way she could look outside . . . no way to see where she was.

She glanced around her. The home was as old-fashioned as the nightgown she wore. Most of the furniture was delicate: velvet cushions and carved woods with intricate, spindled legs. There were figurines and vases and painted chests. Things that could easily be antiques, she supposed, but seemed more

319

like leftovers thrown together into one strange patchwork collection . . . much like the sheets covering the windows. Beside the brick hearth, perfect rows of firewood were neatly stacked.

The light itself came from a partially open doorway, and she hurried toward it, hoping they were alone, that it was just the two of them in this house. She hoped he didn't have a partner.

She held her breath as she nudged the door open with her toe and found herself staring into the kitchen. It was small and cheerful, despite the black sheet covering the window above the sink. The appliances were avocado green, reminiscent of another era.

But there it was, sitting on the counter, the one thing Violet had been searching for: a telephone.

She could hardly believe her luck. She couldn't believe she was actually going to survive this ordeal after all.

The old rotary dial telephone was the same kind her grandmother had once had, and Violet snatched it off the counter as she dropped to her knees, clutching the phone on her lap. She lifted the receiver to her ear and listened.

She waited.

She pressed the button on the base, the one that would end a call, jiggling it up and down.

But there was nothing. No dial tone. No sound at all.

She checked the back of the phone, suddenly feeling the floor drop out from beneath her.

It wasn't attached to anything. There was no cord connecting it to the wall.

She leaned her head back, releasing a silent mewl. *No,* she wailed inwardly. *No!*

She had no idea how many precious minutes she'd already wasted, or how many she had left, but after searching as quietly as she could through the kitchen drawers, she realized she wasn't going to find the cord. Not easily, anyway . . . and definitely not quickly enough.

There was only one choice: She was going to have to take her chances outside.

She didn't have time to search for her own clothes, or for her shoes, so she grabbed whatever she could find.

Anxiety gripped her chest, making it ache, gripping like a vise as she grabbed a pair of woolen socks stuffed inside a pair of old work boots. She thought about taking the boots too, but she knew just by looking at them that they were several sizes too large and they would only slow her down. A coat hanging from a stand beside the door would at least keep her warm. She wouldn't let herself think about who these things really belonged to.

Since the door locked from the inside, Violet simply unbolted it and stepped outside.

She was swallowed by blackness so complete that it sucked the breath out of her. She heard herself gasp at the same time her inner voice silently screamed at her: *Run!*

And she did. Without another thought, she ran. Stumbling and scrambling and running some more.

★ ★ ★

She didn't get far before she found the trap. Or rather, before she triggered it.

There was no way she could've seen it. And no way it could have been avoided. When she hit it—the wire, the thin metal cable that sliced into her shins—she howled into the darkness that engulfed her. That was just before she lost her balance and spilled forward, landing on her face and tasting the rich dank earth beneath her.

And from behind, all the lights of the house switched on, blazing to life.

And she knew: She had caused that. When she'd tripped the wire.

She rolled onto her side, feeling leaves and needles beneath her as she clutched her shins. She spit, trying get rid of the taste of dirt in her mouth, and even without looking, she could feel the blood beneath her fingers and knew she'd cut herself.

Her mind raced. She didn't know what to do, but she couldn't just lie there and wait for something to happen. For *him* to find her.

Beneath the glare of the lights, she saw the car in the driveway. She hadn't noticed it before, when it had been camouflaged by blackness, and her heart sank.

Keys! She jammed her blood-slicked hands into the coat's pockets, hoping, praying she'd get lucky and they'd be in there. But she found nothing, and she cursed herself for not thinking of it sooner. She should've been searching for car keys instead of trying to find a cord for the phone.

Still, she didn't recall seeing any keys, and there was

no time for regrets now.

She clambered to her feet, taking in her surroundings as best she could. All around her, dark tree trunks rose toward the sky like inky shadows, creating an even darker canopy overhead.

She was somewhere deep in the woods.

And if Violet knew anything, she knew the woods.

"Violet? Vi-o-let, where are you?"

It was Caine. She didn't know him well enough to recognize his voice, but he was the only one out here who knew her name. The only one who would be calling for her in the middle of the night.

Hearing his voice only spurred her on, making Violet run even faster. Beneath her feet, branches cracked and she stumbled more often than she should have. Her socks were soaked from running across the damp forest floor, but she refused to shed them. They were the only barrier between her and the rocks and thorns and sticks that threatened to slice her feet. Her bare legs had nothing to protect them and were being ripped and scraped every time she bumped into something spiked or prickly. And she'd fallen more times than she could count.

It was so damn hard to run in the dark.

Still, she kept on. Keeping low and trying to stay quiet as she moved in quick bursts, huddling behind clusters of trees whenever she could.

She would've called out, cried for help, but she knew it was useless. And it would only serve to give Caine something to focus on, some way to find her. A deadly game of Marco Polo.

She already knew he was gaining ground. He had several advantages over her. Most importantly, *he* knew where they were.

And he had a flashlight. Violet had seen its beam, searching and scanning through the trees, cutting through the night. Her heart had nearly stopped when it had come too close. And unlike her, *he* had shoes.

Violet didn't know how long she could outrun him. She had only one advantage. His imprints.

Even without seeing him, she could sense whenever he was drawing near. Her skin, her nose, and her tongue warned her of his presence.

For now, at least, the distance was enough and Violet broke cover and sprinted once more. She raced as fast as she could, trying to ignore the punishing ache in her feet as she moved over the jagged surface. She stubbed her toes and cracked her already bleeding shins against fallen branches in her path. Again and again she tripped.

And again and again she picked herself up to keep moving.

She had to keep moving. . . . It was the only way to survive.

Violet was exhausted, her body fatigued and her spirit crumbling. Her eyes had adjusted enough so she could at least see the ground in front of her and the trees all around her. The sound of her own breathing eclipsed all else . . . crickets, the rustling of leaves overhead, and the far-off calls of night birds.

She pinched her side, massaging the stabbing pain, and panted as she leaned heavily against the rough surface of a tree trunk, desperately seeking her second wind. She couldn't give up.

She knew now they were near water, probably a lake. At first she thought she'd stepped into a puddle. But as she'd waded farther, she soon realized it was getting deeper. Too deep to simply walk through.

Since she couldn't see well enough to know for certain, she'd thrown a rock and had heard it land with a definitive plunk. At the very least, it was an impassible pond.

After catching her breath, she eased away from her hiding place and maneuvered once more through the brush. She shoved aside branches and prickly vines, and brushed away spiders' webs in her path.

When at last she saw the building, she stopped dead, her entire body going rigid. It seemed to appear from out of nowhere, large and looming, blotting out an entire section of forest. Whatever it was, it definitely *wasn't* a house.

Violet stilled beneath the cover of the trees and squeezed her eyes shut, feeling for him, trying to locate Caine in the shadows around her.

He was there. Somewhere. But not so close that she worried he would see her if she crept closer to investigate.

She had no idea if she was making a mistake, if she was

walking into yet another of Caine's traps—like the wire that had encompassed his property. For all she knew, this building belonged to him too. It was the first sign of civilization she'd seen since she'd left the house he'd been holding her in.

But she was growing weary. Hunger and exertion were getting the best of her, and she had to take the chance . . . had to see if there might be help nearby. Maybe inside.

She slipped free from the brush. The heavy jacket draped around her, concealing the stark white of her nightgown as she moved away from the foliage. Her feet were caked in mud, making the socks invisible in the night.

Her voice ached to be free, to call out for help, but she bit it back. What if no one was around? What if no one but Caine could hear her? So she choked on it, letting it die in her throat.

She reached the outer wall of the building and moved quickly, using her hands to guide her along the wooden structure as she searched, feeling her way, for an entrance—a doorway, a window, a crack in the siding, any way to get inside. For too long, she felt nothing, and when she glanced up, scanning the exterior, it seemed to go on forever, reaching all the way to the sky.

Whatever it was, it was enormous.

She rounded a corner, her pulse hammering and blood rushing noisily in her ears. She stayed as close as she could to the wall. She checked over her shoulder time and time again, expecting to find Caine there at any moment, ready to strike.

But she knew he wasn't. She couldn't smell him.

Her fingers fumbled over a variation in the wooden surface. A window frame.

It was above her head, and she balanced on her toes, trying to feel for a latch, but there was nothing. At least not that she could reach.

Her shoulders sagged defeatedly, but she kept going . . . somewhere there had to be a door.

She turned another corner and came to the front of the building where the trees had been stripped away, creating a large clearing. There was something along the perimeter . . . something that looked like fencing. But it was leaning and gapped in places, as if it had succumbed to years of disrepair.

The building itself, Violet realized, was a barn, and she looked up at the huge double doors.

The closer she examined it, even in the dark, the more she realized how run-down it really was. She hadn't noticed the way the paint had flaked beneath her fingers and the way the boards were soft, like they were rotting. She hadn't seen the thick clumps of grasses springing up from the foundation at her feet. It was crumbling . . . a bad sign.

Violet scanned the shadows that stretched ahead of her, searching for another building, maybe a house. But there were none that she could see. Just a wilting old barn.

She staggered forward. It didn't matter; if this was the only shelter she could find, then it would have to do. She needed to stop, just for a little bit. Just long enough to come up with a plan.

Until then, she'd have to rely on her senses to warn her if danger approached. If Caine came near.

ESTRANGEMENT

FRUSTRATION LICKED THROUGH HIM, SETTING
his veins on fire.

*He shifted the beam from his flashlight over the forest floor,
angry that she'd eluded him for this long. He didn't know how that
was possible. She was all alone . . . in the woods . . . in the dead of
night. She couldn't get far. And she couldn't avoid him.*

Yet, so far, she'd done just that.

He was angry now. Furious with himself.

*How had he made such an error? How had he miscalculated so
grievously?*

*She'd tricked him, that's how. She manipulated him into believ-
ing she was the one.*

And he'd believed her.

He slammed his fist against the solid tree trunk, ignoring the fact that he'd just torn his wound open and was bleeding again. He didn't need her, he told himself, words he'd repeated before. There were other girls. Better girls.

But before he could find one of those girls, he had to stop this one. He had to find her and give her one last kiss, silencing her forever.

He stood there, trying to decide which way to go next, trying to tamp down the fury that made him irrational. He had to be clear. He had to think. He didn't know what he would do if she got away, didn't know what his next move should be.

And then he saw it. Something that he'd almost missed as he'd been casting the flashlight's beam across the shadowy terrain. There was something out of place. Something white.

Everything in him went on alert as he lumbered toward it, his feet landing heavily as his eyes searched everywhere, looking for her. Hunting her.

He stopped as he plucked the small piece of fabric from the shrub it was hanging on. He recognized it, of course, this particular piece of fabric. It was a piece of lace from the nightgown, the one the girl was wearing.

Which meant she was close.

He was on the right track.

CHAPTER 24

INSIDE THE BARN IT WAS EVEN DARKER THAN IT had been outside. The doors hadn't been locked, but the rusted hinges were old and protested loudly when Violet finally pried one of them ajar. She'd only managed to create enough room for her to squeeze through before it had creaked shut once more behind her.

She didn't mind, though, the sound—the screaming of the hinges. It would serve as one more warning if Caine were to find her. High above, the commotion she heard sounded ominously like the flapping of wings . . . dozens of wings. She prayed they belonged to birds.

She stumbled along, finding her way in almost total blackness.

The musty scent of old hay and grains and dust swirled around her, and she could feel the crunch of straw beneath her feet. A part of her warned that she'd just backed herself into a corner, while the other part insisted she just needed a few minutes to recover. And this was shelter. She wouldn't stay long.

She crept along the wall, arms out. She passed what she assumed were stalls, but she was too afraid to go inside. She worried about what else might be in here with her: spiders, rats, possums . . . bats. Maybe even something more feral, like coyotes. She really didn't know what kinds of animals made homes in abandoned barns.

Finally she found an alcove behind the long row of stalls at the far end of the barn, and she slipped inside, feeling around for a corner she could hide in. She batted at cobwebs, swiping them from her face, her hair, her coat, and her hands. She did her best to make a small nest of straw so she could sit. Just for a minute.

It was hard to relax as she strained in the darkness, checking to be sure Caine wasn't near. She thought about her parents, and her aunt and uncle. She thought about Jay, and blinked back hot tears.

She wondered if they knew yet. She wondered if they were as scared as she was. She huddled in a ball, wishing it were someone else's arms around her instead of her own. And then fatigue—and the sedatives Caine had dosed her with earlier—won out and her eyelids became heavy.

It wasn't the barn door that woke her, or even the pungent scent of burning rubber. It wasn't the flashlight bobbing over the landscape of the barn's interior, shining light on dust motes so thick it should've been difficult to even breathe.

It was something else that pulled her from the slippery depths of sleep, somewhere she never should have been in the first place. It was the sound of the floorboards groaning with the weight of each hollow step he took over the planked floor.

She was fully awake then, her eyes huge as she peered out from her hiding space and saw his light searching. She waited, knowing that he was stopping at each stall, searching inside, and her heart thundered painfully. Leaping silently to her feet, she stayed low, crouched.

By the peripheral light of the flashlight, Violet could see several things at once. On the opposite end of the barn, there was another way out, a side door. Unfortunately, even if she decided to run for it, he would see her, and most likely catch her before she could get there.

There was also a loft overhead, with a staircase she could surely reach. It was directly ahead of her, just a few short feet away. But even if she made it to the wooden steps, there was no way she could climb to the top without his notice.

"I know you're in here," his voice rang out as if reading her mind, and Violet's blood ran cold. "You can't hide forever."

He was right. She was running short on options.

She searched her immediate area, the alcove in which she'd taken refuge. Not an alcove at all but a tack room . . . or what had once been a tack room. She recognized it from

332

the summer she'd spent working at Chelsea's uncle's farm when they were twelve. They'd made three dollars an hour to muck stalls, which was a fancy way of saying they'd scooped poop for mere pennies.

But she remembered enough about stall-mucking to know there might be something useful here. And Caine was coming closer by the second. She felt dizzy as she dropped to her knees, clumsily groping as she scoured the floor for something, for some sort of weapon.

She found a bucket and a stiffened leather glove, both useless. Her fingers sifted through more cobwebs and dirt as her heart hammered louder and louder, her mouth growing drier and her breathing erratic. She could hear his foot-steps . . . each one louder and heavier and closer. Her skin tightened, tingling everywhere.

Just when she realized she would have to run, when she realized she was out of time, she felt her fingers close around something. A handle. A solid wooden handle.

She had no idea what it belonged to, but she squeezed her eyes shut as she tugged it, willing it to be something use-ful. Something sharp. Something dangerous.

The scraping sound it made when she'd moved it made Violet involuntarily freeze. She knew he'd heard it too; there was no way he hadn't heard it. She'd just given away her location.

The smell of burning rubber got stronger as she pulled on the handle one more time, this time dragging it free from its hiding place, from beneath the filth and the hay that had obscured it from view.

And when she saw it, her heart stuttered.

It was a pitchfork. A rusty old pitchfork.

It was perfect.

"You're not really going to hurt me, are you?" Caine's voice, like his face, was sweet, very nearly angelic, and Violet had to continually remind herself what he really was. What he really intended to do to her.

"Stay away," she warned, holding the pitchfork between them. She'd never been more afraid, or more sure she could actually harm someone. Maybe even kill them.

He lifted the flashlight so that it was too high, too bright in her eyes, intentionally blinding her. She felt off-kilter, but she wouldn't let him get the upper hand again and she lunged forward, thrusting the pitchfork in his direction. "Drop the light. I mean it, Caine." She hated the feel of his name on her tongue. It had been easier when he'd been nameless, faceless. "I don't want to, but I swear I *will* stab you."

He lowered the light, just slightly, and Violet caught a glimpse of that perfect smile. "If you insist."

And then the flashlight hit the ground, and almost immediately they were plunged into darkness as Violet heard it shatter at Caine's feet. Her stomach dropped. She couldn't see him. She couldn't see anything. She had no idea where he was.

And then she took a breath.

She calmed herself, reminding herself just how wrong

she was. Reminding herself that she knew *exactly* where he was. She just needed to stay focused.

A ghost of a smile curved her lips as she realized that *she* had the upper hand now. "What're you gonna do now, Caine?" She took a calculated step forward, clutching the pitchfork, ready to use it. "You can't see me, but I can see you."

There was a lull, a long void, and Violet wondered if he'd even heard her. And then a low moan filled the still air. The sound grew, ripped from Caine's throat until it was a hoarse keening, like the wail of a child.

Violet jumped back, startled by the noises that were coming from him. She heard him drop to his knees as he scrambled for the pieces of the flashlight.

She didn't wait to see if he found them. She took her opportunity to run for the side door she'd seen when the flashlight had been working.

But she didn't get far. As she passed him, Caine clawed at her, his hands desperate, ripping and tearing frantically as he clutched at her coat—at *his* coat. Violet got tangled up and turned around, until the tines of the pitchfork were no longer pointed at Caine. She tried to swing back around so she could strike him—or stab him—but it was too late. She was disoriented and the weapon was useless as his grip on her tightened.

She threw the pitchfork down, letting it clatter to the ground, and at the same time she let her arms go limp and felt them slip out of the jacket, setting herself free. She kept running, leaving Caine clutching the coat and not her.

She didn't have much time; he'd be up and after her in a matter of seconds. She wouldn't make it to the door on the opposite end of the barn—the one she'd seen when she'd been hiding in the tack room—and he was blocking the only other way out.

That left her with one choice . . . up.

Violet scrambled up the steps, which were more like a makeshift ladder than actual stairs, and even without her ability to tell her that Caine wasn't coming yet, she'd have known. She could still hear him, scrabbling around on the floor. Still trying to piece the shattered fragments of the flashlight together, and she wondered why it mattered so much to him.

She knew now that it had been a mistake coming into the barn, that she'd trapped herself. But she still had a chance; she could still get away if she was careful. And smart.

The opening in the loft floor was small, and Violet thought that maybe, during daylight conditions, she might have been able to find something she could drag over to block Caine from coming up. Something to barricade herself inside.

But that wasn't the case. Instead it was even blacker up here than below, something she planned to use to her advantage. She clambered up quickly, her heart in her throat despite her head start.

Once on semisolid ground, on the boards that ran across the tops of the rafters, she tried to move noiselessly. She stayed on her hands and knees, reminding herself how precarious this was, that these planks could be rotting or cracked or just plain weak, like the ones on the outside of the barn. Every movement felt risky, but staying motionless wasn't an option. So she crawled, hoping he couldn't hear which direction she went. Hoping he was too preoccupied with his futile task to notice her. At least for the moment.

Violet heard a violent crash from below, and knew that Caine had thrown the busted flashlight against one of the walls. His rage was palpable, and she huddled farther into the corner, hugging herself as tightly as she could.

If he was desperate before, now he was infuriated. Of the two, she preferred desperation.

She held her breath, listening as he grappled with the steps. He was larger than she was, and his weight made them shudder and groan. She silently prayed they would snap beneath the pressure, even if it meant she'd be trapped up here, all by herself.

But they didn't, and she heard him reach the top at the same time her skin prickled painfully, like a coat of needles.

Unlike her, he stood upright. She knew because when he spoke his voice came from above her. "Come out, come out, wherever you are." Violet hugged her knees tighter, hoping he couldn't see her nightgown—or her—pressed into the darkest corner of the grimy loft. "I promise not to hurt you. I promise you . . . won't . . . feel . . . a . . . thing."

She cringed, shaking all over. Adrenaline tore through

her as she concentrated on one thing. Him. She tracked him by the imprints he bore.

She calculated his position as he walked three steps away from her, and then he turned and walked two more directly toward her. Her heart failed to beat for several immeasurable seconds. Her eyes widened as she felt the tremor of his boot landing squarely in front of her and she could smell every inch of him, basted in burnt rubber. Awash in death.

When he turned the other way, Violet's blood began to pump once more, filling her with a dread so overpowering it threatened to engulf her. This might be her only opening, she realized as with each step he took, the distance between them grew.

She hesitated, unsure that her plan—her only hope—was wise, but recognizing she had no other options. And then, because it was the only thing she *could* do, she fled, moving as quickly as she could, not caring that he could hear her now. Not caring that she was reckless and clumsy.

Just needing to reach the stairway before he did.

Because if she could get out of this damn barn, she might survive.

She was only halfway down the steps, her hands braced on both sides of the ladder, when she felt his hand reach down, his fingers bunching and tangling into her hair. He was bent over the opening, coming through it facedown. But he had enough leverage to stop her, jerking her and making her lose her footing altogether until she was dangling in midair. Her feet swung and she kicked wildly. She crashed against the ladder with enough force to knock the wind out of her.

"Nice try!" he snarled, hauling her up once more. He was stronger even than Violet had imagined, and she fumbled to get ahold of the wooden steps in a desperate effort to keep him from pulling her all the way back up to the loft.

After several failed attempts, she finally managed to slide one of her feet through the rungs and she hooked it there, locking herself in place. He jerked harder, and she shrieked in agony as she felt clumps of her hair ripping free.

"Why are you making this so hard?" he ground out, his large hands reaching down, trying to get a better grip on her.

But Violet refused to be a victim this time. She'd already been rescued by Jay, by her uncle, by Sara and Rafe. She hated that she hadn't been able to save herself then.

This time, however . . . this time there was only her. And she refused to let Caine win.

She reached up, hitting and scratching him, trying anything she could to make him release her. But nothing worked. He was slowed by her efforts, but so was she. She kept her leg wrapped around the ladder, but each time he pulled her, she felt her grip falter.

Finally, she lifted both of her hands and wound them into *his* hair. She squeezed her fists as tightly as she could and she anchored her legs around the steps as firmly as possible. She jerked downward, pulling at him with every ounce of strength she could muster. Pulling him with everything she had.

Until he was falling . . . down . . .

. . . down.

She hadn't realized how easily he would fall until she felt his leaden weight crash against her. He was like a stone, crushing her against the wooden ladder she clung to with only her legs. The splintering sound from the wood was bad, but Violet was much more concerned when she felt his hands grasping at her, clutching for the folds of her cotton nightgown. She realized he'd gotten a handful when she was wrenched downward. Yet even as she heard it tear, he kept tumbling, falling past her.

Her tenuous hold slipped, and then she was plunging too, her arms flailing wildly, a scream frozen in the base of her throat.

The only sound she actually heard was the sickening thud he made when he collided with the hollow wooden floor beneath them. And something else, something she had no time to process before she too landed . . . falling on her stomach, her arms and legs completely ineffective in breaking her fall as dust rose up, choking her and making it impossible to breathe at all.

CHAPTER 25

SUNLIGHT.

Violet blinked, wondering when was the last time she'd actually felt the silvered strands of daylight on her skin. It seemed like forever ago. Another lifetime.

She blinked again and tried to take a breath. She choked on a mouthful of something too thick to be considered air, and she rolled her face out of the dirt.

From nearby, she heard something. An endless, unabating sound.

She coughed again as she struggled to sit up, trying to figure out where she was.

And then her thoughts cleared.

Panic whipped through her and she gracelessly lurched to her feet, unsteady and light-headed.

The sound was still there as if carried on the rays of light that broke through the cracks in the ceiling and walls. Violet searched, knowing what—*who*—she was searching for, even before she found him.

Caine.

And he was there, just inches from her. She jumped back from his broken body, afraid that if she so much as breathed her toes might accidentally brush against him.

She stared down at his wide, unseeing eyes, remembering the sounds from his fall. The solid thud and the other, more grotesque sound . . .

She looked at him now, realizing what it had been. He'd landed on the pitchfork when he'd fallen.

Her hand flew to cover her mouth. Then she heard it.

The sound.

It was a metallic tinkling, like a music box. The kind little girls wind up, the kind with a twirling ballerina inside.

Violet turned in a circle, trying to figure out where the sound might be coming from, trying to pinpoint its location. It was soft and slow, melodic and eerie.

She stepped closer to Caine's body, just needing one last look to convince herself he was actually dead. He'd created his last echo, hurt his last girl. She leaned close, her heart pounding as she gazed into his vacant eyes.

The music grew louder, humming just beneath the surface of her skin, tingling electrically.

And she knew. The echo was his.

She knew then that the music-box sound, the echo that clung to Caine's lifeless form, also clung to her.

She had an imprint of her own now.

Violet had been walking for so long that her legs felt like rubber. In reality, it could have been mere minutes. She knew she was weak, that her stamina was next to nothing.

In the light of day, she'd found a small dirt road that led from the old barn. Like everything else, it had been overrun with weeds and fresh spring grass and clover, but she could still see the tracks that had once been made by tires. And she could still tell which way she had to go.

As she walked, she tried not to listen to the plinking sound of music that followed her, hovering around her. *On her.* But it was impossible, and soon she'd memorized the tune, and despite herself, found herself humming along to it.

She knew that if anyone had been listening, they'd think she'd lost her mind.

Maybe she had. She'd killed a man, after all. How many people could say that? How many normal people had committed murder, even in self-defense?

She looked at her own hands and felt dirty in a way that had nothing to do with the muck and filth that coated them. This was something that went deeper. Something much, much darker.

After what felt like hours, after humming endless loops of the nameless song that only she could hear, exhaustion finally got the best of Violet. She didn't think she could take another step, and eventually she stopped trying, deciding it was best if she just sat for a while in the middle of nowhere and waited.

Violet could hear the cars coming down the tracked road even above the incessant music that shadowed her. She knew they were driving too fast and she jumped up, getting out of their way as she lifted her hand against the sun, shielding her eyes. When the cars were close enough, Violet fell to her knees, sobbing with relief, as everything slipped into slow motion.

She saw her uncle Stephen first, swinging open the passenger-side door of the first car before it had even come to a complete stop. He was running toward her, yelling something to her and shouting orders behind him. Violet heard nothing but the ceaseless tinkling of the imprint she now carried.

The men in the car with him were out now too, weapons drawn as they searched the woods around them . . . alert and ready.

Violet wanted to tell them it was okay, that Caine was dead, but all she could manage were tears of relief. She was safe.

She smiled up at her uncle as he reached her, scooping her up from the ground.

"Violet! Violet! Violet!" Even her name seemed to be set to the music in her head.

She let him fold her in his arms. Let him squeeze her until she felt alive again. Until she could breathe at last.

"Three days," he whispered in her ear. "Do you know the odds? Do you know how afraid we were?" And then, when he finally released her and his eyes met hers, "Is he nearby? Do you know where to find him?"

She nodded. She knew where he was, but she was still too afraid to say the words.

He wrapped her in his arms, leading her to the car. "Your parents are waiting at the local sheriff's office. Just tell me where he is and I'll meet you there."

Violet stopped, and her uncle did too. The music, however, would never stop. "He's dead," she stated quietly. Flatly. "I killed him."

CHAPTER 26

VIOLET'S PARENTS SHOVED THROUGH THE DOOR of the small sheriff's office as the patrol car parked in front. Violet doubted that the deputy driving could have stopped her mom from opening the car door if he'd tried . . . not even the threat of gunpoint would've slowed her down. Once she was surrounded by them, in their arms, Violet found herself crying again, sobbing as first her mom, and then her dad, engulfed her.

Violet clung to them, trying to ignore the wordless tune that cleaved to her as she concentrated on the fact that she'd survived.

"We're so sorry, Vi. We never would've left you alone if

we'd known . . ." Her mother ran a hand through Violet's hair, then rested her palm against her daughter's cheek.

"Uncle Stephen called before you got here. He told us what happened. I'm so sorry you had to go through that," her dad explained sadly. "I'm so sorry you had to do that."

Violet closed her eyes. She didn't want to feel bad about what she'd done. She *didn't* feel bad, she told herself. "It's okay," she said, and meant it. "I had to."

Her mom nodded, lifting her other hand to cradle Violet's face. "It doesn't mean you're okay, baby."

Violet squeezed her eyes shut, wishing the tinkling noise would just vanish. Disappear. "I know, Mom. Believe me," she snapped. And then, because it wasn't their fault, "It'll just take some time for me to . . . get used to it."

Her father's gaze was thoughtful. "Is it . . . ? Do you . . . ?"

Violet nodded. She knew what he was asking.

"Is it terrible?" her mom asked. "What is it?"

Violet opened her mouth to complain, to tell her parents about the continuous noise she'd have to live with forever. And then she realized where she was. That she was standing outside . . . with her parents . . . alive.

"It's fine," she said at last. "It's like one of those windup jewelry boxes with the little ballerina inside. It's like listening to a music box."

Her mother hugged her again, crushing her in that way of hers that Violet had worried she'd never feel again. Violet glanced up in time to see tears glistening in her dad's eyes.

★ ★ ★

347

They didn't get home until early the next morning. Violet had been taken to a clinic in the isolated lakeside community, so she could be given fluids and checked out. That's where Caine had been holding her, in a lake house his family had used as vacation property years earlier. The place hadn't been used in over a decade, not since Caine's father had died when Caine was just a boy.

According to the local sheriff, Caine's father had fallen in a ravine one day while he and Caine had been hiking, and he'd sent his young son in search of help. Caine had wandered in the woods for two days—and two long nights—all by himself before he finally found someone. By the time the rescuers found the ravine Caine described, his father was already dead . . . and, according to the sheriff, his mother blamed the little boy for not trying hard enough. For not saving her husband.

Caine had only been eight years old.

Violet agreed with the sheriff that his story was sad, tragic even, but it didn't change who he'd become. He was a murderer, plain and simple. In the end, he hadn't been the kind of person to feel sorry for, at least as far as Violet was concerned. Given the chance, he would have killed her without so much as a second thought.

At the clinic, Violet had begged for nail polish remover, so she could strip the lacquer reminder from her nails.

But it wasn't until they were pulling into their driveway the next morning that Violet felt the first pangs of panic about returning to her real life. She wasn't sure she could go back in there—into her house. Not after everything that had happened.

She was too worried about the memories it would hold.

She already carried an eternal reminder of Caine . . . of his death.

Violet turned up the volume on her iPod, trying to drown out the persistent music box she heard. It had been hard to sleep last night. Even harder not to dream about him.

But now . . . being here.

Her mom turned and waved her hand in front of Violet's face, vying with the music for her attention. Violet pulled one of the earbuds free. "Your friends are here," her mom announced, smiling in the same way she'd been smiling ever since she'd heard the doctor at the clinic say that Violet was okay. That she just needed some rest and she'd be fine.

Violet had her own opinions about that diagnosis.

When she saw Krystal's car, Roxy, parked alongside Jay's car in the driveway, the mask—the practiced look of serenity she'd carefully donned during the ride home—slipped.

"I know how much they mean to you," her mom explained, her expression painfully hopeful.

Jay stood waiting for Violet outside, and when the car stopped and she got out he watched her silently for a moment, their eyes locked. And then he was running toward her, catching her in his arms and wrapping them around her. Neither of them said anything for a long, long time; they just stayed like that, holding and touching each other, breathing each other in. Jay squeezed her against him, and every time they'd start to relax he'd squeeze her again, his grip tightening even when Violet didn't think it could possibly tighten any more.

"Don't ever do that again, Violet Ambrose. I swear to God, you can never do that again," he said when he finally loosened his grip, keeping his fingers interlaced with hers.

Violet didn't tell him she hadn't done anything. She didn't explain that none of this was her fault, or talk about what had happened during the past several days. Instead, she just lifted her eyes to his. "I won't. I promise."

Behind him, Violet saw the front door to her house open, and she stiffened when Rafe stepped out.

Jay was watching her. "What's wrong, Vi? I thought you'd be happy to see them. It's okay. If Rafe's important to you, then I guess he's important to me too."

Confusion battled inside her, but Violet just stared over Jay's shoulder, her eyes never leaving Rafe.

She didn't know how she felt about her team right now.

It wasn't their fault, she knew. She'd loved getting to know Sara and Krystal and Sam. She was grateful for everything Dr. Lee had done to help her. . . . Even Gemma, as bitchy as she was, deserved a break, Violet supposed. She'd had a rough life, with no one to support and believe in her. Violet might not particularly like her, but she didn't exactly hate her either.

And then there was Rafe . . .

Rafe, who was standing here now. She'd probably never be able to stay away from Rafe entirely.

But she'd given it a lot of thought over the past few days, and she'd decided that she'd be safer—happier—if she steered clear of their unusual organization.

Even if it meant she couldn't use her ability to help any-one. For now, at least, she needed to concentrate on taking care of herself.

"Talk to him," Jay finally said. "He came here to see you."

Violet shrugged, the only answer she seemed able to give, and then nodded. She moved away from Jay, reluc-tantly untangling her fingers from his, as Rafe came down the steps to meet her.

Violet thought he might hug her, an awkward embrace she'd endure, because that's what people seemed to do in a situation like this. Her uncle and her parents had. Even the sheriff, who she'd never met before, had wrapped his arms around her like she was some long-lost relation. She under-stood, she supposed. It was relief. She'd felt it too.

But Rafe, of course, had to be different.

"Dammit, V, I tried to call you. I tried to warn you," he admonished, frowning as if it were all her fault. He started to close the gap, his hand moving uncertainly toward hers.

Violet shoved her hands in the pockets of her hoodie, the one her parents had bought her from a bait shop in the lakeside town . . . the hoodie she'd be burning later so she wouldn't be reminded of her ordeal with Caine. She didn't want Rafe to touch her; she couldn't risk letting his skin brush against hers.

He followed her lead and tucked his hands in the back pockets of his jeans. His casual stance belied the turmoil Violet could feel coming off him like heat. "I . . ." She didn't know what to say. She shrugged.

351

"You don't have to say anything." He watched her intently, his blue eyes somber, sorrowful. "Krystal's inside. She's dying to tell you how she knew where you were. Plus, she made you cupcakes. I think she's been channeling the spirit of Betty Crocker lately. She's been baking cookies and pies. The kitchen at the Center's been like a bakery."

Violet smiled, taking her hands out of her pockets and toying with the hem of her jacket. "My mom told me it was one of you. That Sara called and told them where they would find me."

Rafe shifted nervously, looking down at his feet. "Sara would've come too, but, you know . . . your parents. I don't think they like her right now."

Violet nodded. She understood. "So it was Krystal?" She didn't know why, but for some reason she was disappointed it hadn't been Rafe. She thought they shared some sort of connection and that he would've been the one to find her. "How? Or should I ask who?"

"I'll let her tell you. But I know she felt bad it didn't happen sooner." And then, as if he'd understood what she'd been thinking, he lifted his eyes to hers. "I'm sorry too, V. It should've been me. I should've saved you." This time when he tried to touch her, Violet didn't stop him. His hand came up beneath hers, moving so their skin grazed, their palms barely touching. The jolt was instant, and exhilarating, reminding Violet that she was still alive. That Caine hadn't crushed her spirit.

"Rafe, I can't—" She pulled her hand from his at the

same time she glanced over her shoulder to where Jay was standing, and saw that his attention was focused solely on Rafe.

"I know," Rafe said, more to himself than to Violet.

She turned back to him, her eyes imploring, beseeching.

"Go," Rafe insisted, letting her off the hook. "It looks like it's killing him not to come over here. Besides, I better get back inside before Krystal starts baking your dad a cake or something."

Violet laughed, a first in days. "He'd probably like that." She smiled as she watched Rafe bound up the steps again, but she stopped him before he reached the top. "Rafe," she whispered. "Thanks for being here."

And then Jay was at her side, and she forgot all about Rafe as she slipped back into his arms, so easily, so comfortably, she could've been falling into her own bed. Her face lifted to his and he kissed her. First on the head, like her mother had done, and then on the cheek, the way her dad had. But then his lips found her mouth, and the kiss became something else entirely.

Something that belonged only to them.

EPILOGUE

VIOLET STOOD AT THE CHAIN-LINK FENCING outside the park, curling her fingers through it as she stared at the playground beyond. After a minute, she checked the time on her cell phone.

It was 2:53. She was seven minutes early.

She had no idea what to expect from this appointment. No idea why they weren't meeting at his office, why he'd insisted they meet at the park down the street from the elementary school in Buckley . . . the same one she and Jay had brought her cousins to on a day that felt like it could have been a lifetime ago.

But it was Dr. Lee, and she figured it was just another

form of alternative therapy he was trying out on her.

She sort of thought he might not want to see her any-more, since she'd formally announced she was quitting the team and all. It had been hard to tell Sara, but at least she'd made it easy on Violet. She'd understood, of course. It probably wasn't the first time Sara had seen someone survive something traumatic and come out of it with a new perspective on life.

Gemma had been practically giddy about Violet's decision, unable to hide her smug grin, and Violet had almost taken it back, had almost decided to stay just to wipe that triumphant look from Gemma's face.

Of course, telling the others had been damn near impossible. Especially after everything Krystal had done for her.

Violet knew now how it had happened. Why it had taken so long for Krystal to find her.

He'd told her. *Caine.* Violet was almost certain it had been him . . . even though Krystal didn't see them as corporeal, the ghosts. She couldn't match his human form to his spirit one.

But Violet knew.

Krystal said he'd come to her that night, telling her where to find Violet. Telling her he didn't want Violet to be left alone. Not his girl.

Those were the words he'd used: *his girl.*

Violet still felt sick thinking about it. About him. She didn't understand why he'd helped her, why he'd gone to Krystal to save her . . . especially after she'd killed him. But he had. For whatever reason, he'd sent help.

That made it even harder for Violet to quit them. But she'd done it. And here she was . . . free. Safe.

She stood across a grassy field from the playset, watching the kids take turns on the swings, on the slide, on the monkey bars. The unearthly backdrop of the music box seemed somehow more eerie here, while children dug in the sandbox. She watched as a wispy-haired blonde girl scurried up a wooden ladder.

Violet strained, trying to get a better look, almost sure it was little Cassidy . . . her cousin.

She looked around for her aunt Kat just as a voice interrupted her. "Adorable, aren't they?"

It was Dr. Lee, and Violet turned to see him approach. She frowned. This wasn't the Dr. Lee she knew.

Instead of his pressed jeans and cardigan, Dr. Lee wore a simple black suit over a fitted black turtleneck. The jacket was tailored perfectly, hugging his lean body and his broad shoulders. He looked like some sort of hit man, minus the dark sunglasses.

"What are you . . . ? Why did you want to meet . . . ?" Violet couldn't think clearly. Something was off, and it wasn't her. "What's going on?" she finally managed.

Dr. Lee ignored her gaping stare and stepped up to the fencing. He clasped his hands behind his back and gazed out thoughtfully. "I just thought we should talk, Violet. About your decision to leave the team."

Violet's brows furrowed, knitting tightly. "Okay . . ."

"You should reconsider—"

But she didn't let him finish; she was already shaking her head. "No. Sara said I could take as much time as I wanted."

Dr. Lee's smooth expression never cracked, and his stance never relaxed. "They come here every day, you know. Your aunt and your cousin. She lets Cassidy play while they wait for Joshua to get out of school." He looked down at her now. "Every day."

Violet's stomach tightened. She hated the way he made her feel, his rigid posture, his unflinching stare, his strange clothing. There was something menacing . . . threatening about him. About his statements.

"What are you saying?"

The corner of his mouth inched up. "You asked me once who I worked for, and I'll tell you this: They're very powerful, the men who employ me . . . who employ us. They don't want you to quit, Violet. In fact, they insist that you stay. It's not a request. And if you need me to be more clear, then I will. It's a threat. Against you, against your friends, and against your family." He turned and nodded toward the playground. "You'll continue to be part of the team. You'll continue your sessions with me . . . call it checking in. And you'll tell no one—*no one*—about our conversation today. Have I made myself clear? Do you understand what I'm telling you?"

Violet nodded numbly. Of course she understood. How could she possibly misinterpret any of that? "What about my parents? What am I supposed to say to them?"

Dr. Lee pivoted on the heel of his immaculately shined black shoes. "You'll figure it out. I have total faith in your ability to handle them."

And then he walked away, leaving her standing on the sidewalk, listening to the spectral sounds of the music-box echo.

ACKNOWLEDGMENTS

In the past few years I've come to realize just how many people are involved in the creation of a book, and I have more than a few of them to thank for *The Last Echo*.

As always, I have to thank my stellar, and I mean stellar(!), team at HarperCollins for everything you do for me and for my books. How many brilliant editors does one girl need, anyway? Thankfully I have more than my fair share in Farrin Jacobs, Kari Sutherland, Catherine Wallace, and Sarah Landis, not to mention the fabulous copyeditors, who meticulously remind me that I still don't understand the difference between "farther" and "further" or "lay" and "lie." I also have to thank my publicist Marisa Russell who puts up with my launch-time email barrages without ever batting an eyelash, and Sasha Illingworth for nailing it (once again) with this fabulous cover.

I also want to thank Laura Rennert, my agent extraordinaire, for always having my back. You are simply the best agent in the business and I can't imagine going through any of this without you. Thank you, Laura!

To the Debs, the Tenners, the Smart Chicks, and the Body Finder Novels Fan Site, along with all my other online friends. Thank you for encouraging me when I need it and distracting me when I don't.

To the people who keep me sane on a daily basis, starting

with Shawn (also known as "Mama Shawn") who I have to thank for, well, pretty much everything. Without you, nothing would ever get done and of course we would all starve to death. I also have to thank Tamara, Jacqueline, Carol, and Tammy, not only for your day-to-day support, but also for keeping me sane(ish) during launch season. I hope all of you know just how much I appreciate your friendship.

Then there are my go-to friends, who also serve as my professional resources: Bryan Jeter, John McDonald, and Randy Strozyk. Thank you for letting me pit you against one another in email competitions when I need to know the logistics of a car crash or where a suspect would be held during a murder investigation. You guys are wicked smart, crazy reliable, and just plain awesome!

And of course a special thanks to my family. Thank you for standing by me, even when I have to lock myself away for days (or weeks) at a time. I'm not sure what else I can say, except, I love you all!

Finally, to Josh . . . thanks for keeping me safe and warm. No one else gets me like you do!

Join Violet as she solves murders
by following clues only she can sense.

Read the entire **BODY FINDER** series
by Kimberly Derting